SNOWFLAKES OVER BAY TREE TERRACE

FAY KEENAN

Lots of love and all best wishes,

Fay Keenan xxv

B

Boldwood

First published in Great Britain in 2020 by Boldwood Books Ltd.

Copyright © Fay Keenan, 2020

Cover Design by Alice Moore Design

Cover Photography: Shutterstock

A CIP catalogue record for this book is available from the British Library.

Paperback ISBN 978-1-83889-158-9

Large Print ISBN 978-1-83889-776-5

Ebook ISBN 978-1-83889-160-2

Kindle ISBN 978-1-83889-159-6

Audio CD ISBN 978-1-83889-242-5

MP3 CD ISBN 978-1-83889-773-4

Digital audio download ISBN 978-1-83889-157-2

Boldwood Books Ltd
23 Bowerdean Street
London SW6 3TN
www.boldwoodbooks.com

For the key workers, especially those in the emergency services, who, in 2020, have faced so many challenges with grace, kindness and professionalism. Thank you.

PROLOGUE

A CHRISTMAS SURPRISE

'...And to my great-niece Florence, I leave Number 2, Bay Tree Terrace. I know how much she loved visiting as a child, and it seems only right that, in the absence of a daughter or grand-daughter of my own, the house passes to her to do with as she wishes.'

John Hampshire, of the firm Hampshire, Thomas and Robinson, of Willowbury, Somerset, glanced up at her and smiled. 'Well,' he said as he caught sight of his client's aghast face. 'That's rather a lovely Christmas present, if I do say so myself.'

Florence Ashton was glad she wasn't holding the cup of coffee she'd been given when she arrived, otherwise it would have ended up in her lap. When she'd been summoned to the solicitor's office, she assumed it would be to sign some papers or some such other mundane business. Great-Aunt Elsie's funeral had been a while ago, and the executor of the estate had been a friend of Elsie's that the family didn't know, so there'd been no contact up until the phone call she'd had at the end of last week from the solicitor's office. It turned out she was walking out of there the owner of a pretty, red-bricked terraced house in Somerset.

'Mince pie?' Mr Hampshire passed the plate that his PA had brought in with the coffee in Florence's direction. Gratefully, she took one, shocked at how much her hands were shaking.

'Thanks.' She bit into the one she'd chosen, the warm, spiced and orange-infused filling reminding her of the Christmases she'd spent at Bay Tree Terrace with Aunt Elsie and her mother while her father had been on one of his many tours of duty with the army.

'So how long are you staying in Willowbury?'

Florence swallowed her mouthful of mince pie and took a sip of her coffee. 'Well, given what you've just told me, it would seem I might be moving here.' She laughed. 'Sorry. It's just a bit of a shock.'

'I understand,' Mr Hampshire replied. 'These out-of-the-blue things can take a bit of getting used to. Of course, you don't have to drop everything and move into the house. There's no condition about that. You could just instruct an estate agent to sell it. I know of a good one in Willowbury who'd be more than happy to handle it for you.'

'Oh no,' Florence said hurriedly. 'I loved spending time here when I was younger. And I've been thinking of making a move somewhere else for a while.' She'd been teaching for nine years in York, which was the longest she'd stayed anywhere, and was just starting to think about change.

'Well, give it some thought,' the solicitor smiled. 'There's no rush. It'll take a week or two to tie up the last of the paperwork, and if you're sure then about keeping the house, sorting out the rest of the estate shouldn't take too long.'

'Can I see it?' Florence asked, taking another sip of her coffee. 'I haven't been back to Willowbury in a while.' She swallowed the sudden lump that had formed in her throat. 'Towards the end... Aunt Elsie didn't really want visitors, so Mum popped down for a bit, but she wouldn't allow anyone else to actually stay with her.'

'Of course.' He rummaged in the box file for the door keys. 'After all, it's yours now, so really, you can do as you wish.'

'Thank you.' Taking the keys, with their surprisingly cheery Highland Terrier key fob, Florence stood up on somewhat shaky legs.

'My pleasure,' Mr Hampshire replied. 'We'll be in touch to confirm all the details in due course.'

As Florence left the solicitor's office and wandered out onto the busy Willowbury High Street, she glanced at the sky, which seemed thick with heavy, snowy clouds. Snow was unusual in this part of Somerset, but a small, childish part of her couldn't help hoping for some of the white stuff this close to Christmas. She smiled as she saw the seasonal decorations in some shop windows, and the pagan and alternative colours and shapes of those who celebrated more ancient rituals. Willowbury was a haven for all kinds of spirituality; the centre of the town might have been the ruins of the old priory, destroyed during Henry VIII's time but acquired by the National Trust to be preserved in perpetuity, but there were plenty of corners of the town where the ancient religions and customs found their home, too.

Sprigs of holly and fragrant cut pine branches graced nearly every shop doorway, with the odd sneakily placed frond of mistletoe tucked away in a few, as well. In the air was the heady scent of cinnamon from the festive versions of hot drinks in the cafe on the High Street, the invitingly named 'Cosy Coffee Shop'. Florence decided she'd grab a cinnamon latte from there before heading over to Aunt Elsie's house – there was a real chill in the air and she wasn't sure how warm the terraced house would be.

Heading towards the cafe, she passed the brightly lit window of ComIncense, the health and well-being shop that specialised in herbal remedies and relaxation products. Even in Yorkshire, Florence, a keen follower of politics, had observed the media's interest in the owner of the shop, Holly Renton. Holly had gone up against and then, in a plot twist worthy of a prime-time television drama, had married, the member of parliament for Willowbury and Stavenham, Charlie Thorpe, this summer past.

Glancing through the shop window as she walked by, she could see a tall, striking woman with tumbling red hair straightening the displays in the centre of the shop, and smiled back as the lady smiled Florence's way. *Not exactly your typical politician's wife,* Florence thought wryly, noting the ripped jeans and the flowing coloured tunic that Holly was wearing. But then Willowbury wasn't exactly your typical Somerset town – it had a feel and an atmosphere all of its own, and people flocked from miles around to soak up its alternative atmosphere. And now she was deciding whether to come and live here. For her, it could go from just a nice holiday destination to a permanent place to live.

Florence wasn't, by nature, a risk-taker, but at the age of twenty-nine she was due for a change. She'd taught at the same school in Yorkshire since she'd left university, and, as the daughter of a serving army officer, she was used to never staying anywhere for too long. The past nine years, happy and settled on the outskirts of the city of York, a place she'd come to love, had been wonderful, but literally being given the keys to a new life in a different, but comfortingly familiar, part of the world seemed like a great opportunity. She had a bit of money saved, and no house to sell as she'd been sharing a flat with another teacher since she'd moved out of the family home; she certainly had enough to live on if she couldn't immediately find a job in Somerset. She had to give at least a term's notice if she was going to leave her job, but, depending on the state of Aunt Elsie's place, it might take that long to make it liveable.

All this she pondered as she stepped up the couple of stone steps and into The Cosy Coffee Shop. There was so much to think about, and she'd not even begun to take in the fact that Aunt Elsie had left her a house. But for the moment, a cinnamon- infused latte, and possibly another mince pie, were the foremost in her mind.

As she walked up to the counter and was greeted with a smile by the barista, a sandy-haired man in his late thirties, she determined that all other decisions would have to wait.

'What can I get you?' the barista, whose name was Jack, asked cheerily.

Florence took a deep breath of the coffee-scented air, and gave her order. It felt like the first step of her new life.

NINE MONTHS LATER

1

Florence hadn't expected to sleep well the night before she began her new job. She also hadn't expected, rather than the usual anxiety dreams about turning up to a classroom with no clothes on or shouting at the top of her voice while students ran amok around her, that it would be the noise from the neighbouring terraced house that would keep her awake. And not just any old noise, either. This sounded like the death throes of a Siamese cat being stretched on a rack. She had eclectic musical taste, but at three o'clock in the morning, even Harry Styles strutting his stuff and crooning personally to her would have got short shrift. Pulling her pillow over her ears even more tightly, she prayed that the owner of the electric guitar would garrotte himself on his G-string before she did it for him.

Nine months ago, when Florence had walked into her great-aunt's old house in the eccentric but charming small town of Willowbury, with the intention of living permanently there, it had been with a sense of excitement, laced with trepidation. Aunt Elsie's death had been a great sadness to Florence; she'd spent many childhood summers here in Willowbury with her aunt, and it was only in recent years that life and work had taken over and she'd not seen quite so much of her. It came as a surprise to be remembered in the old lady's will; not just a surprise, but quite a shock when Florence realised Aunt Elsie had left her the house and its contents. In true Elsie Barrett style, she'd left most of her actual cash to the Dogs' Trust but set aside enough for Florence to move in and redecorate. Her great-aunt's decision to make Florence the beneficiary of the majority of her estate had raised a couple of eyebrows in the family, but been met with good grace by those Florence was closest to, for which Florence was extremely glad. But then she had been the one, who, in later years, had tried to keep in touch with Elsie the most, even popping down occasionally to see her for a few days here and there. Towards the end of the old woman's life, though, Elsie had pretty much cut herself off from family, preferring to spend her time alone. Florence, while sad about this, had respected Elsie's desire for privacy, even if she was incredibly sad she'd never actually got to say goodbye to her.

So it was that Florence had made the move to Somerset at the tail end of the summer holidays, with two weeks to spare before the start of a new term, and had been so busy settling and trying to make it a home of her own that she hadn't really noticed the presence of the neighbours on either side of her in the terrace. Perhaps moving to a terraced house in the country wasn't quite as idyllic a prospect as she'd imagined it to be, after all.

'Oh, shut up!' Florence muttered as the noise of the electric guitar ramped up even higher. She hadn't met her neighbours yet; they either seemed to be asleep or out when she was around, and this was not how she had wanted to be introduced to them. The old railway workers' cottages that fronted the road but backed onto the hillside, with six-foot-high stone walls bordering off the back gardens, meant that pleasant conversations over the garden fence weren't really an option, and although their front doors were only a few feet apart, she'd not bumped into the neighbours on either side yet. The brick walls of the terrace were thick but not soundproof, and as the caterwauling grew more strident, Florence's temper frayed further. She hadn't moved three hundred miles for this. Especially not on the eve (well, the morning, now) of a new job.

Just as she was deciding she couldn't take it any longer, the noise stopped. The silence, when it came, nearly deafened her. Her ears were still ringing. 'Thank God for that,' Florence muttered, removing the pillow from her ears and slamming herself face down into it. At least she'd get three hours' sleep before the alarm went off at six. It might only have been an inset day, but it was a new school, a new department and a newish part of the country; she needed to be firing on all cylinders.

Hearing the muffled *thump, thump, thump* of footsteps on what was obviously an uncarpeted landing next door and the flick of the bathroom switch before rather prolonged peeing, Florence sighed. She'd not expected the silence of the countryside to yield quite so much antisocial noise. Resolving to make herself known to the neighbours the next day, she drifted off into an uneasy sleep.

* * *

It seemed only the blink of an eye before the alarm started going off. Flinging the covers back, Florence ambled down the stairs to the kitchen and flipped the switch on the bean-to-cup coffee machine that crouched like some vast black panther on the work surface by the sink. Aunt Elsie would have given the thing very short shrift, Florence reflected, having been a staunch tea drinker all her life, but Florence definitely needed an early-morning coffee shot.

While the machine ground beans and then gurgled, Florence

stretched her arms above her head and brooded on the lack of sleep the night before. If that kind of noise was going to be a regular thing, she'd definitely need to have a word with her neighbours. Or invest in some heavy-duty ear defenders.

When the coffee was ready, she grabbed the cup and headed upstairs to the shower. At least there wouldn't be any students today to run the gauntlet of; she hoped that her new colleagues were as friendly now she'd got the job as they'd appeared at her interview.

In a short time, she was ready, and as she left the house she dithered for a moment. Was it worth knocking on her neighbour's door now and making a firm but polite complaint about the noise last night? Then again, whoever it had been making that noise would doubtless still be in bed; after all, it was only eight o'clock, and they'd been playing until gone three.

She glanced up at the front of the house and noted that the curtains on the front bedroom window were, indeed, still closed. *Lucky that you can have a lie-in,* she thought mutinously, forgetting that she'd been having a fair few of them herself over the school holiday, at least before she'd made the move. No matter what the teaching profession said about working conditions and workload, six weeks off, or at least working from home in the summer, were a definite bonus.

She decided that a note might be a better course of action. After all, she hadn't even met her neighbours yet, and she didn't want to antagonise the people she shared a wall with. Perhaps, if she popped one through the door before she went to work, she could go round and introduce herself later, try to establish if the nocturnal noisemaking was going to be a regular thing.

Heading back into the house, she cursed as she realised that the only pen she could find in her kitchen was of the pink and sparkly variety. She nonetheless scrawled a hasty note.

Slamming the heavy front door, that she'd painted a pale lavender shade, shut, she popped the note through the door of the adjoining house. Then, hurrying around to the back of the terraces, she unlocked her car and headed off for the short drive to Willowbury Academy. The great thing about living in Aunt Elsie's old house was that she was only ten minutes' drive from work, which would come in very handy during the dark nights of the Autumn and Winter Terms. Not that it was dark or gloomy at all on this sunny September day, she reflected as she drove.

Willowbury in the early autumn was a lovely sight. The small town, with its array of crystal shops, alternative booksellers, ancient pub, butcher and newly opened, more mainstream independent bookshop was incredibly picturesque and would have been even without the newly planted tubs of winter pansies that adorned the shops and the hanging baskets full of violas that rustled gently in the still warm breeze. She'd loved the place as a teenager, and now she was a resident, she was looking at it with even more fondness.

Lost in a reverie, it wasn't until she was two tyres over the zebra crossing in the middle of the High Street that she noticed someone had stepped off the pavement to cross.

'Shit!' Florence slammed on the brakes of her ancient Astra Estate, which, fortunately, she'd just had MOT'd. Heart thumping, she felt her face start to flame as a tall, fair-haired man loped over the stripes, throwing her an ironically raised hand in acknowledgement as he passed in front of her car. Florence smiled weakly, mouthing 'sorry' through the windscreen, but unsure if he'd actually seen her attempt at an apology.

'Get a grip, Ashton,' she muttered as she put the car in gear and pulled away, checking before she did that she wasn't about to run over any more pedestrians. 'You can't go mowing people down just because you didn't get any sleep.'

Irritated, she again wondered who the hell was making the racket next door, and, resolve hardened, was determined to seek them out. After all, she needed all of her energy if she was going to tackle a new job and a new house; irritating neighbours just weren't an option.

2

Sam Ellis had always suspected that his weakness for Ginsters pasties would get him killed one day. Just off shift, he'd pulled up on the side of the road opposite the Co-Op in Willowbury, driven by the urge to grab a carb-laden pastry before heading home for a shower and bed. The night shifts with the Somerset Air Ambulance were always hardest on him; he'd never quite got used to the rotations, and Ginsters were the only thing that would make the exhaustion better. He knew he'd have been better off having some of the granola dust that his sister Kate was always trying to foist on him whenever he visited her, but there was something about the way the pastry stuck to the roof of his mouth after a long shift that he just couldn't resist. Perhaps he'd been too distracted by the anticipation of the pasty to look properly before he stepped out onto the zebra crossing, or perhaps the driver of the ancient Astra who'd slammed on its brakes just in time hadn't had their mind on the road, but whatever it was, as he raised a hand in the driver's direction, he realised that he'd just had a very near miss.

Even with this knowledge, though, the lure of the pasty was too great. Not even waiting until he got home, he tore off the wrapper sank his teeth into it, revelling in the salty meat and vegetable goodness for a bite or two, before dumping it down on the passenger seat, where it joined about five other pasty wrappers. He'd have gone spare if someone had left the cockpit of the air ambulance in that state, but in his own car he was far less fastidious.

The drive home took only a couple of minutes more, and as he pulled into the designated parking space behind the row of terraced houses where he lived, he felt the tiredness overwhelm him. Experts on night working had advised him to try to treat his working day just like any other; not to go straight to bed when he got home, but to potter around, eat at leisure and unwind for a few hours, just as he would when he was working during the day, but he hadn't quite managed to get into a routine as yet.

Of course, it didn't help that Aidan was king of the antisocial hours, and Sam never knew whether he was going to be awake or asleep when he got home. More often than not, Aidan was out and about when Sam got back and, being quite a private person, Sam didn't mind this. He was used to sharing accommodation from his days on ship, so the notion of personal space was one he wasn't too bothered about. The fact he had his own room was good enough for now.

For now was as close as Sam had to a life's mantra. After all, who knew what tomorrow would bring? That was something he'd learned the hard way over the past couple of years.

Letting himself in through the front door, he smelt the rank odour of Aidan's hand-rolled cigarettes and resolved to remind him that they'd agreed on a no-smoking-in-the-house rule. The trouble was, Aidan, like him, had his coping mechanisms, and Aidan often had more need of them. Letting Aidan get away with smoking a few roll-ups seemed a small price to pay, given what he'd been through.

As he closed the front door behind him, he noticed a note that had been shoved through the mottled brass letter box. Stooping to pick it up, he smirked a little at the pink sparkly gel pen it had been written in, before his expression creased in irritation. The note read 'Please can you keep the noise down in the early hours of the morning, as I have to get up for work very early. Thank you, Florence Ashton (number two).'

It seemed that cigarettes weren't the only antisocial habit Aidan was indulging in. He had a passion for the electric guitar, and although Aidan was a grown man and more than able to fight his own battles, Sam added it to the list of things to discuss with him. What was one more irritation, after all?

Wandering through to the kitchen to make a quick cup of tea to take up to bed with him, Sam noticed the washing-up still in the sink from two days ago when he'd last had dinner at home, and a row of empty lager bottles by the back door waiting to be put out into the recycling bin. Some of them had been his, but most of them belonged to Aidan.

He sighed. Things were going to have to change around here. He felt too drained from a night shift that had involved a long, protracted wait on a local football pitch before a high-speed dash to the helipad at the top of Bristol Royal Children's Hospital with a young casualty to enter into a discussion on housekeeping right now, but he resolved to raise things with Aidan the next time they were both home and vaguely awake.

As the kettle boiled and he sloshed the water into a mug with a tea bag in it, the last clean one in the cupboard, Sam shook his head. This wasn't quite how he'd imagined his life would be at thirty-two years old. But then, he hadn't imagined ever leaving the navy, either. If it hadn't been for Aidan, he'd probably still be on a ship somewhere.

Wandering up the creaky wooden stairs to the still uncarpeted landing, Sam noticed that Aidan's bedroom door was still open. As he poked his head quickly around the door, he saw Aidan slumped on his bed, a half-empty bottle of whisky beside him on the chest of drawers, and the amp, still plugged into the guitar, humming away in the semi-darkness of the room. It was light outside now, but Aidan's curtains were still closed. Sam sighed. It wasn't the first time he'd come home to this.

Creeping across the bedroom floor, taking care to avoid the worst of the noisy floorboards, he turned the switch on the amp and glanced at the bed. Aidan was out for the count, still fully clothed and snoring his head off. Sam assumed he'd had another one of his frequent bad nights. Slipping out of the room again, he pulled the door closed and then padded off down the landing to his own room.

He realised, as he put the tea down on his own bedside table, that he still had the note from the neighbour in his back pocket. Taking it out again, he reread it, and then put it alongside his tea. He'd deal with it when he'd had a good sleep, he thought. Hopefully he'd be able to tackle Aidan about it before he had to head out to work again, and then he'd pop round to see the writer of the note and apologise.

It's not your problem, a little voice in the back of his mind told him, as he slipped off his shoes and unbuttoned his jeans. Aidan was a grown man and should be able to conduct himself sensibly. It wasn't as simple as that, though, Sam knew. Things were never simple as far as Aidan was concerned.

As Sam rapidly undressed down to his boxer shorts and lay back against the pillows, sleep overcame him, leaving his tea to go tepid, then cold, in the chilly air of his bedroom.

3

Florence had grown used to moving around constantly as she was growing up – her family had been posted to seven different locations in fourteen years, including Germany at one point – so she had no trouble acclimatising to a new job. As luck would have it, the year-long part-time post at the newly built Willowbury Academy had been advertised in the *Times Educational Supplement* fairly soon after Florence had inherited Aunt Elsie's house. Although she was not a great believer in providence, this opportunity still seemed too good to pass up, and after a successful interview in the early spring of that year, she'd accepted the post when it had been offered to her.

As she settled into her new department's office and chatted with her colleagues, she kept having to remind herself that it was the West Country accent that was dominant now and not the lilting Yorkshire tones she'd spent nearly a decade enjoying. She was sure there was going to be a whole new set of teenage slang words to memorise as well, and hoped that she'd be up to the task.

While she was filling out her planner for the next day's teaching, and familiarising herself with where the set texts were, her thoughts were interrupted by a cheery 'Hello!' as another colleague came into the office.

Glancing up, she saw the new arrival was a friendly-looking but slightly harried woman with a cascade of long, unruly dark hair, messily tied back in a loose ponytail. Struggling with a box of books and her oversized handbag, she slung them down on the conference table to the side of the door and let out a huge sigh.

'Christ, I didn't think I was ever going to get away from home this morning!' she exclaimed, digging in her handbag for a coffee mug and wandering over to the sink on the back wall of the office. 'Nick's supposed to be taking our son Jacob out to Crealy Park today, but Jake was still in his PJs as I left.' She grinned. 'Good luck to them!'

Florence got the impression that this was one of those women who clung onto organisation by her fingernails, but couldn't help smiling as, coffee made, she headed back towards her.

'Josie Sellars,' the woman said. 'We didn't meet when you came for interview as it wasn't one of my working days, but it's nice to meet you now.'

'Florence Ashton,' Florence replied. 'It's nice to meet you, too.' Dredging up some of the information that the Head of Department had given her at her interview, she continued, 'You live in Willowbury, don't you?'

'Yes, that's right,' Josie said as she pulled her laptop from her bag and flipped the lid. 'It's quite handy for this place, only ten minutes by car, which is a definite result. Do you know the town?'

'I've just moved here,' Florence replied. 'Into my aunt's old terraced cottage at the foot of the hill.'

'Oh, you're Elsie Barnett's great-niece, aren't you?' Josie grinned. 'She was the scourge of the local coffee shop – it was about two years before darling Jack managed to get her Earl Grey right.'

'All I found in her cupboard when I moved in were boxes and

boxes of Earl Grey,' Florence laughed. 'And a bottle or two of gin, of course. She loved both.'

'Were you close?' Josie asked as the familiar tones of her work laptop jingled the air.

'I spent a lot of summers in Willowbury when I was a kid,' Florence said. 'And she was, believe it or not, great fun when she forgot to be strict.'

'Well, she must have enjoyed having you to leave you the house.' Josie sipped her coffee thoughtfully, then flushed slightly. 'Sorry – I tend to speak without thinking.'

'No, it's fine,' Florence said. 'I was as shocked as anyone, but it was a lovely gesture. Although it's going to take some work to bring it into the twenty-first century. Aunt Elsie must have stopped decorating in the nineteen sixties!'

'With a bit of luck, being only three days a week here you'll get plenty of time to sort it out,' Josie said. 'Although part-time teaching isn't quite all it's cracked up to be as I've found out over the past year or so. You still tend to take the same amount of work home with you.'

'I don't doubt it,' Florence laughed. 'But at least, with this place being so new, there are only five, rather than seven, year groups to worry about at the moment. And I love teaching years seven to eleven anyway, so I'm sure it'll be fine.' There were plans to increase the size of the school to include a sixth form as the numbers of students increased.

'Speaking of which, we'd better get a wriggle on.' Josie stood, picked up her coffee mug and her teacher's planner and glanced at the itinerary for the inset day. 'Oh great,' she muttered. 'Just what we need on the first day back, an hour of health and safety and admin, followed by some outside speaker, who, doubtless, will patronise us to the nth degree about how to do our jobs.'

Florence looked at her own copy of the itinerary. 'I've heard this bloke before,' she said, clocking the outside speaker's name. 'He came into my old school last autumn after our exam results took a dive. He's quite entertaining, actually.'

'Glad to hear it,' Josie said drily. 'After all this time in the classroom, admittedly with a few years off to be a dreadfully disorganised stay-at-home mother, I do tend to be a little jaded about so-called experts, but I'll try to reserve judgement this time.'

Picking up her own cup of coffee and a notebook (she hadn't had time to grab a new planner from Admin yet), Florence felt a lot more relaxed. Josie seemed like a lot of fun, and she was beginning to feel more settled in her new school already.

* * *

An hour later, after a lengthy update from the School Business Manager about new buildings on site and the precautions that staff and students needed to take, Florence was looking forward to escaping the auditorium, where all the school's staff was seated, largely grouped by department. Ironically, teachers aren't the best at sitting still and listening to other people for great chunks of time, and as she glanced around the hall, she could see several of her new colleagues doodling in their planners, sending surreptitious text messages or muttering under their breath to the person next to them.

Always a tough crowd, she thought, feeling a pang of empathy for the visiting speaker, who was due up after the break.

Gagging for another cup of coffee, especially after being kept awake for so long the previous night, she was glad when the session broke and it was time for caffeine and tray bakes. She was definitely going to have to make sure that her annoying next-door neighbours had got her hastily scribbled note when she got back tonight.

Lost in thought, she jumped when Josie's voice broke into her reverie. 'How are you doing?' Bearing Florence's travel mug, which she'd taken to get refilled in the school dining room, and a large slice of flapjack – 'you'll come to rely on these when term really gets started!' – Josie settled down at the lunch table where Florence had taken a seat. 'How are you finding it?' Josie asked, once they'd both taken a sip and a nibble.

'OK so far,' Florence replied. 'I wish I'd got a bit more sleep last night, but the coffee's definitely helping.'

'Was it the usual pre-teaching anxiety dreams?' Josie grinned. 'I always end up either stark naked in front of a class or shouting at the top of my voice while they all run riot!'

'Not exactly,' Florence admitted. 'Although, with my luck, I'll end up having those tonight. It's my neighbours. They're rather... energetic in the early hours.' At Josie's suggestively raised eyebrow, Florence burst out laughing. 'No, not like that! One of them plays electric guitar, and last night he obviously forgot to plug in his headphones before he started. I can't say I share his taste in music.'

'Even if you did, late at night is no time to be playing it,' Josie said stoutly. 'Have you had a word?'

'Not yet,' Florence sipped her coffee. 'They never seem to be at home when I am, but I've put a note through their door. I can't imagine Aunt Elsie putting up with that kind of noise, although she was pretty deaf in later years.' So much so, Florence thought, that she needed to install a dog flap on her back door to let Hugo the Highland Terrier out at night when she couldn't hear him barking.

Poor Hugo had died just before Aunt Elsie, and part of Florence wondered if she'd died of a broken heart. She'd been more devoted to Hugo than any human companion she'd ever had, so far as Florence knew. Given that she'd only ever known Aunt Elsie as a somewhat irascible older lady, she couldn't imagine her as part of a romantic couple, anyway. She certainly hadn't been hugely keen on her great-niece consorting with the local boys when Florence had come to stay, and had raised an eyebrow at the holiday romances Florence had embarked upon while staying with her.

'Well, everyone knows everyone in Willowbury, so if they continue to be a hassle, give us a shout and I'll see what I can find out.' Josie glanced at her watch. 'We'd better get back to the auditorium – this speaker guy's going to be on soon. Since you've said he's all right, I'll blame you if I fall asleep!' Josie's eyes twinkled.

'Thanks,' Florence rolled her eyes. Finishing off her flapjack, she picked up her coffee cup and headed back to the hall. She felt a prickle of excitement about starting this new phase of her career, and she hoped the rest of the afternoon would be good preparation for actually meeting the students tomorrow.

4

Sam woke to the sound of an insistent rapping on the front door. Rubbing the sleep from his eyes, and still clad only in his boxer shorts, he swung his legs over the bed and reached for the T-shirt that he'd shed before crashing out. He could have just ignored it, of course, but some sense of discipline still remained from his navy days, and he felt it best to deal with whoever it was head on.

Peeking out through a crack in the blackout curtains in his room, which just happened to look directly down to the front door, he noticed a blonde mane of hair tied back in a loose ponytail.

'All right, I'm coming,' he muttered as he saw her raise her hand to the smeary brass door knocker again. Still in his bare feet, he jogged downstairs and through the rather chilly hallway, toes feeling the cold of the Victorian tiles of the hall.

Whipping back the chain (the visitor didn't seem like much of a threat from upstairs), and pulling open the door, he came face to bleary eyes with a serious-looking, but nonetheless very attractive, woman. She looked to be in her late twenties at a guess, and was casually dressed in skinny jeans and a checked shirt, which was unbuttoned over a tighter black top.

'Can I help you?' Sam asked, rather more gruffly than he'd intended.

'I hope I'm not disturbing you,' the woman replied, after a brief moment's hesitation where she was clearly trying to curb her surprise about the fact Sam had opened the door in only his boxer shorts and a T-shirt. Sam was also sure he wasn't imagining a sliver of irritation in her voice, though. 'I just wanted to have a word about the noise.'

'Noise?' Sam repeated. His brain still felt fuzzy from being pulled away from sleep. Then he twigged. 'The note. Did you write it?'

'I did.' She didn't elaborate further.

The pause, for some reason, irritated Sam. He felt as though he was a small boy again, under the scrutiny of his form tutor for talking during registration. 'Sorry,' he said. 'I've just woken up. I was on a night shift. Did someone disturb you last night?'

'Well, if it wasn't you, then it must be someone else who lives here,' the woman replied, giving a tight, tense smile. 'Is there any chance I can have a word with them?'

Sam's heart thumped uncomfortably. 'I'm afraid he's not here at the moment, but I can pass on the message when I see him.'

'Thank you,' she said. 'It's just that when you've got to get up for work early, being kept awake by someone playing the electric guitar until three in the morning is a bit of a problem. The walls on these houses might be thick, but they're not quite Metallica proof!'

Sam smiled apologetically. 'I understand, and I'm sorry. I'll have a word with my... er... housemate and get him to plug in his headphones if he decides to give a late-night concert again.'

'Well, as I said, it's a bit much when you've got to get up for school.'

'I get that, really,' Sam said. Perhaps it was lack of sleep, but he was still irked by her slightly schoolmistressy tone, although at least he now knew why she sounded that way. 'I'll have a word,' he repeated.

'Thank you.'

There was an uncomfortable pause. Fleetingly, Sam wondered if he should ask her in for coffee, but he was still knackered and she, understandably, didn't seem to be in an overly sociable mood.

'Right. I'll be off then. See you around,' she continued.

'Wait,' he said as she turned. 'Since we're neighbours, shouldn't we introduce ourselves? I'm Sam Ellis.'

'Florence Ashton,' she said, and, with a little hesitation, she thrust forward a hand. 'Nice to meet you. Even if I am having a moan!' She finally smiled, and Sam was surprised, especially in light of his irritation, to find how the smile lit up her face very attractively. Suddenly, she didn't seem so much like a schoolmistress any more.

'Let's hope next time we talk it'll be under better circumstances,' Sam replied. 'And I will have a word with him, don't worry.'

'I'd appreciate that,' Florence replied. 'And I'm sorry if I've woken you up, too. Night shifts must be rough.'

'They take a bit of getting used to,' Sam said. 'Especially when you get woken up.' Despite his words, his tone was teasing.

'I can't imagine what *that* feels like!' Florence said, with a note of irony in her voice.

'Fair point,' Sam replied, but smiled anyway. After all, if they were going to be neighbours, he ought to keep her on side. Telling Aidan to keep his guitar playing down was one thing, but actually getting him to do it was quite another, after all. Aidan often used noise to block out the things he really didn't want to hear or think about.

'Well. See you then,' Florence said, turning on her heel and wandering down the pathway. Sam, still standing at the door, grinned more broadly when she opened the gate and came back up her own path, which was separated from his only by a three-foot-high wall.

'You could have just jumped over,' he said in amusement as she put her front door key in the lock. His heart gave a lurch as she grinned back, and this time, the smile reached her eyes.

'Maybe when we know each other better,' she said lightly. 'I wouldn't want to go arse over tit in front of a stranger.'

'Fair enough,' Sam replied.

Pushing his own door shut, he glanced at his watch. He only had an hour and a half before he had to get down to base for his shift; it wasn't worth trying to get any more sleep.

Sam rubbed his eyes and headed back upstairs to take a shower, trying to ignore the clunk and clank of the ancient hot water system. He knew he'd have to have a word with Aidan before he left, just in case he decided to give Florence another impromptu recital in the small hours of tomorrow morning. As much as he told himself that sometimes Aidan couldn't be held fully responsible for his actions, it still frustrated him that he was the one taking the flak for them. Again.

If this living arrangement was going to work, he was going to have to make sure that Aidan knew exactly what he could and couldn't do, or relations with those around them were going to get very strained indeed.

Stripping off his boxer shorts and T-shirt and shivering slightly in the chilly air of the bathroom as he waited for the water to warm up, Sam tried to get himself into the right frame of mind for this shift. It wouldn't do to be unfocused while he was working; a lack of concentration for Sam would mean more than inconvenience; it could be the difference between life and death.

Stepping under the shower, he tried to purge all tiredness from his bones and all stress from his mind. It nearly worked.

5

Florence returned to her house feeling somewhat mollified by Sam's response. She couldn't help being curious about the guitar-playing anti-socialite next door. Perhaps he or she was a shift worker like Sam? After all, there was plenty of industry in Somerset that employed people all through the day and night – several large supermarket distribution centres lined the southern stretch of the M5 motorway, as well as having the nuclear power station, Hinkley Point, well within driving distance.

She found, to her surprise, that having met Sam at the door, she was far more preoccupied by him than the initial reason for going around there. His sexily dishevelled, literally just-got-out-of-bed dirty blond hair topped a face that had striking blue eyes, a strong, square jaw and a generous mouth, which had, eventually, smiled when they'd discussed the noise issue. She also hadn't failed to notice a well-constructed torso, which had been hinted at by the slight tightness of his white T-shirt, and long legs beneath blue and white checked boxer shorts. Not a bad-looking guy, she had to admit. He certainly made the conversation easier, as well, once he'd realised why she was there.

Something else was nagging at her. Sam looked familiar, although she was sure she hadn't met him before. Perhaps sleep deprivation was making her imagine things.

That said, it had been a while since Florence had had a steady man in her life, and apart from a couple of casual dates, she was surprised to realise that she missed having someone to go out with. Seeing Sam in his night clothes, with the subtle but warm scent of sleepiness and yesterday's cologne emanating from his bed-warmed body, she felt a tentative attraction. Although shagging the next-door neighbour could be awkward, she conceded. Imagine having to open the front door every day and risk bumping into that person if it all went pear-shaped!

Putting those thoughts firmly from her mind, she wandered through to the kitchen at the back of the house and pondered on dinner. She was a good, plain cook, but, still keyed up after her first day at school, and feeling nervous, despite her years of experience, about meeting her new classes tomorrow, she couldn't summon up much enthusiasm for food. She did fancy a glass of wine, though. She'd ordered a bottle of Chablis with her last online food shop, and it was sitting unopened in the fridge. One glass wouldn't hurt, she thought.

She pulled open the top cupboard where she'd put her glasses and then poured a generous glug of the perfectly chilled wine. The day was still warm, and her south-facing back garden was accessible through French windows at the back of the kitchen, so she decided to drink her glass of wine on the patio and then think about what she wanted to eat.

Throwing open the doors, the late-afternoon sunlight, mellow with the promise of autumn, warmed her upturned face. Although her new home was on the edge of a reasonably busy road, she couldn't hear much of the traffic noise from the back, which was definitely a blessing. The leaves on the mature beech trees that

marked the boundary at the end of her long, generously propor-
tioned garden rustled in the breeze.

Sooner or later, she'd need to get a lawnmower and cut the large
expanse of grass that had been growing steadily since she took on
the house. She'd paid a gardener to tackle it when she'd moved in,
but even though she owned the house outright now, it still seemed
an extravagance to employ a gardener on her part-time salary.
Besides, the exercise would do her good after time in the classroom.
Aunt Elsie would have been horrified at the thought of her great-
niece wielding a lawnmower, but needs must.

The rest of the garden was in reasonable shape; there were long
flower beds running parallel to the boundary walls on each side of
the property. On the left, where her house butted up against Sam
and his housemate's, was a row of hydrangea bushes, mature and
on their last flowering before the autumn frosts would get them.
Alternate pink and lilac, she knew that Aunt Elsie loved the flowers,
so she was determined to keep them in good check. On the other
side stretched an equally impressive bed of old English roses, which
again would take some upkeep, but their large, flamboyant blooms,
whose scent emanated more strongly as late afternoon progressed,
were louche and elegant in the golden September sun.

Making a mental note to buy herself a book on tending roses,
Florence's attention was drawn by the sound of muffled voices, both
unmistakably masculine, drifting from the open window of Sam's
house. From the tone of the voices, they clearly knew each other
very well, as conversation seemed to be flowing easily between
them, even though she could only make out snatches of words. Her
hearing, honed by years of picking up on illicit pupil conversations
while teaching, was excellent. The words 'meds', 'sleep' and 'routine' jumped out at her, and it was then that she started to feel a bit
guilty for eavesdropping, even though that thought was ridiculous,
as she was, after all, sitting in her own garden. The conversation

was obviously serious, though. She started to wonder what their relationship was. Were they friends? Family? A couple? An avid watcher of people, Florence was definitely curious.

A door slamming, or perhaps being caught by the breeze as it drifted through the open window, signalled the end of the conversation, and the voices ceased. Shortly after that, she heard what she assumed was the side door to the house next door being opened and the sound of a car starting up, then nothing more.

She glanced at her watch and realised that it was probably about time to start thinking about dinner. Putting what she'd just heard out of her mind for now, she finished the rest of her wine and headed back into the house.

As she was perusing the contents of her fridge, her phone pinged from the worktop where she'd put it when she'd got home. Still short on inspiration for food, she wandered across to it and swiped for the message. It was her new friend, Josie, from school.

Hey! Forgot to mention today that I'm going to be directing the town's Christmas show. Can I count on your support, since you're a fellow part-time slacker? Might get you out to meet some new people! Jx

Florence grimaced slightly. She loved teaching drama in her English lessons, and was a total Shakespeare fiend, but the last thing she wanted to do was to actually stand up on stage and act. Besides, she really wasn't any good at that. She could pick apart a text to the nth degree, but when it came to performances, she was strictly a backstage girl.

But it *would* be nice to get out and do something in the community, rather than just going to work and coming back to Aunt Elsie's house. Perhaps if she made it crystal clear that behind the scenes was where she was best, it would be all right.

Texting something along those lines to Josie, she wondered

what the production would be about. She imagined some hokey alternative nativity was on the cards, but with Willowbury being just about as New Age as it was possible to get, perhaps it would be something entirely different. All the same, she was, she had to admit, curious to find out. And at least the thought of that, rather than facing the students on her first proper teaching day, would hopefully ensure calmer dreams tonight.

Finally deciding on a carton of fresh soup from her fridge and some crusty bread, she poured another glass of wine and settled in for the evening. Hopefully, now she'd spoken to Sam, it would be a quieter one.

6

As usual, Sam hadn't had time to go shopping, and, as usual, Aidan hadn't even considered that they needed to. Consequently, when Sam opened the cupboard above the cooker, looking for something to sustain him before his next night shift, all he found was a can of tomato soup and a packet of cream crackers. Sighing, he opened the can and chucked it into the only clean saucepan from the cupboard below. They really needed to sort out a more regular form of shopping than a madcap dash to the local Co-Op, topped up by random visits to the wealth of takeaway establishments that Willowbury incongruously offered., alongside all of the health and well-being, spiritual and New Age shops.

Resolving, once he'd had his soup, to get online and schedule a delivery from one of the bigger supermarkets, while he was waiting for the soup to warm through, he absent-mindedly nibbled on a cracker. He wasn't sure what his team leader would think about his choice of sustenance before a night shift, but, he reasoned, he was pretty sure he'd left a microwaveable lasagne in the fridge of the air ambulance base's kitchen anyway; he could always eat that, if there was enough downtime.

Once the soup was warm enough, Sam poured it into a bowl and took it to the kitchen table. Taking a spoonful, he realised too late that he'd heated it to thermonuclear temperatures as it nearly took the roof of his mouth off. He stood abruptly and grabbed the nearest glass from the draining board, downing the cold water swiftly in an attempt to stave off blisters. That was all he needed. He didn't even like tomato soup anyway, and now the bloody stuff was leaving him with third-degree burns.

Waiting a couple of minutes for the cursed stuff to cool, he stirred the spoon in the bowl absent-mindedly, forming figures of eight in the red mixture and ruminating on the fact that, while he was quite partial to a Bloody Mary, in whose juicy, alcohol-fuelled loveliness he could imagine himself back on ship floating around the Pacific and enjoying the company of his former squadron, canned tomato soup was about as far from this dream as it was possible to be. But then, *he* was about as far from that old life as it was possible to be, even if he was still flying heli-copters.

The ability to take off to sea and leave the land behind was something that he'd never really got over giving up, and much as he appreciated the security that living with Aidan in a house in the country now offered, he still felt incredibly landlocked by circum-stances. In the air, flying to a job or back to the base in Norton Magna, he could forget it for a while, but in the downtime, it came creeping back to him; the disillusionment, the restlessness, the frus-tration that a promising career in a job he loved was now beyond his reach.

Dispiritedly, he finished the soup as quickly as the warmth of it would allow, and then took a couple more cream crackers from the packet.

And, to cap it all, after their next-door neighbour's impromptu visit this afternoon, he'd have to make sure he had a word with

Aidan about plugging in his headphones when he indulged in a little late-night guitar playing.

Florence, that was her name, wasn't it? In his too-rudely awakened brain fog, it took him a second to remember. If Willowbury was anything like his parents' place, he wouldn't see his neighbours from one year's end to the next anyway, even if they did share a party wall. But the memory of her blonde hair and her friendly eyes, even when she'd been complaining about the noise, had stayed with Sam and if he was in a better place emotionally, he might even have considered asking her out. But what with the naval discharge, the move to a new place, the new job and the complications that sharing a house with Aidan entailed, there wasn't time left over for anything else. And how awkward would that be, anyway, starting something with the next-door neighbour? When the break-up came, as it inevitably would, they'd be stuck trying to avoid each other coming and going. It was far better to put her out of his mind and focus on what was important at present; doing his job and making sure Aidan kept out of trouble.

Standing up from the kitchen table, he took his now empty bowl to the sink, where it joined the rest of the crockery that had overflowed the decrepit dishwasher. They'd run out of tablets for that, too, and washing-up liquid.

Sam glanced at his watch. Not enough time to do the washing-up before he had to leave for work but perhaps enough to put an online shopping order in. Grabbing his phone, he logged onto the supermarket's site and started to fill his virtual basket. The one thing he wouldn't be adding to the list, he thought, was a replacement can of tomato soup.

7

The first couple of weeks of the new term sailed by for Florence, who was too busy getting to know her classes and, in the downtime, beginning to make a start on renovating the other rooms of Bay Tree Terrace, to think of much else. Josie had turned into a friend as well as a colleague, and they'd met for coffee a couple of times on their days off in the Cosy Coffee Shop. Over a mug or three of steaming fair-trade latte, Josie had outlined her plans for the Willowbury Christmas production.

'It's going to be a seasonally appropriate version of Shakespeare's *Much Ado About Nothing*,' Josie said. 'I've pared it down so that it'll run for just over an hour, and thrown in a ton of Christmas references. The masked ball is going to be a Christmas party, and of course, the stage'll be covered in mistletoe so that the two couples have good excuses to snog a lot.'

'Sounds great,' Florence said. 'Count me in for backstage support – I've become pretty good with a paintbrush, if scenery needs doing.'

Josie shot her a sidelong glance. 'Actually, I was rather hoping you'd help me with the auditions. Read some parts for me when the hordes arrive, that sort of thing.'

Florence nodded. 'Sure. Anything to help.' She didn't notice Josie smiling slightly into her latte. Little did she know that Josie had a lot more than just shifting scenery in mind for her new friend.

* * *

A couple of days later, Florence had one of the more unusual experiences of her teaching career when a high-priority email pinged around the staff, asking those on break duty to assemble on the school's playing field at the start of break time. Her eyes widened when she saw the reason why. She'd seen plenty of heavy military machinery up close, but never one of these. A small surge of excitement thrilled through her as she fired off a brief reply to the email, letting the head teacher's PA know she'd be on duty.

Half an hour later, she wasn't feeling quite so sanguine.

'I feel like an ambulance chaser,' Florence grumbled as she wrapped her coat more firmly around herself to combat the chilly breeze that was blowing directly down from the Mendip Hills and onto the school's playing fields. 'Are you sure we're allowed to be here, just watching?'

'Of course,' Josie said, as airily as the autumn wind itself. 'After all, there's no casualty on board at the moment, so we're not gawping over someone who's hurt, or worse. And how many times in your life have you seen one of those things landing or taking off, anyway?'

Florence conceded that Josie was right on that score. There was something quite exhilarating about being so close to a helicopter, after all.

The school field had a cordon of members of staff who'd been asked to ensure that no students got in the way of the craft as it was preparing to take off. Florence had been aware that it had landed on the generous playing fields of the school during her Year 8 lesson, from the deep, whickering throb of the rotor blades as they'd passed over the building. No amount of brand-new double glazing could keep out the low rumble of that noise, she'd realised. The class she'd been teaching had momentarily been distracted by the sight of the bright yellow air ambulance setting down on the fields behind her classroom, and even she'd stopped what she was doing to watch it for a few minutes. The rest of her lesson had been rather scrappy, to say the least, but eventually the children had lost interest when there wasn't a blood-soaked casualty to gawp at. Teenagers' taste for the macabre never ceased to amaze her.

Thankfully, it had turned out that the casualty was stable enough to go by road, so the students were denied their potential gore fest, and the injured party was spared their curious eyes. So now, as the Somerset Air Ambulance was waiting for clearance to take off, the school's staff had been requested to keep students back from the fields, in case any of them decided to make a break for it.

The pilot, who had spent a bit of time talking to staff and students, was around the other side of the helicopter. From her distance of about fifty feet, Florence could see his broad back, and his rather unruly dark blond hair. He had his back turned to the school, and to her, so she couldn't see his face, but she could see he was holding his audience of students, and the teachers who were keeping watch on the other side, captive with whatever he was saying.

'Tell me you're not having *Top Gun* fantasies,' Josie said wryly, following the line of Florence's gaze.

'Of course not,' Florence replied hurriedly. 'And anyway, that was planes.' Actually, it was rather more *Fifty Shades of Grey* than *Top Gun* that she had in mind. She might have had a giggle at the rest of the film, but Christian Grey's piloting, however fanciful, was actually quite sexy.

'Well, it looks like he'll be off in a minute,' Josie said as the small group of students who'd been chatting and their teacher made their retreat back across the field. 'I have to say, this wasn't quite how I envisioned spending my break time, but it's a damn sight better than marking Year Seven's assessments!'

'So we've just got to keep everyone back until he's taken off, now, then?' Florence said.

'Yup. Hopefully it won't be too much longer. I am getting a bit chilly.'

Florence watched as the pilot turned and came back alongside the helicopter, and as he glanced towards where she was standing, she gave an involuntary gasp, and felt her stomach flip. No... it couldn't be. Hurriedly, she turned away before he could recognise her.

Josie, hearing Florence's sudden intake of breath, gave a laugh. 'Now what did I tell you about fantasising? Although he is pretty fit, I'll give you that.'

'Er... right.' Florence was far too embarrassed to confess that it wasn't exactly fantasy that had caused her to gasp. Rather more that the pilot who was just about to get that impressive machine up into the air was, in fact, the next-door neighbour she'd had to confront about the three a.m. music sessions before her first day at school. And, of course! Now she realised where she'd seen him before. He was the person she'd nearly run over on the zebra crossing at the start of term, too. She ducked her head, hoping the high collar of her coat would disguise her from any attention he might have paid her.

'What's up?' Josie, who had a nose for a good scandal, peered curiously at Florence, who knew she'd gone a most unbecoming shade of puce, despite the autumn breeze.

'Nothing,' Florence responded, sounding like the teenagers she'd been teaching.

'Yeah right!' Josie grinned. 'Have you got the hots for our sexy helicopter pilot? Love at first sight, is it?'

'Not exactly first sight,' as the words came out of her mouth without thinking, Florence cursed herself. There was no way Josie was going to let *that* go.

'You'd better be free at lunchtime,' Josie said. 'And then you can tell me where you've seen that gorgeous hunk of flying manliness before.'

'Let's just keep an eye on the kids, shall we?' Florence said archly, scanning the crowd for any incidents of poor behaviour that could divert Josie's attention from a potential interrogation. Sadly, the children were all too excited to see the helicopter up close to consider messing about, for once.

As the pilot shut the door of the helicopter, Florence could see that he was checking a number of switches and, within a minute or so, the rotor at the back and the large one on the roof of the helicopter had started to spin, slowly at first and then with increasing velocity until the blades became a blur, and then, oddly, seemed to stand still, they were moving so fast. The breeze that started as a whisper whipped up until Florence was brushing her hair back from her eyes. Then the roar started.

'I told you it was worth waiting for,' Josie raised her voice above the engines. 'I might be a country bumpkin, but how often do you get to see a helicopter taking off up close?'

Florence was reluctant to take her eyes off the air ambulance but managed to glance around to make sure that the staff cordon was still in place, and that no overexcited students were trying to do a James Bond and storm the helicopter before take-off.

The noise was growing louder, and Florence could feel the earth under her feet vibrating as the air ambulance reached full power. Then, graceful as a dancer leaping onstage, the helicopter started to lift, until it hovered a couple of feet above the ground. It floated there for a moment, and Florence could see the pilot doing a few final checks before the helicopter rose further. Then, in an almost stage-like nod to its audience of students and teachers, the pilot turned the helicopter around to face the gathered spectators at the edge of the school field. He hovered the craft ten feet above the ground for a few seconds, allowing students to take photos and videos, before turning the craft back around and rising further into the air, its vibrant yellow stingingly bright against the grey September sky. In another few seconds, it had risen at great speed and, as Florence watched, it sped across the sky, vanishing from sight in a matter of moments.

A murmur of disappointment rumbled around the spectators as, perfectly on cue, the bell rang for the next lesson change-over, breaking the spell and restoring all of them back down to the now still earth.

'Come on, you lot,' Josie called to the nearest group of students. 'Time to get back to lessons.'

Amidst mild rumbles of dissent, the students shuffled off to where they should be for the last period before lunch.

Josie looked at her watch. 'Right. Just time to swing by the office and grab a coffee to take with me to class Seven Oh-bloody-hell-not-them,' she said, giving Florence a martyred grin. 'And at lunchtime you can tell me all about your first encounter with that stunning pilot.'

Florence sighed. Josie could make a drama out of anything, and, really, there wasn't much to tell. Not that the truth would deter Josie from making a good story out of it, she was sure.

8

'Oh God, not this one again. Really?' Air ambulance paramedic Haleh 'pronounce it like the comet' Constantine groaned as Sam tapped the screen on his phone and the cabin was filled with a recognisable beat.

'Pilot picks the music,' Sam said wryly as 2Pac's 'California Love' rolled its way, once again, through the cockpit. At the end of a call-out, if they weren't going on to another job but were returning to base, Sam liked to take down the operational tension a notch or two by playing music on board and, when they happened to be flying back over a particular landmark, dropping their height by a little so that the landscape swept past them in sharper focus. This after-noon they were heading back from Weston-super-Mare after the patient had been transferred by road to the Bristol Royal Infirmary. It was their second callout of the shift, having been summoned to the playing fields at Willowbury Academy after a pensioner had fallen down the stairs of their terraced house that backed onto the school's playing fields. The SAA had the capacity to hop from job to job, so after stabilising the pensioner, they'd been called to a sports centre in Weston after a rugby training session had resulted in a neck injury to one of the players. Once again, the expert medical team had stabilised the casualty enough to send them by road ambulance to the Bristol Royal Infirmary, so they were flying back to their base at Norton Magna to replenish their supplies.

Now that the cloud had cleared and the sky was blue, this was a trip that would take no longer than about twenty minutes and as Sam had already logged height, direction and air speed with Air Traffic Control, the team was looking forward to a cuppa and a cake back at base. It had been Haleh's birthday at the weekend, and she'd brought in enough pastries and cakes to feed an infantry division.

Given the short distance between the job and base, there wasn't much opportunity for an extensive in-flight playlist, but Sam had been riffing a lot on the rap music of his youth lately. It amused him, as an adult, that as a somewhat diffident, white, middle-class, teenage boy, he'd been so enamoured of 2Pac and the other mid-nineties rap giants, but he still had a lot of affection for them and their genius.

'Not exactly a fair rule,' Neil Sims, the duty doctor who was currently sitting in the front seat next to Sam commented. 'It's not like any of us can jump into your chair and take over.'

Sam grinned at Neil, who, in addition to being the chief medic on board, also doubled as technical crew. Neil was responsible for running through the pre-flight checks alongside Sam and knew almost as much about the operation of the helicopter as he did.

'I reckon technical crew should get a choice of playlists as well, sometimes,' Neil added.

'No way,' Sam laughed. 'The last time I let you have control over the back-to-base playlists, there was so much Radiohead, I nearly threw myself out of the door!'

'Nothing wrong with Radiohead; keeps our patients sedated

longer than this crap,' Neil, who was drier than the Serengeti in August, deadpanned.

'Precisely my point,' Sam said, still grinning. 'You don't want your pilot asleep on the job, do you?'

A guffaw from behind him, where Haleh and the second of the paramedics, Darren, were sitting, made Sam glance back.

'Behave or I'll throw a bit of Marilyn Manson onto the next playlist.'

'I wouldn't mind that, actually,' said Haleh. 'Back in the day I went through a bit of a goth phase.'

'I can't imagine you smothered in black lipstick and looking miserable,' Sam teased the seemingly perennially cheerful Haleh. She was the voice of calm and positivity in the team, and Sam really enjoyed working with her, as she could always put any job into perspective, no matter how terrible it seemed at the time. She'd got the team through some dark trips back from the more traumatic jobs, and somehow always had a way of being able to see the light in the darkness. He was glad she was part of the team.

Sam looked down as the varying green patchwork of fields flowed beneath them, bisected by roads where the traffic seemed to move at a snail's pace from the view of the helicopter. The sky was a vibrant, cloudless blue, in contrast to the countryside beneath, which, in addition to the fields, was broken up occasionally by clumps of forest, scattered with evergreen and beech trees, turning a vibrant copper in the late-autumn season.

They approached the magnificent contours of Cheddar Gorge at a leisurely pace, flying low enough so that a couple of dog walkers on the top flat looked up and raised their arms in greeting, and even the mad-looking collies they were with looked up, intrigued by the noise. Then it was across the M5, a long, straight expanse of motorway that led to the Devon border and the home of the Helimed Control Centre in Exeter, who co-ordinated all of the incoming jobs.

'You reckon we'll make it back without another callout?' Haleh's voice came over the radio system.

'Well, since we've done two jobs already, I'm not sure we could get back out without going home first,' Neil replied. He was helping Darren to compile a checklist of current onboard supplies, ready to replenish before another job. 'If Helimed Control calls one in before we get back, we'd better decline.'

'Great,' Sam said. 'I could do with a coffee before we head out again, if we need to.' He glanced back at the instruments and adjusted slightly to accommodate for the increased wind speed this side of Cheddar Gorge. The West Country weather could be capricious, and it was essential to stay on top of conditions at all times. 'Let's hope the tourists don't cause an accident on the motorway before the end of the shift.' The M5 was notorious for accidents caused by visitors to the counties of Somerset and Devon; not a week went by when at least one stretch of it wasn't closed to clear up.

'Amen to that,' Darren replied.

The crew fell into a companionable silence as they approached the base and Sam began his landing checks. On a day like this, when a casualty was likely to have a good outcome, it was easy to feel optimistic, to appreciate the positives of the job they all did. Sometimes it wasn't quite so easy, when it was too late to treat someone, and the darkness would creep in post-operation. But, on this beautiful Somerset day, all was optimism.

9

When Florence got home from school, the ever-present box of books to mark under one arm and her laptop case slung over the other shoulder, she hurried more quickly than usual through her door, just in case she encountered Sam on the doorstep. Since she'd realised he'd been the man she'd nearly mown down on the zebra crossing, she'd been more than a little embarrassed at the prospect of seeing him again. She'd also promised to cast an eye over Josie's pared down *Much Ado* script that evening and, at some point, she had to eat. She certainly had enough to take her mind off the images that kept persistently running through her mind of Sam in his pilot's uniform on the school field, and then taking off into the skies above. That, combined with the persistent memory of his appearance in his sleepwear at the front door was enough to make her want to see him again. Although she was never going to admit to having nearly run him over; not in a million years.

Sitting down to a big bowl of her favourite macaroni cheese three quarters of an hour later, she swiped open her Kindle and began to read through Josie's script. A seasonal adaptation of the famous tale of enemies-to-lovers Beatrice and Benedick, and love's-young-but-thwarted-dream Hero and Claudio, Florence immediately noticed that Beatrice and Benedick's roles had been beefed up, and Claudio and Hero's pared down to avoid Shakespeare's somewhat anachronistic, and rather brutal, treatment of the latter. In fact, apart from one or two little scenes of conflict and then resolution, the focus was much more on Beatrice and Benedick.

She found herself laughing out loud at the early scenes, which took all the comedy moments from Beatrice and Benedick's relationship and set them against the backdrop of a wintry Willowbury, then smiled as Josie skilfully interwove the Shakespearean with her own adaptation, having them bickering with each other, falling under the spell of their friends' chatter, stumbling foul of the 'Willowbury Whisperers', who did their best to split up Hero and Claudio, and then, happily, all ending well and in a passionate kiss under the mistletoe. The ringleader of the 'Willowbury Whisperers' was the Don John figure, the mischief-maker of the play, but, pleasingly, he got his comeuppance and was dunked in a pan of mulled cider at the end.

It was part pantomime, part *Shakespeare Retold*, but was guaranteed to be very entertaining. It also seemed to fit the slightly odd world of Willowbury to a T, bringing in elements of Winterfest, the celebration of all things frosty, which took place in the town every year. It would, she was sure, go down a treat with the locals.

After making a couple of notes on a scene or two, Florence emailed Josie with her thoughts and then put her plate in the sink, wishing she'd got her act together and arranged to have the kitchen of Aunt Elsie's cottage refitted before she'd moved in.

Wandering upstairs, she didn't feel quite like settling into her evening's marking just yet; not on a stomach full of macaroni cheese, anyway. Suddenly curious to investigate the only place in the house she'd not fully checked out yet, she stepped down the landing until she was standing underneath the hatch to the house's loft space. As a child, the loft had always fascinated Florence, even though she'd never been allowed up there. 'Imagine if you put a foot down and stepped through the ceiling!' Aunt Elsie always said when Florence had mithered her to go up.

Reaching up to grab the cord that would pull the counter-weighted steps down from the loft, Florence felt in her back pocket for her phone, so she could use it as a torch. The blast of cooler air from the roof space as the hatch came down to reveal the concertinaed steps to the loft cautioned her that she should probably check out the roof insulation at some point, too. But tonight she just wanted to take a quick look inside the space she was never allowed to go into when she'd been Aunt Elsie's guest.

As she ascended the steps, she shone the phone torch around her, trying to get a sense of the loft space. Perhaps one day it would be nice to use the space for something other than storage, if she could afford to pay for the conversion. She noticed there was a pile of cardboard boxes off to one corner, but before she could investigate further, her phone rang. Swiping the screen to talk to her mum, who was just calling to check in, she forgot all about the contents of the loft as she headed back downstairs.

10

Sam drove back home after his shift finished in the late afternoon and felt relieved that, for once, the kitchen cupboards were going to be full. He was ravenous, as he often was when he returned to base, and he was looking forward to a decentish dinner, a couple of beers and an early night. It took him a few days to adjust back to working daylight hours, but he finally felt as though he was coming out of the other side of the night-shift pattern he'd been working.

He loved his job, despite the interminable waiting around that often seemed to follow a callout. He wasn't fazed by having to carry casualties, having gained an awful lot of his flying hours ferrying injured soldiers on and off ships. It was easy to divorce himself from the often upsetting realities of the job by focusing on the technicalities; the many checks that had to be carried out before he was able to take-off; the permissions that must be gained in order to leave the ground. There was a kind of elegance, a balance to it that enabled him to keep a clear head despite what may have been going on behind him in the treatment area of the helicopter. That wasn't to say that he was cold-hearted; seeing broken bodies being loaded into the back, especially when they belonged to children or the equally vulnerable, was harrowing, but, much like the medics themselves, or the other emergency staff that attended, it was essential to protect his own mental health in these high-stress situations; the processing always came later.

As he went through the post that had been delivered earlier that day, he laid aside the letters for Aidan to peruse when he surfaced. Since Sam had spoken to him about the late-night guitar playing, Aidan had, mercifully, remembered to plug in his expensive new headphones. At least Florence wouldn't be storming around complaining again. Although, Sam thought unguardedly, he'd quite like to see her again; if not within the context of a neighbourly complaint.

He wondered how she was settling into her new school. He didn't know where she was teaching, but as he'd landed the air ambulance on the field behind the newly built Willowbury Academy, thoughts of her had crossed his mind. He quite liked talking to people when he had to land in a more public place, and the Willowbury students had seemed polite and well mannered, if a little excited about having the helicopter landing on their football pitch. It was funny, he thought; he'd caught sight of a blonde teacher with a ponytail about a hundred yards from where he'd landed, but she was too far away to recognise. He wondered if it had actually been Florence. Willowbury Academy was certainly convenient for her house, although he did wonder about living and working in the same town; what teacher would want to be sprung doing something silly by their own students?

Among the letters and junk mail, Sam noticed a brightly coloured flyer advertising auditions for something called the annual Willowbury Dramatical Spectacular. Glancing at it, he shook his head. He was no actor. But, on further inspection, it seemed that the proceeds from the performances would be going to a charity that he knew very well; the self-same charity that he worked for. Although he absolutely wasn't going to get roped into doing any acting, he did wonder if perhaps he could help to publicise it in other ways. The Somerset Air Ambulance, like all of the UK's air ambulance services, was totally funded by donations from the public to enable it to run. Perhaps he could get some flyers and magazines for them to hand out with the tickets? It would give him an excuse to get involved with the community without having to dive straight in and get caught up in the details of staging the production.

Making a mental note to grab some of the promotional materials from the base the next time he was at work, he wandered through to the kitchen and opened the fridge. Since the online shopping order had arrived during the afternoon, Aidan had put it all away, and Sam was surprised to note that he'd actually arranged the fridge rather well. It was a far cry from the early days, when he'd be unable to sustain his attention on even the simplest of tasks. But then, a lot had changed since the early days, Sam thought, and even more since the time before. But there was no sense in focusing on that; what was done was done. It was all about going forward now.

With that sobering thought suddenly uppermost in his mind, Sam pulled out a fairly decent looking pre-prepared shepherd's pie from the fridge, along with a bottle of lager to drink while it was baking, and settled down at the kitchen counter to go through the rest of the post.

As he was carelessly opening envelopes and taking in their contents, he realised he'd opened one of Aidan's in error. It was a letter from the local health authority, and, despite himself, Sam found his eyes scanning it. Aidan was under the care of the GP but had been referred to a counselling service for some cognitive behavioural therapy. This was the most recent in a line of talking therapies, intended to complement the medication that Aidan would, in all likelihood, be on for the rest of his life. Sam noticed that the date was for next Friday. Scrawling a hasty note on the envelope, he placed it in Aidan's pile of mail. With Aidan, routine was key, and Sam intended to make sure he kept to it as much as possible. When he didn't, life became a whole lot more complicated, and complications were something neither Sam nor Aidan needed any more of after the last two harrowing years.

11

The Saturday of the auditions for the Willowbury Dramatical Spectacular dawned bright and chilly, and as Florence threw on jeans and her favourite cosy jumper, she felt a thrill of excitement at the turn in the weather. Though she loved the summer, what she really adored was the autumn frost; the crispness of an early morning where the mist rolled over the crystalline blades of grass in the fields and the nip of the cold against noses and fingertips was energising. It helped that the run-up to Christmas was always the best term, as well; the students were madly keen to show some seasonal spirit, even if the requests to watch films in class tended to start in mid-November.

This morning in late October seemed to herald the change from the Indian summer of recent weeks to more usual autumn weather. As she opened her bedroom curtains and looked out into her back garden, Florence's gaze was drawn to the sheep grazing at the top of the hills that her house backed onto, and there was a cooler scent in the air when she threw open her window. Having spent a fair amount of her life in Yorkshire, she wasn't afraid of cold weather.

A ping from her mobile phone on the bedside table drew her

attention away from the early-morning rural scene outside her window, and she padded across to check it. It was a message from Josie, just double-checking she was still OK to help out with the auditions. Texting back a quick affirmative, Florence wandered down to the kitchen to grab some breakfast and a coffee.

Willowbury had its fair share of eccentric and unusual characters, and she wondered how many would show up to audition for Josie's revamped play. One thing was certain; it was going to make for an interesting morning.

* * *

'I'm not sure about this, Josie,' Florence said, looking in trepidation at the musty hall, the aged upright piano tucked in the corner, and the rickety-looking stage area at the front. 'I mean, I know the play all right, but I haven't been on stage since I was a sheep in the school nativity play!'

'Oh, it'll come back to you,' Josie said, unconcerned. 'It's just like riding a bike.'

'I broke my arm riding a bike when I was six,' Florence muttered, wondering if it was too late to back out. 'That stage looks like it's seen better days, too.'

'I wouldn't worry,' Josie pulled open one of the dusty curtains that blocked out the light from the hall. 'Anyway, this is just a temporary rehearsal space. The actual production's going to be in the visitors' centre on the priory site, remember?'

'If they finish it on time,' Florence replied. 'At this rate, we could be performing in the ruined nave of the priory on the shortest day of the year!' She'd been intrigued when she'd taken ownership of Aunt Elsie's house to see that the priory, that had been broken apart during the Reformation, had finally been acquired by the National Trust, after much toing and froing on the economic viability of such a project. It had been something that the local MP, Charlie Thorpe, had been keen to push through during his first term of office, and there had been much rejoicing when it had been achieved with a combination of local petitioning of the trust and his intervention on the town's behalf. Now to be saved in perpetuity, like all buildings taken on by the National Trust, no time had been wasted in earmarking a clear patch of ground on the site to build a visitors' centre, which would also double as a performance space for community projects. The building was nearly finished, but there were jobs left to do before it could be signed off. The performance would be the debut show, and so Josie was keen to involve as much of the community as possible.

'That's the spirit!' Josie replied, her optimism seemingly undentable.

'I'm serious, though,' Florence said. 'I'm happy to stand in and read some parts, but I'm strictly behind the scenes when you've got everyone you need on board. I'll paint as much scenery as you want, but I'm not going on stage.'

'Look,' Josie said patiently, 'I know you don't want to be part of the cast, but I need a few people to show willing for the others. This town is full of wannabe acting divas, I'm sure, but I need someone who actually knows their stuff to make the others raise their game. So, what do you reckon? Humour me. Do it for a mate?'

Josie, once she got into full-on persuasive mode, was irresistible.

'I'll read some lines,' Florence conceded, 'but only until someone better comes along.'

As if on cue, the door to the hall opened and a stocky, muscular, sandy-haired man walked confidently through. Looking to be in his mid-thirties, he wore a broad smile and a collarless linen shirt, and had a twinkle in his eye.

'Good morning,' he said cheerily as he approached where Josie and Florence were setting up some chairs for the audition space. 'Am I in the right place? I'm here for the casting.'

Florence chanced a look in Josie's direction before watching her friend shake the man's thrust-forward hand.

'Yes, that's right,' Josie replied. 'I'm Josie Sellars, the director, and this is Florence Ashton.'

'Nice to meet you,' the man replied. Hesitating slightly, as if he expected recognition, he added somewhat regretfully afterward, 'I'm Tom Sanderson.'

Florence couldn't help but notice the upward inflection as he announced his name. Perhaps they were in the presence of someone who she ought to recognise? Josie hadn't mentioned anything about any thespians of note living in Willowbury, and, Florence reasoned, she hadn't been living there long enough to find out for herself. Perhaps this guy had some sort of claim to fame?

Josie, who was looking quizzical at the mention of his name, suddenly beamed. 'Oh, of course. I remember you. Weren't you on *Britain's Got Talent* a few years back?'

Tom looked pleased. 'Yes, that's right. Simon... you know, Simon Cowell, said I had great potential for the West End.'

Florence wondered, in that case, why he was still lurking around Willowbury, if London had come calling. She only just stopped herself from asking before Tom cut back in.

'Of course, an audition for RADA helped, but I was keen to explore my roots here, give something back to the community, so to speak.'

Ah, that was more like it, Florence thought. She was finely tuned to blarney and excuses; she wouldn't have lasted five minutes as a teacher if she hadn't been able to suss out the truth from the convenient fibs, and it was clear to her that Tom's story was perhaps hiding a subtler, less flattering truth. However, she didn't think too much of it; after all, she'd be working behind the scenes on backstage details, and Josie, as director, would have to deal with actorly egos more than she would. And she'd never been a fan of TV talent shows.

'So, Tom,' Josie began, 'as you know, we're casting for the lead roles for *Much Ado About Christmas* today. It's a mash-up of *Much Ado About Nothing* with some seasonal and local references, mostly told in updated English. Do you know the original play at all?'

'Indeed, I do,' Tom replied portentously. 'I played Claudio at university, but, as I've got older, I've a yen to play a more substantial role. Benedick, perhaps, or Don Pedro.'

He obviously fancied himself as Kenneth Branagh in the making, Florence thought; all the way from his perfectly cultivated goatee (with a trace of ginger) to his designer brogues. What a pity he didn't seem to have Branagh's charisma.

'Well, perhaps you'd like to read for Benedick this morning, and we'll go from there.' Josie looked down at her clipboard, where she had several copies of two of Benedick's key speeches from the play. She passed both scenes to Tom. 'Have a quiet read for a few minutes, and then feel free to present one of these to us when you're ready.'

Tom took the papers and squinted down at the small print. Florence surmised that reading glasses would have been his preference, but vanity had prevented him from bringing them to the audition.

'And, Florence, once Tom's ready, would you read Beatrice if needs be?' Josie said, a mischievous look in her eye.

'Sure,' Florence muttered. 'So long as you don't expect me to actually act!'

'Not fond of the stage?' Tom interjected, glancing up from the script.

'Not if I can help it,' Florence replied. 'But since I've taught this play to a lot of students over the years, I said I'd lend a hand.'

'Oh, a valiant pedagogue!' Tom chuckled. 'How noble of you in this day and age. You have my sympathy.'

'Oh, there's no need for sympathy,' Florence shot back just as quickly. 'I love my job. It's all I've ever wanted to do.'

'Glad to hear it,' Tom replied. 'After all, we need dedicated professionals.'

Rather getting the feeling that she was being patronised, Florence looked back down at her copy of the script. Suddenly, she could think of far better things to be doing on a Saturday morning than standing in a damp-smelling village hall listening to would-be actors. But a promise was a promise.

* * *

To her surprise, despite Tom's pompous manner, he was actually quite a decent actor, and Florence found herself getting into the role of Beatrice as they played the first scene with the two of them baiting each other after Benedick and the other soldiers return from the 'Christmas Shopping High Street Wars'. She could see how Tom could make a very good stab at the role, and that Josie, much to her own surprise, seemed to be thinking the same.

'Thanks so much,' Josie said as they got to the end of the scene. 'That was great.'

Tom bowed with only a trace of irony. 'A pleasure.' He looked at her expectantly, and this seemed to get Josie's back up a little, despite his good performance.

'I'll be posting the cast choices on the Facebook page I've created for the production by the end of the day,' Josie replied. 'So be sure to check it out and see if you've made the cut.'

'I shall do,' Tom replied, obviously nonplussed by this abrupt dismissal. He glanced from Josie to Florence and back again. 'I look

forward to working with you, and bringing this production to life.'
And with that, he walked out of the door.

As the rickety door to the hall banged closed behind him,
Florence burst out laughing. 'Is he for real?'

'Sadly, yes,' Josie replied. 'But, the thing is, he may very well
be the best we've got.' She looked speculatively at Florence. 'And I
have to say, your reaction to him worked brilliantly. Are you sure
I can't twist your arm to be onstage rather than behind the
scenes?'

'Nope,' Florence said firmly. 'And I don't care how well it worked
with Tom – I'd throttle him for real if I had to play Beatrice to his
Benedick!'

'The audience would love it,' Josie said slyly.

Florence, pretending to occupy herself with reading the script,
chose to ignore her.

* * *

At five to twelve and after innumerable auditions, which included
six main speaking roles and a handful of more minor ones, Josie
and Florence were just about to call it a day. The auditions had
ranged from the wonderful – a young drama student doing her A
levels at nearby Stavenham Sixth Form College, who would be
absolutely perfect as the play's version of Hero – to the frankly
appalling efforts of the handsome but rather wooden mobile black-
smith, whose anvil would have had more charisma than he did.
However, Josie seemed confident that she could cast all roles
successfully by the time Florence's stomach started rumbling for
lunch, except for the key role of Beatrice, the play's quick-witted
heroine.

They were about to switch off the lights and go their separate
ways when the door to the hall opened. Glancing up from the list of

names that Josie had handed her, Florence was surprised, and a little flustered, to see Sam Ellis standing in the doorway.

'What are you doing here?' she asked, then blushed at her rather ungracious tone. 'I mean... have you come to audition?'

'Not likely!' Sam replied, ignoring Florence's rather direct first question. 'I thought I'd drop off the flyers for the air ambulance unit, in case anyone wants to gift aid a donation after the performance.'

Smiling, Josie took them from him. 'Thanks.' She looked quizzically at Sam for a moment, and then recognition dawned on her face. 'Are you the pilot who landed on the school field the other day?'

Sam nodded. 'Yes, that's right. We've used it a few times for call-outs around there.'

'I thought I recognised you,' Josie replied. 'Don't you recognise him too, Florence?'

Florence, face feeling hot, nodded. 'I should do,' she said, 'since we live next door to each other as well.'

At Josie's surprised twitch of the eyebrows, Florence realised she'd never got the chance to fill Josie in on her connections to Sam, that lunchtime after the helicopter had landed on the school field. Josie was clearly hurriedly filling in the gaps now.

'Well, isn't that a coincidence?' Josie kept smiling as she turned her gaze back to Sam.

Don't, Josie... Florence thought. But she was beginning to discover that with Josie, there was no such word as don't.

'Are you sure we can't persuade you to do a quick audition?' Josie teased as she placed the flyers down on the table. She waved a copy of the script at Sam. 'After all, you're quite new to the village and it would be a good way to get to know people.'

Sam laughed apprehensively, seemingly unnerved by the steamroller of Josie's persuasive charm heading towards him. 'No, honestly, drama's really not my thing. Besides, my shift patterns involve working a lot of nights, so I wouldn't really be available for rehearsals or performances.'

'Oh, you don't have to be in the main cast,' Josie said airily, glancing down to consult her list. 'I need— I mean, the production needs a few non-speaking soldier roles, and I'm sure you'd look great in uniform.'

Florence giggled, wondering if Josie knew how flirtatious she sounded. Sam glanced at her, and she found herself colouring in response to his irritated expression.

'Come on! Humour me and read a little bit of the scene where Benedick talks about love,' Josie thrust a piece of paper into Sam's hands. 'Just for fun.'

Sam looked as though he was just about to refuse point blank, when Florence stopped smirking and found her voice. 'Don't push him, Josie, if he doesn't want to. I'm sure he's got more important things to do than be in our production.'

Perhaps it was her slightly challenging tone, but at her words, Sam straightened up a little, and his clear blue eyes glinted. 'Don't you think I'm up to it?' he asked.

'Well, I know you're really busy,' Florence replied. 'I can tell from the way you're hanging around your house all the time when you're not working.'

'Christ, you're as bad as my...' Sam trailed off, then, with a game smile turned to Josie. 'Let's give it a go.' He cleared his throat, glanced at the piece of paper and smiled. 'I remember some of the original story from school.'

Was Florence imagining things, or was Sam blushing as he read the scene to himself?

'When you're ready,' Josie prompted, a trace of amusement in her voice.

Sam cleared his throat, glanced up at the two women and

began: 'I really do wonder why men seem to make such idiots of themselves when it comes to love? You wouldn't catch me dressing up or writing poetry to impress a woman. Honestly, I can't believe Claudio's wasting his time trying to get Hero to marry him!'

Sam struck a suitably irritable tone for Josie's interpretation of Benedick's great diatribe on the nature of love, and Florence was quietly impressed. As he continued on with the rewritten and modernised speech, she found her eyes drawn to his face. Half reading, but glancing up every so often to gauge the reaction of his audience of two, Sam seemed to be relaxing, and perhaps even starting to enjoy it.

As he reached the end of the speech, Josie put her clipboard down on the table beside her and clapped.

'Brilliant! Far better than anything we've seen so far. Present company excluded, of course.' She glanced at Florence. 'Wouldn't you agree, Beatrice?'

Florence stared at Josie, agog. 'Er... what?'

'You heard me.' Josie's eyes twinkled. 'The question is, do we even need to discuss who's going to play Benedick? I mean, let's face it, there's not been a lot of other choices.'

'Thanks,' Sam said drily. 'But, as I said, my shift patterns involve a lot of nights, so I don't think I could commit to the play, anyway. It was fun auditioning, but I really don't have the time to spare.'

'That's a shame,' sighed Josie. 'You're far and away the best male we've had. Ah well.' She glanced at Florence. 'Looks like you'll be alongside Tom Sanderson, then.'

Florence suppressed a grimace. 'Do I really have to be Beatrice? Can't you find someone else?'

'Afraid not,' Josie grinned. 'You were here all morning, right? Beatrice is the only role we didn't have anyone suitable for, except for you, of course. Besides, you're the only one under forty but over twenty-five who's actually any good. And you're too old to play

Hero, so Bea it is.' She looked back at Sam. 'But you're not off the hook entirely. I'm going to put you down as Tom's understudy, so if he does get a last-minute call-up to Broadway, you'll be on stage. Got it?'

Sam looked dubious. 'Does that mean I'll have to learn all the lines?'

'Yup, but attendance at rehearsals isn't mandatory – I'm sure, living next door to Florence, she'll be able to keep you posted about any, er, developments.'

Thanks, Josie, Florence thought. She was still embarrassed about nearly running Sam down on the crossing, although she had to concede that at least things had been a lot quieter next door lately.

She knew by now that it was useless to argue with Josie once she had her mind set on something. Out loud, she merely said, 'That's fine.'

Sam shook his head. 'I had no idea that dropping off a bunch of leaflets would mean I got strong-armed into being an understudy.'

'Count yourself lucky,' Florence quipped. 'I only came to give Josie moral support, and I've been cast as bloody Beatrice!' Her laughter seemed to put Sam a little more at ease, and as he smiled, she again found herself thinking how attractive he was. Clean-shaven, and in a pale grey jumper that looked enticingly like it might be cashmere, and dark blue jeans, there was no disputing his attractiveness. And there was that morning she'd seen him in his flight suit, of course, when the air ambulance had landed on the school field. She couldn't help drawing another *Top Gun* comparison at the memory. Sam looked just as good in his uniform overalls as Tom Cruise had as Maverick, and had the distinct advantage of being a fair bit taller.

'Anyway, I'd better get going,' Sam said. He gave Florence a slightly quizzical look, and at that moment, she definitely knew that he knew she'd been checking him out. 'Is there anything I need to do, as the understudy?'

'Well, if you could learn the lines and turn up to as many rehearsals as you can, that would be good, although I have a feeling that nothing short of a bomb under him could keep Tom off the stage!' Josie smiled, but Florence, who was still watching Sam closely, noticed that he didn't return the smile; instead, it seemed as though Josie had unwittingly touched a nerve.

'Right,' he said abruptly. 'Well, keep me posted.' He left the two women to it.

'Was it something I said?' Josie asked Florence.

'Who knows?' Florence replied. 'I wouldn't worry. If he's only the understudy, I'm sure we won't need to see much of him.' Although, she thought privately, she wasn't sure who it would have been easier to act opposite: Tom, whose luvviness was bound to irritate her, or Sam, who she felt distinctly attracted to.

'Shame about his crazy work shifts,' Josie said. 'If I had my way, I'd have cast him as the lead instead of Tom. But it can't be helped.'

As Florence, too, said goodbye and wandered back to her house for a late lunch, she couldn't help mulling over Sam's sudden change of mood when Josie had joked about Tom. Perhaps he didn't like to be lumped into the same category as such an obvious twerp as Tom, although he didn't seem like the oversensitive type.

Trying to drag her mind away from the sight of Sam's torso in that wonderfully form-fitting cashmere jumper, she tried to think instead about scheduling the kitchen fitters. Aunt Elsie's house needed a lot of work, and the kitchen was the most urgent. She wanted to get it done before Christmas, if possible, but was getting fed up with looking at flooring, tiles and units. Resolving to make some actual decisions this weekend, she put Sam, and his odd behaviour, out of her mind.

12

A week later, about half an hour into the first read through of the Willowbury Dramatical Spectacular, Florence was amazed that Josie was still smiling. Having announced the cast list via the Facebook page she'd set up after the auditions were complete, the first time they'd all been in the same room together had certainly been eventful. It had all started amiably enough, Josie having bought enough coffee and pastries to fortify most of the West End, but soon it was obvious that certain members of the cast, including Tom Sanderson, he of the *Britain's Got Talent* audition, had very definite ideas on interpretation. Florence thought she'd scream if she heard the words 'when I was in the Bristol Theatre School production...' one more time. This was hardly a large-scale, professional production, after all; it was just supposed to be a bit of festive fundraising entertainment to benefit the very worthy cause of the Somerset Air Ambulance.

'OK, let's take a break,' Josie said about an hour and a half into the read-through, by which time, given all the interruptions, they'd only read about half of the play. She nodded in Tom's direction to acknowledge yet another point he was making, and then suggested they take fifteen minutes to stretch their legs before resuming.

'Christ, Josie, I don't think I can do this,' Florence said, the minute Tom and most of the rest of the cast were out of earshot. 'I mean, it's not that your script isn't great, but if Tom makes one more suggestion for interpretation or emphasis, I think I'm going to feed it to him!'

Josie rolled her eyes. 'I know, but it's only the first time we've all come together. He's just trying to throw his weight around. Ignore him.'

'That's all very well for you to say – you don't have to cosy up to him in the second half.' Florence took a defiant bite of one of the Danish pastries. 'God, that new guy at Fairbrothers' Bakery knows how to make the best flaky pastry,' she mumbled in appreciation.

'Hopefully he'll stick around for a while,' Josie replied. 'Fairbrothers tends to get through their staff quite quickly.'

'You mean they have a high turnover?' Florence quipped weakly. She was struggling to find the humour in working with Tom, which she knew was going to be important as the nights grew shorter and the production got into full swing.

Josie rolled her eyes. 'I hope you can inject a little more humour into your lines than that, after the break.'

Thankfully, a bit of fresh air seemed to knock some of the stuffiness out of Tom, and during the second half of the read-through he was noticeably quieter. At the end, he lingered while Josie and Florence put the chairs away and washed up the coffee mugs.

'I think that went well,' he said brightly, grabbing a couple of the chairs and stacking them in one corner of the hall.

'Hmmm…' Florence murmured non-committally.

Tom hesitated, as if he was working up the nerve to say something else. This reticence seemed so unlike the blustering thespian of the first part of the rehearsal that Florence immediately felt a little defensive.

'I was just wondering, though, if you might be, er, open to doing a few extra rehearsals, just you and me, as well as working with the rest of the cast,' Tom eventually blurted out.

'Well,' Florence started, shocked by his sudden request. 'Shouldn't we just try to build a rapport between us all for the early ones? It seems a bit unfair to sneak off behind their backs and rehearse on our own.' She smiled what she hoped was an encouraging smile in Tom's direction.

'Ye-es,' Tom replied doubtfully. 'It's just... can I be frank, Florence?'

I thought you were Tom, Florence thought mutinously, before zoning back into what he was saying. 'Of course.'

'I just don't feel, as a professional, you understand, that you're quite committing to your role in our paired scenes. I know this is only a small-town production, but I'm just not feeling Beatrice.'

Florence nearly choked on the last, surreptitious bite of the lone Danish pastry that was left over from the read-through. 'Er, I'm sorry?'

'Oh, don't apologise,' Tom replied, seemingly completely misinterpreting her surprise for compliance. 'It's early days and you're not, as you admitted yourself, one for treading the boards. I just thought that it might benefit you, help you to really get under the skin of the character, if I gave you some one-to-one coaching between official rehearsals. What say you?'

Florence just gaped at him, now completely at a loss for words. Fortunately, at that moment, Josie, who'd been eavesdropping casually while getting the rest of the hall back into shape, sailed in and rescued her.

'I don't think there's any need for that just yet, Tom,' she said briskly. 'As we've all just agreed, this was only the first read-through.

Plenty of time to develop the appropriate rapport when we're all a lot more secure with the script.' The tone that was so successful with her rowdier classes seemed to work its magic on Tom, who looked suitably chastened.

'Of course, of course,' he attempted what he clearly thought was a hearty laugh. 'I was merely trying to be constructive. No offence intended, Florence.'

Florence smiled briefly. 'None taken, Tom. I'll be sure to read up on the role before our next rehearsal, being as I am a mere amateur.' She noticed Josie giving her a cautionary look and decided not to go the whole hog and rein in Tom in the manner she would an errant student.

'Good, good.' Tom glanced from one woman to the other, then, with a brief inclination of his head, walked towards the exit.

'Did he seriously almost just bow?' Florence exploded. 'That's the icing on the frigging cake, that is!'

Josie burst out laughing. 'Just ignore him. For all of his bluster, I'm sure he just wants the best for this production.'

Florence snorted. 'Like hell. He wants to turn it into the Tom Sanderson show. Bloody Kenneth Branagh wannabe. If he was really any good, he'd sure as hell not be hanging around here for this "small-town production".' Irritation about being browbeaten by Josie in to playing one of the leads, and now being criticised for that performance by a pompous arse like Tom, finally bubbled over. 'I've half a mind to resign from this bloody play myself.'

'Oh, please don't do that,' Josie said in alarm. 'You're the only one in Willowbury who'd be any good at playing Beatrice. It's not like I was fighting actors off with a stick, you know.'

'I know,' Florence said, slightly mollified. 'But I swear, Josie, if he keeps trying to rile me, I'll bloody lamp him myself.' Her learned Yorkshire vowels crept in when she got cross, and she felt even more irritated.

'If it looks like you're going to murder him, I promise you, as your director, I'll step in,' Josie said solemnly. 'But, look on the bright side; he does have a lot of stage experience. You might actually learn a thing or two!'

Florence didn't dignify that with a response. Suddenly, she thought how much more preferable it would be to have been acting opposite Sam Ellis in this production. She was sure, whatever his faults were, that criticising her performance wouldn't have been one of them. She was faintly horrified to find herself hoping that Tom might get run over by a bus on Willowbury's zebra crossing before the performance.

13

The following Monday, having had Sunday to relax and catch up with some schoolwork and put the whole debacle with Tom into a calmer perspective, Florence returned home in rapidly darkening skies that presaged rain. As she grappled with a big box of exercise books and her house keys, the stocky, dark-haired man on the other side of the terrace wall put the bag of groceries he was carrying down hurriedly and drew closer to the wall.

'Let me help you with that,' he said, reaching over the low wall and relieving Florence of the box just as it was about to slip from her grasp and scatter the exercise books all over the still damp garden path.

'Thanks,' Florence said gratefully, handing over the books and slotting her key into the Yale lock on the front door.

'No problem.' The man regarded her intently for a moment, before handing her back the box after she'd pushed open the door. 'I'm Aidan, by the way.'

'Florence.' She put the box down on the doormat and turned back to shake his proffered hand. 'It's nice to meet you. You must be Sam's, er, housemate, right?'

Aidan smiled. 'Guilty as charged. And guilty of something else, too, I think.' He raised an eyebrow in her direction.

'Oh yes?' Florence feigned ignorance. She'd dealt with enough shifty-looking school kids in the classroom to know when a confession was coming. 'What would that be, then?'

'It was me who kept you awake with the guitar playing, I'm afraid.' He shook his head, and Florence couldn't help again making the naughty schoolboy comparison. 'I'm sorry about that. Sam's bought me a really good pair of headphones now, so it won't happen again.'

Florence nodded. 'That's very generous of him – I'll have to make sure I thank him the next time I see him.' She looked more closely at Aidan, trying to assess what exactly the relationship was between the two men who lived on the other side of the wall. They certainly didn't look anything alike; Sam was tall and willowy, with ruddy blond hair and piercing blue eyes. Aidan was shorter, about her height in fact, which, while not short for a woman, was considerably shorter than Sam's over six feet. Aidan's colouring was different, too; wiry dark brown hair, warm-looking skin with a reddish tinge, and a stockier, possibly more gym-honed body, as if he was used to doing a whole lot more exercise than his housemate. She also noticed what appeared to be the tip of a scar peering out from his hairline, just above his left ear.

'He, er, said you'd been over to complain about the noise – I just wanted to let you know it won't happen again.'

'Thanks,' Florence replied. 'That means a lot – I'm a teacher, so I tend to need a good night's sleep to survive a day in the classroom with my rowdier students!'

'I can believe it.' Aidan paused. 'Sam, as well as me, felt really bad about the fact I'd woken you – gave me a right bollocking for it. Although,' he paused mischievously, 'I think he was overdoing it a bit. He used to be in the navy and got really used to shouting orders at people!'

Florence laughed. 'He seems a bit too laid-back for that sort of thing.'

She remembered the first time she'd met Sam, when he'd been on his doorstep with attractively rumpled just-got-out-of-bed hair and felt her cheeks burning a little. Then she remembered the abrupt *volte face* after the morning of the auditions when Josie had joked about Tom Sanderson getting a bomb under him. What if Sam had actually witnessed people being blown up in war zones? What a stupid thing for Josie to say, if so. Not that she'd have known, of course.

Zoning back into the conversation with Aidan, who appeared to be unwilling to break away just yet, she smiled. 'Must be tricky sharing a house with him, then!'

'Oh, he's not so bad,' Aidan replied. 'He's kept me on an even keel at times, too, although I'd never admit it in front of him.' He bent over suddenly and rummaged in his brown paper shopping bag for something. Finding what he wanted, he straightened back up and Florence was touched to see a small rose plant in his hands. 'I bought you this to say sorry for keeping you awake,' Aidan said. 'I noticed you had a lot of rose bushes in your back garden and figured this one could join it in the spring.' He handed it over to her. 'I was going to pop round later and give it to you, but since we're back at the same time...'

The small, antique rose plant had delicate pink flowers and tiny, just emerging thorns. 'Thank you,' Florence said, surprised and touched. 'There really was no need, but it's very pretty.'

There was a pause between them, as Florence, wondering what else to say, fixed her gaze on the pink flowers in her hands. 'I, um, guess I should get inside and crack on with this marking.' She glanced at the box of books, still sitting inside her front door.

'Looks like you've got a fun evening ahead!' Aidan quipped. 'I should probably get the rest of this shopping inside, too. Sam hates it when stuff's just left on the counter and he has to put it all away after a long shift.'

The casually intimate way he said that convinced Florence that they must be a couple, and she found herself feeling a little bit disappointed. They were both pretty good-looking, after all; a shame she clearly wasn't either of their cups of tea. Not that she was looking for a relationship right on her own doorstep, of course.

'Have a nice evening,' she said. 'And thanks again for the rose.'

'No worries. You too.' And with that, Aidan rummaged in his own pocket for his keys. 'Let us know if you need anything; we're happy to help.'

'Thanks,' Florence said. As she went through her front door, stepping over the box of books to put the rose bush on the hall table, she found herself smiling; perhaps sharing a wall with Sam and Aidan wasn't going to be a nightmare, after all. And maybe Sam might have a straight friend or two whom it might be more appropriate to lust over. She stopped that thought as soon as she'd started thinking it; she'd dated a couple of guys from the forces over the years, and it had never ended well. Whatever, she thought, Sam and Aidan certainly made a good-looking couple.

14

All thoughts of Sam and Aidan were banished as soon as rehearsals got under way in earnest for the play. Thankfully, Tom, possibly mindful of needing to keep the peace, decided to keep his opinions to himself for the next few sessions. In fact, things were starting to come together. Florence, despite her doubts about keeping her temper with Tom, found that her antagonism lent her performance as Beatrice an added edge, and it was not just Josie who commented that their scenes seemed to have an extra *frisson*. As the weeks drew closer to Christmas, and the decorations started to appear in shops along Willowbury High Street, Florence found herself looking forward to the production.

Florence and Josie had taken to having a post-rehearsal drink in the pub on Willowbury High Street, The Travellers' Rest. It was an atmospheric, ancient place, having been a coaching inn in Queen Elizabeth I's time and, bedecked with holly, pine sprigs and other decorations of the season, was a great place to have a glass of mulled wine and dissect the progress of the play so far. Inevitably, talk got onto work-related matters, as always happened when two teachers spent time together, and it wasn't long before Josie was regaling Florence with anecdotes from her long teaching career.

'So, I think probably the most embarrassing thing so far I've had to deal with was when I realised that the mother of one of my Year 8 students had basically seen me naked,' Josie, sitting at the bar sipped her post-rehearsal glass of Pinot Grigio and winced. 'And not just a seen-getting-changed-in-the-swimming-pool-locker-rooms kind of naked, either!'

Florence nearly choked on her own glass of wine. 'Oh go on, you'll have to tell me now.'

Smiling wickedly, Josie took another sip of her wine before she continued. 'Well, a few years ago, Nick and I were even more strapped for cash than usual. Jake had only just started school, but I was struggling to find a job that would fit around his school hours.'

Florence wondered for a moment where this was going. With Josie, she could never be quite sure.

'Lovely Jack Winter, who owns the Cosy Coffee Shop, who I'd got to know quite well when I was still a stay-at-home mother, offered me a job, but to be honest I'm not the greatest at carrying huge piles of plates around, so I decided to do something a bit more exotic.'

'What, burlesque dancing?' Florence suggested.

Josie laughed. 'Not quite, but you're close. There was an art class in Stavenham town hall that had just been set up, and they were looking for life models. I'd done a bit of the same back when I was at university a few times, so I figured I might as well do it. After all, it's not too bad, sitting still for a couple of hours while people try to get your likeness on paper. Anyway, it was a few years ago now so I didn't think anything of it.'

'So what happened?'

'There I am, getting my official on for Parents' Evening last year, when this woman walks in and sits down. I'm chatting away about her precious offspring's literary prowess – or, frankly, the lack thereof – and she suddenly gasps. I'm there wondering if I've hit a nerve, and frantically mentally back-pedalling, trying to work out what it was I'd said, when she blurts it out. She was given one of those blessed life drawings by a mate a couple of Christmases ago, and I'm hanging in pride of place over her bed!'

Florence burst out laughing. 'Oh god! How do you follow that?'

'Well, as you can imagine, it put me totally off my stride. Thankfully, she told me how much she liked it. I can't imagine what little Eddy would have thought, had he been there at the appointment.'

'Has he said anything to you?' Florence was imagining just how that particular classroom conversation might go down. Badly, she assumed.

'Nope,' Josie said, not without a trace of relief in her voice. 'I'm guessing she didn't enlighten him about who it is who's hanging on his parents' bedroom wall in the buff. After all, it's enough to put the poor kid off English, and other things, for life!'

'Well, I'm happy to say that, as far as I know, none of my students has ever seen me starkers, although I dread them catching me at the local swimming pool,' Florence said. 'I do worry, living so close to the place, that I'll get witnessed doing something un-schoolmistressy.'

'Oh, students crop up in the most ridiculous of places,' Josie said airily. 'Most of the time when you've got a drink in your hand, I find.' Surreptitiously, she glanced around the crowded bar. 'Seems like we're OK today, though!'

Florence also relaxed a little, until Josie followed up with her next question. 'So, has Tom offered you any more one-to-one rehearsals?'

Florence grimaced. 'Either I've improved to his so-called stan-dards, or he's given up trying.' She took a sip of the deliciously cinnamon-and-spice-flavoured mulled wine that Josie had replenished from the bar a few minutes before.

'From what I can see, as your director, you're doing fine,' Josie said gently. 'I know I talked you into this part, but, honestly, it's been lovely to see you getting into your stride.'

'Now you're talking like one of my old Drama teachers!' Florence joked, to hide how pleased she was by the praise. 'But that doesn't mean I'm going to take him up on the one-to-ones, even if he does ask me again.' She frowned. 'You don't think he was, er, hitting on me when he suggested it, do you?'

Josie burst out laughing. 'To be honest, I think Tom's far too in love with himself to consider sharing his luvvy life with anyone else.' She paused. 'Besides, I don't think you're his type.'

Florence felt a little stung. 'What makes you say that?'

Josie rolled her eyes. 'Let's just say he's far more alert when that gorgeous next-door neighbour of yours pops in to rehearsals. It wouldn't surprise me if Sam's more Tom's cup of Earl Grey than you, darling!'

'Really?' Florence smiled. That would be something to rib Sam about, the next time she saw him. Relations had improved between the neighbours in the past few weeks, and she regularly saw Sam leaving for his shifts and said a cheery hello.

'Oh, I'm almost certain Tom's gay,' Josie replied. 'But, either way, the two of you are creating a great chemistry on stage.'

'I'm glad that my restraint in not braining Tom is paying off,' Florence replied.

'Try not to do that until the play's over, please,' Josie said briskly. 'I'm not sure we'll get another Benedick in at such short notice. Although...' she grinned mischievously.

'Don't even go *there*,' Florence muttered, knowing immediately that Josie was drifting back to Sam in her mind. 'Besides, I don't think he'd be remotely interested in me,' she added, half to herself and forgetting Josie's incredible antenna for inner musings.

'Why ever not? You're a good-looking girl, you know. And you're also pretty good company.' Josie raised an eyebrow. 'And neither of you would exactly have to walk far to do the walk of shame!'

Florence laughed. 'That's not what I was getting at, Josie. I, er, met the man *he* lives with recently.'

'Really?' Josie took a hefty swallow of her wine. 'You could have fooled me – the chemistry that was crackling off you two when he dropped off those leaflets.'

'You have a very vivid imagination,' Florence said. 'But, believe me, I'm definitely not his type.'

'Ah well,' Josie replied. 'Looks like you'll just have to pretend with Tom, then!'

'Ugh!' Florence snorted. 'Believe me, the thought of snogging Tom in the final scenes of this blessed play is enough to make me start wondering if lesbianism is a better choice.'

'And, on that note, I'd best get home,' Josie said, finishing the rest of her wine. 'I'll see you at school tomorrow.'

'Sure thing,' Florence replied. She vowed to return home to an afternoon of simpler pleasures, like finally making a decision on those blasted kitchen cabinets.

15

Florence busied herself over the coming weeks with schoolwork, redecoration and learning her lines for the play. Before she knew it, it was late November and the play mere weeks away. She and Tom and the rest of the cast had made good progress, though, and even Sam, with Aidan in tow, had managed to make a few rehearsals. Before they knew it, they had been co-opted by Josie into the non-speaking roles of Don John's men, which suited them both as all they had to do was turn up, dress up and stand there at various points, unless something terrible happened to Tom, of course.

Thankfully, Tom's tendency to try to impose his views on interpretation on everyone from Florence to the priory's feral cat, who kept curling up in the corner of the room during rehearsals, had waned since Sam and Aidan had been popping in. Whether it was the desire not to appear like a massive show-off in front of the other two, or he'd just given up trying to turn the Willowbury Dramatical Spectacular into some West End production with himself headlining, Florence wasn't sure, but she was grateful. It meant that she and Tom could more sincerely act the tender moments of the Beatrice and Benedick scenes, at least.

In fact, the cast was getting on so well that they had been adjourning to either The Cosy Coffee Shop if it was too early for a drink or The Travellers' Rest pub if it was later in the day. Florence felt that she was starting to settle into Willowbury, and she couldn't help noticing that Sam and Aidan, despite their non-speaking roles, would hang around for the post-rehearsal drinks as often as they could. Florence found herself walking home with them after the drinks, too, and she decided she quite liked getting to know her neighbours. Aidan was naturally gregarious, whereas Sam was a little quieter, a little more reserved and seemed content, often, to let Aidan lead the conversation.

Florence still wasn't entirely sure what the relationship between them was, but they accepted her into their world easily. She was sure she wasn't imagining Sam shooting her the odd surreptitious glance when he thought no one was looking, though. Perhaps she'd got her assumptions wrong? Perhaps they were just housemates, after all. She found a part of herself sort of hoping that was the case.

'Peace! It's time to stop talking,' Tom interjected into Florence's thoughts as she found her attention wandering offstage and to the audience space where Sam and Aidan were chatting to other cast members. 'Er... Florence...?'

'Sorry,' Florence's attention snapped back to the lines she was meant to be delivering before realising that Tom was leaning in for the stage kiss that was demanded by the script at the culmination of the play, when both couples are, in Shakespeare's version, due to marry. Josie had seen fit to ensure that Hero and Claudio's reunion did not end immediately in a marriage, as it does in the original play, but instead had them tentatively reunited at the end, hoping for a reconciliation, but it was wedding bells for Beatrice and Benedick, and Tom seemed more than keen to channel his inner Branagh for that moment. They'd not got around to actively rehearsing this scene before, and Florence had been absolutely dreading it.

'OK, everyone, let's leave it there,' Josie said. She raised a hand as Tom started to interject, and instead she drew the whole cast together. 'That was a really good run-through. I reckon we'll be word-perfect by next week, if we can all keep our attention focused,' she gave Florence the side-eye, and Florence blushed, knowing that Josie knew exactly why she'd got distracted.

'Anyone coming for coffee?' Florence asked, keen to get attention off herself.

'I've got to get home, sadly,' Josie sighed. 'I'm on childcare duty since Nick's going off to watch the rugby this afternoon.'

As the rest of the cast said their goodbyes and left, Florence found herself wandering towards The Cosy Coffee Shop with Aidan and Sam. As they were nearing the café, Aidan made his excuses, too, leaving just her and Sam to themselves. With a flutter of nerves, Florence took a deep breath.

'Looks like it's just you and me, then,' Sam smiled. 'If you want to hang out with only me, of course.'

Florence found herself smiling back. 'Sounds good. I really need the caffeine after a hard morning's rehearsal.'

'But you seem like a natural,' Sam said as they drew closer to the cafe. 'Even allowing for a prat like Tom.'

'Oh, he's not so bad once you get past the bluster,' Florence said. 'He's just really invested in this play. It might as well be at the Old Vic; the effort he's putting into it!'

'I thought you'd appreciate that kind of attention to detail,' Sam teased. 'Being a teacher, shouldn't you encourage that in all your students?'

'Well, yes,' Florence admitted, adding rather sheepishly, 'but the problem is that the longer I teach, the more subversive I get about my own behaviour. I guess it's a consequence of having to follow rules, and getting the students to do the same, all day. I get a bit rebellious when I'm out of the classroom.'

'Really?' Sam raised an eyebrow. 'I can't imagine you being the rebellious type, somehow. You seem too... too...'

'Too what?' Florence replied. 'Too much like a boring teacher?'

'No, no, not at all,' Sam stammered. 'Just that, well, you seem quite, er... Oh God, I've got myself into a hole, haven't I?'

Florence, realising that Sam thought he really had put his foot in it, decided to let him off, and laughed. 'Don't worry about it. You were in the navy. Didn't you ever feel like cutting loose and being a bit naughty, deliberately not making the effort just because you didn't have to?'

Sam's brow furrowed slightly. 'Well, on leave abroad we did tend to have quite a good time. I suppose you get so ingrained in routines, it's nice to break out of them sometimes.'

'Exactly,' Florence said. 'Let's go and get that coffee, and you can tell me all about your wild nights on shore leave!'

Sam laughed. 'I think I'll have to know you a whole lot better before I tell you anything about that!'

As they crossed the threshold into The Cosy Coffee Shop, Florence found herself thinking that she'd definitely like to get to know Sam better. It would be nice to have a friend on the other side of the party wall, instead of just an acquaintance she waved at when they happened to leave the house at the same time, or chatted to only at rehearsals.

'I *so* need this!' Florence said gratefully as Sam wandered over to their table with two steaming americanos and a couple of slices of cake on a tray. 'I've not had a lot of sleep again this week.'

'Nothing to do with, you know, the guitar playing, I hope?' Sam replied. 'I've not checked recently to make sure he's not been prac-tising at three in the morning again.'

'No, nothing like that this time,' Florence sighed. 'It's mainly schoolwork keeping me up. Even though I'm only working three days a week, the marking is still insane. A new school means that everyone's keeping an eye on how you perform, even if they claim they're not, and so I'm making sure everything is done as well as I can do it.'

'Don't you think you're being a little bit hard on yourself?' Sam asked. 'I'm sure your colleagues are probably just trying to get through their days, too. I bet they're not judging your every move.'

Florence smiled. 'Maybe it's just me, then. I just want to do the best job I can. After all, this is only a temporary contract in the first instance, so I'm trying to prove I'm worth making permanent.' She shook her head. 'But I'm boring myself. What about you? How's your week been?'

'Oh, same old, same old,' Sam said lightly.

'Really?' Florence raised an eyebrow. 'I'd have thought that, in your line of work, nothing was ever routine.'

Sam took a sip of his coffee. 'Well, it's true enough that I never quite know where we'll be going from one shift to the next,' he conceded, 'but now I've got to know the helicopter, that, at least, doesn't have that many surprises.'

'Have you always wanted to fly?' Florence asked, aware of the sudden warmth in Sam's eyes.

'Always,' Sam replied. 'It's kind of in my blood. Dad was a navy pilot, and my grandfather before him, too. It's all I ever wanted to do.' His eyes assumed a faraway expression. 'The first time I went up in a glider, I knew that I wanted to fly. And when I joined the navy it felt like I'd come home.' Embarrassed, he looked down at his hands. 'For ten years I lived that life and ended up in the front seat of the helicopters, flying on and off the ships and feeling that incredible buzz.'

'Why not the Royal Air Force instead?' Florence asked. 'If flying's your first love?'

Sam grinned. 'Family tradition, I guess. And I've never been one to get seasick!'

Florence glanced at his face, still animated, but obviously reliving his memories. 'So why did you stop?' she asked. 'You sound like you loved it.'

'I did,' Sam said. 'More than almost anything.' He looked at her. 'But things change, don't they? You can't always keep doing the thing you love.'

Florence was torn. There was something in Sam's voice that suggested a deeper story, a deeper reason, but she didn't know if she should probe him for it. Then, figuring that he could only clam up, she thought she'd risk it. 'So, what happened?'

Sam paused, and it seemed to Florence that he was weighing up what, if anything, to tell her; that he was somewhere else for a few moments, reliving another time and place. Eventually, he answered. 'My brother, who bucked the family tradition, joined the army when he left school. He was always the more rebellious one, and he didn't want to just follow in the footsteps of everyone else. He was deployed twice to Afghanistan. Near the end of that second tour, he got blown up by a roadside bomb in Helmand. That was just over two years ago.' Sam said softly.

Florence gasped, thinking back again to Josie's flippant comment about bombs, and knew, instantly, that Josie would never have made it, had she known about Sam's brother's experience. 'Oh my god. Did he...'

'He was hurt badly, but they managed to airlift him out.' Sam shook his head. 'The physical injuries were bad, but they put him back together. The mental scars ran deeper. He was the only survivor from his unit, and he witnessed the rest of them lose their lives. He was discharged from the army on medical grounds. I left the navy as soon as I found out so that I could do what I could for him once the immediate treatment had come to an end.'

'So how is he now?' Florence asked. She remembered colleagues of her father's who had been through similar experiences during the Troubles in Northern Ireland, and his sense of pride and sadness when he spoke of them.

Sam paused, as if he was wrestling with something. 'Mostly, he's making a good recovery,' he said. 'But at times it takes him over. The doctors keep adjusting his medication, experimenting to see what will work long term, but it's a numbers game. He sees a counsellor regularly as well, which helps.'

'Do you spend a lot of time together?'

'You could say that,' Sam smiled. 'But even so, it's not easy to keep an eye on him. The meds can affect him differently at different times. Often they mess with his biorhythms so he becomes quite nocturnal. That's why you've been hearing a lot of early-morning guitar playing recently.'

Florence was lost. What did Aidan's guitar playing have to do with Sam's brother? She'd imagined that his brother, wherever he was, would still be under the supervision of a Forces medical unit. Then she felt embarrassed; she should know better than to assume anything like that. Then it clicked.

'*Aidan's* your brother, isn't he?'

Sam looked surprised at the question. 'Well yeah. Why? What did you think he was?' As he saw Florence blushing furiously, the penny dropped and he burst out laughing. 'You mean you thought we were... a couple? Just because we live together? Isn't that a bit of a leap? He's going to piss himself laughing when he hears that!'

Florence, face flaming, couldn't help laughing. 'Well, the way he was acting when he gave me the pot of roses, saying how you didn't like things left messy in the kitchen, and his tone of voice when he spoke about you, he sounded like one half of an old married couple. I just assumed you were... you know. And you look nothing alike,' she added, slightly defensively.

'I'm going to have a word with him when I get home,' Sam grinned broadly. 'He's made me sound like an OCD loser in front of the neighbour.'

'I wouldn't go that far!' Florence laughed. 'Although it was kind of cute, the way he talked about you.'

Sam looked deeply into Florence's eyes for a moment. 'Well, I can assure you that Aidan and I are definitely brothers; he's absolutely not the great love of my life.' Sam shuddered theatrically. 'And yes, you're right, we look nothing alike.'

'Well, I can't be blamed for making an honest mistake then,' Florence said, beginning to recover her equilibrium. She was ignoring her pulse, that, irrationally, had sped up on the discovery that Sam wasn't Aidan's partner. That didn't mean he wasn't gay, though, she kept trying to remind herself.

Sam grinned in abashment. 'Yup. I guess I was a bit too on the defensive that day you knocked on the door to complain to come clean with you. But, no, he's actually my baby brother.'

Florence laughed. 'You certainly kept that one quiet.'

'Well, I'm not keen on telling random strangers my business, even if they do live next door.'

'I hope you don't see me as a random stranger now,' Florence replied. 'After all, if Tom gets a call-up to the West End, we're going to be on stage together.'

'Heaven forbid!' Sam said, gulping the last of his coffee. 'I mean, I'm quite happy to learn lines, but I really don't fancy actually standing there saying them in front of a load of people, including my colleagues from the SAA.'

'I'm sure it won't come to that,' Florence said. She glanced at her watch. 'Anyway, I'd better get home. I said I'd get online and take a look at some costumes for the female members of the cast, and Josie's expecting results by the next rehearsal on Monday evening.'

'Look, Florence…' Sam suddenly looked unsure of himself.

'Yeah?'

'I'm sorry that I didn't level with you about who Aidan was earlier. You're a nice person, and I should have trusted you.'

'It's OK, Sam,' Florence said softly. 'It sounds like you two have been through a lot in the past couple of years. No harm done, except a broken night's sleep.'

The pause between them was loaded with something that neither could quite identify, until, with a nervous laugh, Sam got up from the table. 'Can I walk you home?' he asked.

Florence grinned. 'If you're sure it's not out of your way!'

'I think I can manage a slight detour to your door without being home too late myself.' Sam loaded up the two coffee cups and cake plates and returned them to the counter, where Jack Winter, the owner of the shop, took them from him gratefully. The lunchtime rush was just starting to gain momentum and, from what Florence could see, Jack was working single-handed today.

As Sam sauntered back to their table, she stood and, with a flush of pleasure, smiled as Sam held the cafe door open for her. He really wasn't as standoffish as she'd first thought, she mused as they fell in step beside one another on the walk home. In fact, if she wasn't careful, she could even end up falling for him, and that just wouldn't do. After all, she was busy enough already with the house, school and the play; a relationship would be completely out of the question.

Just before they reached the paths to their respective front doors, Sam paused and turned back towards Florence. 'Um...' he began, then bit his lip.

'What?' Florence smiled, charmed by his obvious and sudden nerves.

'I was just wondering... but, honestly, it's no bother if not...'

'What's no bother?' Florence didn't know whether to be amused or irritated by the tone she could hear in her own voice; sometimes the school teacher encroached outside the classroom, especially when someone was being diffident or reticent. She'd spent enough time over the years trying to worm things out of students, from homework excuses to more serious concerns.

'There's an open morning at the Somerset Air Ambulance base next Sunday. I just wondered if you might like to come down and see what we do. I mean, the play is being put on to raise funds for us, and it seems like a nice idea, if you can spare the time. I could, er, show you round if you like.' Clearly still nervous, he rubbed the back of his head with his right hand. 'The company which maintains the helicopter is bringing a spare down for people to look around and, operations permitting, there'll be a chance to see the ops room and some of the other aspects of our work. Those not on duty have been asked to come in and lead a couple of demos, that sort of thing. It's pretty small scale because obviously we're still going to be fully operational, but if you fancied it...' he paused, before adding hurriedly 'Unless you've got other plans, of course.'

Florence's heart thumped. Was Sam asking her on a date? Was that what she wanted? Or was this just an offer from a neighbour, because he wanted to show her where the money from the play was going to go? 'Er, I'll have to check my diary, but if I can make it, that sounds great,' she said. Then, without thinking, she added, 'I'll see if Josie wants to come too. As the director, I'm sure she'd be really keen to see the base.'

Was it disappointment that flickered over Sam's face when she added that? Florence wondered. It was a momentary expression, and then it was gone.

'Great,' he said, after the minutest of pauses. 'Well, let me know and I can show you, er, *both* around.' There was another pause. 'Well, have a good rest of the weekend,' he said finally, making a move towards his own front door.

'You too,' Florence replied. As she pushed the key into the lock, she glanced round to see Sam looking in her direction, barely a foot and a half away, and blushed. 'Take care,' she added as she opened the door.

She found herself thinking about that exchange long after she'd closed the door and settled in for the rest of the day with her marking, and later, a film and a glass of wine. Had she made a faux pas by suggesting she bring Josie with her? Had Sam really intended on seeing her alone? He was so diffident sometimes, she just couldn't read him. Those perfectly erected barriers that must come from a life of professional training, like her teacher voice, bled over into other aspects of his life, or at least that's what it felt like. Surely, if he'd intended just to spend time with her, he'd have asked her out on a date?

Eventually, she decided to just ask Josie if she fancied coming anyway. Sam had been infuriatingly ambiguous and she didn't want to assume anything. She sent Josie a quick text to see if she was, indeed, free next Sunday and let that be the decider. She also felt cautious about reading too much into the time she and Sam had spent together. She'd snogged too many squaddies in her time as an army brat to even consider getting involved with someone from the military, even if Sam was no longer in the navy. That kind of commitment to a job ran deep, and she knew it never really left those who worked in the Forces. Sam might be handsome, and charming, but there was clearly baggage there, and baggage was absolutely the last thing she needed.

16

The Saturday before the SAA open day saw Willowbury celebrating something a little different; its annual celebration of all things frosty, Winterfest. Although these days it was held in the late autumn rather than the depths of winter, it was still a sight to behold. For one Saturday a year, the High Street gave itself over to stallholders selling all manner of weird and wonderful items, and every other person Florence encountered on the day was wearing some kind of velvet hat or cloak. Although, perhaps these days the commercial interests of the town had made this event a little more about money than it used to be, it was still a great chance to see the residents of Willowbury out in force.

Florence could hear the bands that had set up at either end of the High Street as she strolled out to take in the atmosphere on Saturday afternoon. As she joined the crowds who were wandering up the High Street, she was assailed by the scents of a variety of types of street food, from cauldrons of spicy broth and curry to the smoky aroma of burgers flipping on a flaming griddle. On either side of the street were stalls selling a variety of craft items, including tie-dyed clothing, hats adorned with brightly coloured flowers, and rails of velvet coats, patchwork skirts and hand-knitted jumpers and scarves. Unlike the laid-back, weekend-long celebration of the summer, Willowfest, which took place in the grounds of the priory in the centre of the town, this homage to winter felt like a hive of activity, as if visitors knew that night would soon fall and the temperatures with it.

Huddling into her coat against the rapidly cooling afternoon air, Florence smiled as she spotted a couple of her students, carrying huge sticks of candyfloss and pointing out some of the weirder and wackier items on sale. She herself was tempted by a large, multi-coloured double-bobbled hat from one of the stalls outside ComIncense, the health and well-being shop, but decided that it was a little out of her price range for something she probably wouldn't have the nerve to wear outside of her own garden anyway. She did buy a new pair of fingerless gloves, though, as the fuchsia pink wool really caught her attention. Then, since it was Christmas shopping season, she bought a second pair for her mum as a present. If she didn't see them before Christmas, she'd pop up in the New Year and deliver them herself. Her parents hadn't yet finalised their plans for the festive season, as they loved a last minute deal and may well chose to go away for it, but Florence figured she'd hear any day now what their movements were. Her brother had emigrated to Australia some time ago, so family gatherings were few and far between. They were all excellent communicators though, and used Skype and FaceTime regularly to keep in touch.

'Hey,' a voice called from just behind her as she turned away after paying for the gloves. 'This is all a bit mad, isn't it?'

Smiling as she recognised Aidan's tones, Florence wandered up to him. 'It's a town tradition,' she said. 'I remember being here for Winterfest as a kid and finding all the hats and incense really weird. Aunt Elsie found it all a bit much when she got older, but I like to think she enjoyed it when she was my age.' Florence couldn't really imagine Elsie cutting loose and dressing in velvet and a bobble hat, but there was a lot about her great-aunt she didn't really know, despite inheriting her house.

'Not to mention the random guys wearing antlers,' Aidan observed as a tall, bearded gentleman wandered past in a green cloak and a pair of what looked suspiciously like real deer horns on his head.

'Oh, you'll get used to it,' Florence smiled. 'It's not known as the pagan capital of England for nothing, you know.'

Aidan shook his head. 'Sam'll be sorry to have missed this.'

'What time's he working until?' Florence tried to make her voice sound more casual than she felt, as she remembered Sam's somewhat nervous invitation to the SAA base tomorrow.

'He's due off at seven, but, as usual, it'll depend on the jobs.' Aidan grinned. 'I'll tell him you said hi.'

'Thanks,' Florence ignored the suggestive tone in Aidan's voice.

The two of them wandered up the High Street together, taking in the sights and sounds of Winterfest and smiling at some of the other members of the cast when they saw them out and enjoying the afternoon. Florence couldn't help noticing Aidan's eyes darting around, glancing in all of the spaces between the stalls and the way he seemed a little uneasy in this mass of tourists and locals all out at once on the High Street. Given what Sam had told her last weekend about Aidan's experiences in Afghanistan, and his subsequent PTSD, she assumed that hyper vigilance was something he had to manage. Not wanting to draw attention to it, but also aware that as the crowd grew denser Aidan's tension seemed to be rising, she paused in their walk together.

'Shall we head back down to the Travellers' Rest for a drink?' she asked. The pub was at the bottom of the High Street, on the corner, and the two of them would be walking against the flow of people on the way down, but at least the crowd was thinning out a bit.

Aidan smiled at her, although she noticed his eyes flicking to the area behind her as he did. 'That would be great.' He turned swiftly, shoving his hands in the pockets of his leather biker's jacket, and headed down the street. Florence caught up with him, matching his pace. She knew a little about the effects of PTSD from the training she'd done at school, as some students had the condition because of early-childhood experiences, and she could see how being in such a noisy, vibrant crowd might affect someone, if it suddenly became overwhelming. While she knew that this crowd, however alternative, was harmless, to Aidan it could well mean something different.

When they reached the doors of the pub, Florence was relieved to see that the bar itself wasn't too busy, and they could easily find a table by the window. 'Can I get you a drink?' she asked as they commandeered the table.

'Let me,' Aidan said. 'What would you like?'

'Just a Coke, please,' Florence said. 'I've got a few bits of marking to finish tonight if I'm going to play truant tomorrow and go and see the air ambulance base.'

'Sam said he'd invited you down for the open day,' Aidan said. He gave her a knowing look. 'He didn't bother mentioning it to any of the other cast.'

Florence blushed, remembering how she'd suggested to Sam that Josie might like to come down to Norton Magna with her. 'I'm sure he would have done if he'd had the chance.'

Aidan smiled. 'Right.' He wandered off to the bar, seemingly more at ease now they were off the crowded High Street.

Florence pondered Aidan's words; perhaps Sam really had only meant to invite her? Had she put his nose out of joint by suggesting she bring Josie with her? He was so difficult to read, unlike Aidan, who seemed to wear his emotions on the surface pretty much all the time. She had the feeling that he must always have been that way, even before what had happened in Helmand. He just had a more open way about him.

As Aidan returned with the drinks and sank onto the bench seat opposite her, Florence once again marvelled at how different the two brothers seemed. Aidan must have noticed her scrutiny, looking up from his drink and regarding her quizzically.

'What're you thinking?' he asked.

Florence shook her head. 'Sorry. I know it sounds bonkers, but I only found out that you and Sam were brothers yesterday. I guess I'm trying to look for the similarities, like I do when I teach siblings.'

Aidan grinned. 'What did you think we were, then?'

Blushing, Florence recounted the conversation between herself and Sam, when she'd fessed up to thinking they were a couple.

'Really?' Aidan snorted with laughter. 'I like to think I'd have better taste than him! I've seen the state he leaves the bathroom in!'

'Oh, I don't know,' Florence said without thinking, and then buried her face in her glass before Aidan could see her blushing.

'Well, as I said, he's not invited anyone down for an open day before, so I'd keep an eye on him if I were you.'

'No comment,' Florence said, once she'd recovered her equilibrium. She glanced up again at Aidan, who was now looking out of the pub's large front window and onto the High Street. 'Are you all right?'

Aidan nodded. 'I assume Sam also filled you in on why he's taken it upon himself to move in with me.'

'He mentioned some of what happened to you, yes.'

Laughing slightly self-consciously, Aidan replied, 'I'm not great in crowds these days.' He was still watching the passers-by. 'Sometimes it's difficult to switch off that sense that there's a threat around every corner, but equally I can't spend my life staring at four walls at home.'

Florence's heart went out to the man sitting opposite her. 'I can't imagine what you've been through,' she said softly.

'It's getting easier, day by day,' Aidan said. 'Some days, like anything, are better than others. But I've not come out this afternoon to think about that.' He visibly perked up again, and Florence followed his gaze and saw Tom Sanderson wandering past the window. She waved at him as he glanced in, and, in a moment or two, he'd come through the door and joined them at their table.

'Hi,' Tom said. 'I'm so glad I saw you. I've had just about enough of traders trying to sell me recycled yak wool scarves and organic quinoa soup this afternoon.'

'Better have a drink, then,' Aidan said, glugging back the rest of his pint of cider. 'Can I get you one?'

'That would be great, thanks.'

Tom settled into the chair opposite Florence, but as Aidan gestured to her own glass, she shook her head. 'I really should get back home and get some work done.' Wriggling out from behind the table, she smiled at Tom. 'I'll see you at tomorrow's rehearsal?'

'Absolutely,' Tom said. 'I'm dog-sitting my parents' Jack Russell this weekend, so I might have to bring him with me. The little bugger's got a habit of chewing my shoes if I leave him alone and needs to walk about six miles a day!'

'Sounds like my Great-Aunt Elsie's dog,' Florence said. 'She always said little dogs had more stamina than big ones.'

'No kidding,' Tom rolled his eyes. 'I've been taking him up Willowbury Hill, which seems to tire him out, thankfully.'

'Well, I'll leave you to it,' Florence said, as Aidan returned with the drinks for himself and Tom. 'I'll see you soon,' she added to Aidan by way of parting.

'Enjoy tomorrow morning, if I don't see you before,' Aidan said.

'I will.'

Wandering out of the pub and back onto the High Street, Florence glanced back through the window and saw Aidan and Tom chatting animatedly about the upcoming play. She felt a bit guilty about running out on them both, but since they seemed to be getting on fine without her, she soon got over it.

17

On Sunday, Florence felt her stomach flipping a little as she drove the twelve miles to the Somerset Air Ambulance base for the second of their twice-yearly open days. They usually held these days in early summer and then again in late autumn, as a way of raising awareness about the unit, as well as thanking those who continued to support them financially with their donations. As all of the air ambulances in the UK were completely charitably funded, these days were part of an ongoing campaign of public relations and were opportunities not just to raise awareness but also the funds to keep the show on the road, and the rotor blades turning. She hadn't seen Sam since the previous Saturday's rehearsal and coffee after, but he had texted her with the best time to turn up on Sunday. Josie had booked a weekend away with her husband which meant she wouldn't be back in time to accompany Florence, but Florence hadn't mentioned that in her text back to Sam.

Today was a beautiful late November day; the leaves on the trees were turning and falling, but the hills of Brent Knoll and Crook

Peak were still a vibrant green in the sunlight. The sun was low in the sky, casting everything in a golden glow.

When Sam had suggested she come down to the open day to see what exactly his job involved, for a moment he'd looked endearingly shy. Her heart had melted at the thought of someone who had to be so in control, so authoritative in his job, feeling self-conscious or nervous about showing that to her. She figured he must really want to impress her, or at least to let her into his world.

And it was a world, she had to confess, that she knew nothing about, apart from having watched a couple of films and caught the end of a documentary called *Emergency Helicopter Medics* some years ago. 'It's not like it is in the movies!' Sam had laughed when she'd admitted this to him over the coffee they'd shared the previous weekend. 'We don't fly flat out and burn fuel to the bottom of the tanks, just to look good!' He'd virtually pissed himself laughing when she'd admitted that her favourite film as a kid had been that 1980s classic tale of arrogant US military flyboys, *Top Gun.* She hadn't even been born when it had been released in the cinema, but her dad had loved it, and still did, she'd told him, so she'd ended up loving it too. The thought of Tom Cruise playing volleyball in a pair of tight Levi's 501s still made her break out in a sweat, and the flight sequences took her breath away - to quote the title of the film's signature song.

Oddly though, despite her love of *Top Gun*, she'd never really been one for flying. She'd been offered the chance to take a helicopter ride as an impressionable eight-year-old but had shaken her head, terrified at the prospect. Years later, she assumed it was because she was more frightened about the associations those huge military craft had. Helicopters in army green, to her child's mind, took soldiers away from the people who loved them, and she was already heartbroken every time her father had to go away again. As an adult, she'd sat in a military Lynx helicopter that had been flown down for a country fair in the village where her parents lived, while a pilot friend of her father's had talked her through the various controls and what it was they did, but she'd jumped out again without any inclination to actually fly. She could just about remember the basics of how they worked, all the same.

She was feeling an entirely different set of emotions as she drove up to the brand-new air ambulance base at Norton Magna this morning, though the nerves in the pit of her stomach were remarkably similar. Sam had advised her to get there early to avoid the crowds, as the prospect of a flight in the emergency helicopter was too good a chance to pass up for a lot of locals. It was bit like when the local multinational cider farm, Carter's Cider, opened its doors to the public; people came from far and wide, as well as locally, to have a gawp at a place they wouldn't usually get the inside track on, and a free glass of cider, of course.

Florence drove the long, broad road to the part of the airfield, almost at the back, where the SAA hangar resided. The site was open and flat, with acres of close-cropped green grass bisected from time to time by runways old and new. The sun shining down on this late-autumn day gave the grass a lush hue, and the hangar rose, slightly imposingly, out of the ground, with the iron doors in front opening out onto a tarmac area, where, Florence presumed, the helicopter took off from.

She parked the car and grabbed her jacket from the passenger seat, glad she'd brought her thicker winter one instead of just a light raincoat. The wind on the flat field of the base was whipping up her hair, but the overall sensation she got, much to her surprise, was one of incredible peace and tranquillity. The only sounds were a couple of crows cawing in the trees that lined the right-hand perimeter of the base, separating it off from the golf course on the other side and, above and slightly to the right of the hangar, a vintage Tiger Moth aircraft chugging through the cloudless blue sky.

As Florence wandered towards the rear of the hangar, she saw Sam heading in her direction. Her heart thumped in her chest when she saw him in the dark blue boiler suit with the SAA logo on its left-hand pocket.

'Hey,' Sam said as he, too, caught sight of her. He jogged over to her. 'Glad you could make it.'

'Me too,' Florence replied. She drew in a quick breath as he leaned over and kissed her, rather shyly, on the cheek. Whether it was because his colleagues had just opened the doors and were milling around or he was genuinely nervous about her being here, on his turf, she wasn't sure, but she was struck by the sweetness of the gesture.

'Will Josie be joining you?' Sam asked.

'Er, no,' Florence replied. 'She's away for the weekend.' Was she imagining it, or did Sam's smile get a little broader at the news she'd come alone?

'I'm glad you managed to get here early,' he continued as he led her across to the hangar where the operational helicopter was kept. 'The crowds'll be coming in soon, and I'll be caught up answering my share of questions, as well as doing a couple of the flights in the spare aircraft.'

'Sounds like it's a good PR exercise,' Florence remarked. 'After all, apart from seeing you flying through the skies, I bet most people don't really know the true extent of what you do for a living.'

'It's usually a good day,' Sam replied. 'This is my first autumn one, although I was around for the early summer one.'

'You've got a lovely morning for it,' Florence said, although she wrinkled her brow. 'I assume it is, anyway.' She glanced at the blue skies above.

'It's not bad,' Sam replied. 'Got to be mindful of the wind, but it should be OK once we get going. 'Speaking of which...' he trailed off tantalisingly.

'What?' Florence asked, pausing in her step as he did.

'I need to give the helicopter the company brought down for the visitor flights a quick whiz around the base before the crowds arrive, make sure it's all in working order. It's an older model, the one we had before Leonardo upgraded us last year, and the company are paying for the fuel so we won't be out of pocket. Do you fancy coming with me?'

Florence felt a flutter of nerves. Did she? Well, to be fair, she kind of figured she was going to get up into the air at some point today but had thought it would be alongside a few other visitors. Was she up for a solo flight with Sam? Her mouth made the decision before her head could step in. 'Sure.'

'Don't panic,' Sam laughed, obviously sensing her hesitation. 'This is only going to be up, round and back down again. I know some people get a little nervous about flying.'

'I'm OK,' Florence said hastily, although in truth she wasn't just nervous about the flight itself; she knew Sam was, obviously, a more than competent pilot. It was equally the thought of being alone in the helicopter with him. She fancied him more than she was prepared to admit, and adrenaline plus attraction was bound to equal passion. Was she ready for that?

'Come on then,' Sam said briskly; then his face softened as he saw her expression. He stopped and took her hand. 'I'll make sure you come back to the ground safely, I promise.'

'I know,' Florence nodded. 'I trust you.' The current from Sam's touch seemed to fizz through her, and she was disappointed when he released her hand.

The two of them walked towards the large yellow helicopter that was standing on the runway, a safe distance away from where the operational air ambulance helicopter was based. Florence was stunned, up close, at how big the thing was. Stinging yellow in colour, to stand out against the sky in all weather, it looked state of the art, despite being the previous model.

As Sam opened the front door of the helicopter, Florence marvelled at the space it had. She stepped up and seated herself beside Sam, who'd scooted round to the other side and was explaining, as she settled, how to buckle up and release the harness, and where the emergency exits were. He also explained what to do in the event of an emergency, although this was accompanied by a reassuring and disarming smile.

'OK,' he said, and his voice sounded strangely disembodied in the ears of the headset she had also put on, under his watchful eye. These weren't the audio-enabled helmets that were found in the operational helicopter, but rather a set of headphones and mouthpiece that she slipped on and adjusted to fit her head, much like a very expensive set of musical headphones. Sam gestured to the intercom cable hanging from the cockpit roof above her right shoulder and she clicked the wired jack into it. 'Are you ready?' His voice came to her again through the headphones.

'As I'll ever be.' Her stomach turned over again as he turned his head towards her and nodded before turning his attention back to the instrument panel in front of him.

'Norton Radio, Golf, Sierra, Alpha, Alpha, EC135, 2 POB. Charlie copied 1013 set, engine rotor start.' Florence felt reassured by Sam's voice in her ears.

Just as quickly, Air Traffic Control responded. 'Golf, Alpha, Alpha, Charlie correct, start own discretion, 2 in the visual circuit.'

Florence glanced at Sam, glad that he, at least, understood the throwing around of acronyms, even if she didn't. The language of flight was fascinating, and she felt like a tourist in a new place, drinking it all in but not completely understanding what was happening around her.

Sam ran through the pre-flight sequence. 'Norton Radio, Golf, Alpha, Alpha, taxi runway 24.'

Florence took a deep breath as she felt the helicopter throb to life. She tried to focus on the feeling of the beat of the rotors through her body but felt her eyes being drawn back again and again to Sam. She watched his face, his hands as they busied themselves over switches and his eyes glanced at dials. His concentration seemed absolute, but at the last moment, he turned his head and smiled at her.

'OK?' he asked.

She nodded.

Air Traffic Control came back again over the radio. 'Golf, Alpha, Alpha, taxi and line-up own discretion, no traffic to effect.'

'Golf, Alpha, Alpha, taxi and line up 24,' Sam replied. Still looking at her, he explained. 'This is a non-urgent flight, so I'm just telling ATC that I'm going to ground taxi to the runway and line up.'

The helicopter began to lift into a hover along the tarmac, and Florence's heart flipped again as she felt the strange sensation of leaving the ground; there was no going back now. Her right hand clenched in her lap where, a moment ago, it had lain relaxed.

'Are you sure you're OK?' Sam glanced over at her again. 'You look a little bit pale.'

'I'm fine,' Florence replied, hearing her own voice coming back to her over the comms.

'Golf, Alpha, Alpha, ready for departure.'

'Golf, Alpha, Alpha, no traffic to effect, take off pilot's discretion,' ATC responded.

'Golf, Alpha, Alpha,' Sam repeated. He looked across at Florence again, as if asking her for silent confirmation.

She nodded. This was it; she needed to trust him.

The helicopter tilted forward, building airspeed as it rose. There was a swift, exhilarating acceleration upwards as Sam squeezed the cyclic back, raising the nose of the helicopter slightly and making the aircraft climb away while still accelerating.

Florence almost forgot to breathe. The rush was like nothing else she'd ever felt.

'Wow...' she murmured. 'This is... is...'

'An English teacher, lost for words?' Sam's teasing tones seemed reassuringly normal after all of the technical phrases he'd been uttering for the past few minutes.

'Ha, ha,' Florence replied, turning to him and grinning. 'But this really is something else, you know.' It struck her, once they were in the air, just how peaceful and calm the flight felt. She knew the conditions were good, which must make a difference, but rather than the full-throttle acceleration and high-octane speed she was expecting, everything felt calm, slow, sedate, now they were in the air, as if the helicopter was a bumblebee in flight.

'I know.' He glanced at her and gave a heartbreakingly attractive smile. 'Even after all those flight hours, it's still almost the best feeling on earth.'

Florence saw, just for a moment, a deeper intensity burning in his eyes, and she felt her stomach disappear for entirely non-flying-related reasons. Her gaze drifted from his eyes to his mouth, down his body, snugly clad in his flight suit, to his hand on the collective lever to the left of him. This was a man completely at home in the air; it was his space, his territory. She felt a surge of desire, which fought with the nerves in her stomach caused by the flight, watching him handle this craft with such ease and expertise.

As they began to glide through the sky, turning in a long, lazy arc from the airfield, Florence saw the countryside beneath them, the vibrant green fields interspersed with houses and bisected by roads, all looking like some town planner's model.

'This can only be a quick one, I'm afraid,' Sam said, and

Florence was sure she didn't miss the teasing undercurrent in his voice. 'I've got to put down and make sure it's ready for the slightly more crowded flights later.' He turned to her again. 'What are you thinking?'

Florence smiled. 'That I've never been so exhilarated, and so terrified, in my life.' She shook her head. 'It's such a strange feeling.'

'It's a bit like riding a bike,' Sam said, grinning. 'You're connected to everything much more closely than in a fixed-wing aircraft, and the controls are much more intuitive. You kind of get used to it, but you should never take it for granted.' He glanced at the controls in front of him and a look of mischief flickered over his face.

'What are you up to?' Florence asked.

'Hold tight,' Sam replied. He manipulated the helicopter into a hover, then worked with the yaw pedals until the aircraft slowly began to rotate on the spot, while remaining stationary in terms of height, like a dancer performing a pirouette.

Florence's eyes followed the path of the nose of the helicopter, and she laughed. 'That's a good trick.'

Sam laughed, too. 'I'm glad you approve.' Steadying the aircraft, he pulled in the collective for a moment more, gaining a little more height before conducting another, wider turn so that they were facing back towards the runway. 'We'll have to leave it there, I'm afraid,' he said as he gradually began to descend the helicopter towards the tarmac. 'Unless you fancy coming back up as part of a crowd later.'

'I think that's about all I can take for one day,' Florence said. She was impressed by Sam's expertise but still couldn't quite shake the nerves that surrounded flying for her.

'No worries,' Sam replied. 'Besides, when I'm up here, I'm supposed to be all about the job – professional distance and all that.

Difficult to maintain that when I keep wanting to look at you. Would be worse with a cabin full of extra passengers!'

Florence felt herself blushing; Sam had seemed so naturally reticent up to this point. Perhaps, with headsets on and in control of this aircraft, he felt a little freer to be more honest about his feelings. Whatever the reason, she glowed inside with pleasure.

As they neared the ground again, Sam began his landing exchange with Air Traffic Control, and in very little time he'd set the helicopter carefully down on the tarmac once more. Florence was surprised at how smooth the landing was, given that her only flying experience up until this point was on the budget airlines, when landings had been, a lot of the time, incredibly bumpy, especially on a windy day.

Sam went through the shutdown checks and Florence sat back in her seat, watching him ensure everything was safe and as it should be. She felt oddly content, just observing him paying attention to the details that guaranteed a safe finish to the flight. Again, she felt a bit like a stranger in a strange land, but she was instinctively reassured.

When it came to unbuckling the harness, her fingers fumbled with the mechanism and she found she couldn't quite manage to do it. She jumped as Sam leaned over from his seat and undid it swiftly and easily. The touch of his hand, even through her clothes, sent a jolt of electricity through her.

'Thanks,' she breathed, spine tingling as he, very close to her now, looked her straight in the eyes.

'No problem.' Sam smiled. His lips hovered a little way away from hers and the pause seemed to go on forever. They drew a millimetre or two closer, and were within a heartbeat of a kiss, when the radio system crackled to life again.

Florence jumped, mentally kicking herself for it as Sam smiled ruefully.

'That's my cue to get off my arse and get this thing ready for the visitor flights later,' he said, moving away again.

Florence wriggled out of the straps and waited for Sam to come round and open the door for her – she wasn't sure what she should touch and what she shouldn't. When he did so, she stepped down from the helicopter on legs that weren't exactly wobbly just from the flight.

'If you head back to the hangar, Hannah, our charity rep, is there to show you around,' Sam said. 'If you want to see the inside of the place, that is.'

'I'd like that.' Florence looked up at him, feeling like she was still pitching a bit from being up in the air. 'Why do I feel like I'm never going to get my air legs?'

Sam laughed. 'It takes time.' He paused for a moment, then reached over and took her right hand in his. 'But did you like it?'

'I did,' Florence breathed. She drew closer to Sam, who, unlike when he'd asked her to come to the open morning, now seemed injected with a whole lot more confidence and authority. She figured it was because he'd been in control in the sky, and he'd been showing her something he loved and was good at. She was sure he was standing a little straighter. Her feet seemed to have a mind of their own as she moved to within a hair's breadth of him again, and her left hand snaked its way up his arm to his shoulder and then to the back of his neck. 'Thank you for sharing it with me,' she murmured as she tilted her face to his and, finally, their lips met.

The kiss was sweet, and his lips were a warm contrast to the breeze that was curling around them. As she gently explored Sam's mouth with her own lips and tongue, Florence felt an incredible sense of rightness; as if she'd been waiting for him, as if being in the air had unleashed some kind of passion that had been simmering under the surface ever since they'd been spending more time together.

him once or twice, as he seemed keen to come and visit and support the new school. As a teacher, she tended to be sceptical about politicians, but, to give Charlie Thorpe the benefit of the doubt, so far she'd only heard good things about him and his record in office.

Checking her watch, Florence realised that she'd better grab something to eat before she spent some time planning and marking for the next few days at school, and then went to the rehearsal. The performance was taking place the following Saturday, but Josie wanted to make sure everything was present and correct the weekend before so that there was no last-minute rushing around. All the tickets had been sold, and it was only now that Florence was beginning to feel nervous. After the kiss with Sam, as well, she felt her stomach fluttering with a few more butterflies that weren't all brought on by the prospect of being on stage in less than a week's time. She couldn't decide if she was relieved or disappointed that she wasn't going to be playing Beatrice to his Benedick but had to put up with Tom instead. One thing she was certain about, though; after that blissful, but brief kiss just now, she definitely wanted to feel Sam's lips on hers again.

18

That evening, all was going surprisingly well, and Florence found herself almost looking forward to the performance of *Much Ado About Christmas,* when the bomb, at least figuratively, dropped. She was just reading and rereading a few lines from the masked ball scene before the rehearsal was due to officially begin when her mobile pinged. Her brow furrowed as she pulled it out of the back of her jeans. Her face fell further when she read the message.

'Shit!' Florence's uncharacteristic expletive made even Josie look up from the notes she was making on the script. Last-minute changes to lighting and some of the actors' intonation were occupying her a little more than they should.

'What is it?' Josie asked. 'Is everything OK?'

'I've just had a text from Tom,' Florence said. 'He spent last night at Weston General Hospital having his ankle plastered. He put a foot down a rabbit hole and fractured his ankle when he was walking that bloody Jack Russell he's been looking after.'

'What the actual fuck?' Josie nearly dropped her script. 'You're joking, right?' As if on cue, her own phone pinged, with a carbon copy of the same message. 'Well, that's that then,' Josie said as she scrolled down the text. 'He says he's going to be in plaster for at least six weeks.'

Florence's heart sank. 'So now what?'

'I don't know.' Josie pushed back her unruly auburn curls from her forehead and took a sip of her coffee. 'God, I wish this was something stronger.' She grimaced. 'We've sold every single ticket, and the press is coming to the dress rehearsal to take some publicity shots for the *Stavenham and Willowbury Times*. What bloody awful timing.'

'Can we reschedule?' Florence asked. 'Shall I give the priory wardens a ring and see if the performance space is available in eight weeks' time?'

'I don't think we can risk it,' Josie said. 'The rest of the cast has other commitments, and they've blocked their diaries out for this week. I know for a fact that George is off on a cruise with his wife at the end of January.' George Stevens, a kindly retired bank manager, was playing Leonato and had provided the cast with several trays of exquisitely baked flapjacks to sustain them during the long winter rehearsals. 'Not to mention, it's a Christmas-themed adaptation – that's not going to play well with the New Year blues!'

Florence slumped in her seat. She was gutted. Not just for Tom, who wouldn't cope terribly well with being in plaster for six weeks, but also for herself. Since they'd cleared the air and come to an understanding, she and Tom had really cracked the roles of Beatrice and Benedick, and now they weren't going to get the chance to showcase their work.

'We do have one other option,' Josie said, eyes sparkling with sudden enthusiasm.

'Oh yes?' Florence said warily. She'd quickly grown accustomed to Josie's often misplaced enthusiasm for hare-brained solutions, even if some of her more out-of-the-box ideas did work occasionally.

'Well, isn't it obvious?'

Florence sighed. Josie's love of drama, and not just the Shake-spearean kind, was also widely known. 'Just tell me.'

'It's a no-brainer, really,' Josie said. 'I don't know why I didn't think of it straight away.'

'Just spit it out, Josie.'

Josie's eyes gleamed. 'You and Sam have been hanging out a lot, haven't you? Why don't we just call him in? He is the understudy after all.'

Florence's stomach lurched. 'What? Sam? Don't be daft.' Hurriedly, she tried to think of reasons why that wouldn't be the best idea. 'I mean, OK, we've been getting on well lately, but we've not done any actual acting. He won't have a clue about the blocking, the choreography... it'll be a disaster.' Not to mention their kiss this morning – acting alongside him might have been a nice fantasy after the kiss had happened, but it might also end up being horren-dously awkward.

Josie cocked her head to one side and regarded Florence. 'I think he's our best shot for getting the play on, don't you?'

'Well, yeah,' Florence conceded, 'but will it actually work, putting him in one of the lead roles less than a week before the first performance? He'll freak.'

'The lady doth protest too much, methinks.' Josie's tone was teasing, but there was a determined glint in her eye.

'Wrong play,' Florence muttered. 'And he totally won't go for it. We virtually railroaded him into agreeing to be understudy for Tom anyway. He'd never have expected to actually be onstage in a speaking role.'

'Well, the least we can do is ask him' Josie replied. 'Have you got his number? I'll give him a ring.' Josie's tone was her tried-and-tested 'this will broker no disagreement' that Florence had heard her use on a particularly recalcitrant Year 9 class when she'd observed her a couple of weeks ago. She pitied poor Sam, who was only seconds away from having this news broken to him.

Florence pulled out her mobile and was just checking through her contacts for Sam's number when the door to the performance space opened. She nearly dropped her phone when Sam himself poked his head round the door, a smile on his face and a bag of custard doughnuts in his hands.

'I thought you might like a bit of sugar while you're busy rehearsing,' he said, putting the bag of cakes on the table.

'You might not feel that way when Josie asks you what she's got to ask you,' Florence said slyly, but she helped herself to a doughnut before Sam could change his mind.

'Oh yes?' Sam looked warily from Florence to Josie, whose eyes were glinting with a combination of amusement and trepidation.

Quickly, Josie filled Sam in on Tom's unfortunately timed accident. Sam's face transitioned from sympathy to horror in the space of three sentences.

'Are you having a laugh?' he said when Josie paused. 'I mean, learning the lines is one thing, but actually standing onstage playing the role?'

'But you did say you were taking a week off to help Aidan redecorate the kitchen and living room,' Florence insisted, deciding in for a penny and all that, and somewhat infected by Josie's steamrolling persuasive tone. 'So you won't get called into work, and you should have plenty of time to learn the blocking as well as polish up the lines.'

'Well, yeah, I have got a week off, but I'd planned on painting walls, drinking beer and sleeping late every day, not prancing around in someone else's costume pretending to be in love with you!'

'I'm hardly over the moon at that prospect either, you know,' Florence replied tartly. 'I mean, at least Tom was a semi-pro. How do I know you'll be able to remember lines and move at the same time?' Embarrassment because this wasn't the way she'd imagined their first conversation since their kiss that morning going, and nervousness because she was genuinely worried that they'd both be making fools of themselves onstage on Saturday, made her voice shriller than it should have been, and for a moment she really did feel as though she was channelling Beatrice.

Both of them looked over to Josie, who, to Florence's chagrin, was grinning broadly. 'You two sound like you've already psyched yourself into the roles,' she said. 'See? All you have to do is work on the blocking and it'll be fine.' She looked down at her notes as both Sam and Florence tried to protest. 'And if it makes you feel better, we'll do a press release for the local media that lets everyone know about the eleventh-hour change of cast, and I'm sure the audience will be right on your side.'

Florence gave an exasperated sigh, but even as she did, at the back of her mind and in the pit of her stomach she was feeling a tingle of anticipation. Would it *really* be such a bad thing to be acting alongside Sam? All right, so Tom was the professional, and they'd perfected their snippy Bea-and-Ben banter over the past six weeks until both were able to anticipate the other's lines and moves almost with their eyes closed, but she was always one for embracing the unpredictable, and she was nothing if not adaptable. *Dad, you have a lot to answer for,* she said silently.

'It sounds like we've not got a choice,' she said, finally, realising that Sam and Josie were looking for a response from her. 'And,' she paused, turning to Sam with a game smile, 'it's not as if you haven't come to any rehearsals at all. I'm sure it'll be fine.'

'Fine,' Sam conceded. 'I'd better phone Aidan and tell him not to expect me back for a while then, hadn't I? We seem to have some rehearsing to do.'

'That's the spirit!' Josie said, the relief evident in her voice now that her two leads had come to an agreement of sorts. 'After all, it's hardly The Globe. The audience aren't expecting RSC standards from any of us, thank God!'

Florence's stomach, turning somersaults until thirty seconds ago, gave an almighty rumble. She reached for another doughnut from the bag of cakes that Sam had brought along with him and bit into it, spilling sugar all down her black T-shirt. Heedless, she polished it off, ignoring the glances that Josie and Sam were giving her.

'Well, when you've quite finished stuffing your face, I suggest we get rehearsing, don't you?' Josie grinned and helped herself to a cake, too.

A little while later and Sam was being walked through the blocking in the makeshift stage area in the performance space of the museum. This was just as tricky as learning the lines, as Tom, Josie and Florence had worked out weeks ago where they should be standing for each scene, and, even trickier, how they should move during and after speaking.

'That's it, and just a little closer to where the altar space is meant to be... yes, good.' Josie glanced at her copy of Act 3 Scene 2 that she had on her clipboard and then motioned for Florence to give her line.

Florence took a deep breath. Josie was really throwing her in the deep end by skipping all of the ensemble scenes and focusing on the Beatrice and Benedick moments. If she didn't know better...

'When you're ready, Florence,' Josie repeated, raising one eyebrow.

'Um, sure, sorry.'

Florence felt Sam slipping closer to her as Josie had directed, taking on that persona of Benedick when he becomes less playful soldier and more earnest lover, before swearing to do potentially the most dreadful deed of his life for the woman he realises he loves. It was a scene that had reduced Florence to tears when she'd watched Kenneth Branagh and Emma Thompson do it on film, and she hoped she could do justice to it in this small stage version.

As Sam delivered his lines, falteringly at first, but then with increasing confidence, Florence felt the hairs rise on the back of her neck. For a moment she could feel him really becoming his version of the character, and as he drew closer to her, preparing to give Josie's version of the 'I do love no one in the world so much as you' line, she felt Beatrice under her skin, too, responding to Sam's Benedick with heart and soul.

'OK, and just break there,' Josie's voice intruded into Beatrice and Benedick's private world before the moment got too intense. 'Let's just run through the end scene, and then you two can go and learn some lines on your own before the dress rehearsal tomorrow evening.' She sighed. 'I hope you-know-who doesn't have a blue fit when he finds out Tom's been replaced.' She was referring to the notoriously grumpy, but devastatingly attractive Chris Charlton, who was playing Don John. Much like his character, he didn't take kindly to last-minute changes of costume, let alone personnel.

'He'll just have to lump it,' Florence said. 'After all, it's me who has the lion's share of the stage time with the replacement!'

'Thanks,' Sam said drily. 'Talk about filling a man with confidence.'

Florence flushed. 'Oh, you know what I mean. Anyway, we'd better go and rehearse a bit more. Your place or mine?'

Sam grinned. 'Better go to mine – Aidan will doubtless want to be the willing audience.'

Florence felt a faint sting of disappointment – there was a part of her that wanted to be alone with Sam for a couple of hours, just to get to grips with the mammoth task ahead of them, but all the same, she realised that it was important to Sam to keep an eye on

Aidan. 'OK then.' She grabbed her coffee and turned back to Josie. 'I'll see you back here at six o'clock tomorrow?'

'Yup. Don't be late,' Josie replied. 'I'll need you two to pull out all the stops if we're going to reassure the cast.'

With that, Sam and Florence headed off to cram in as many lines as they could before running the gauntlet of a full dress rehearsal the following evening. Florence couldn't help feeling a flutter in her stomach that wasn't entirely due to nerves about the impending performance. The thought of kissing Sam again, even if they were in role, was a tantalising one.

19

'OK, let's go from Act 2 Scene 4,' Florence said. She glanced up at Sam from where she was sitting by the roaring fire in the living room. Aidan, who was playing the part of their audience, grinned from the sofa where he was ensconced.

'Great idea,' Aidan said. 'Isn't that the bit where you get to give each other a massive snog at the end?'

Florence blushed. She wasn't sure if Sam would have said anything to Aidan about what had happened after the helicopter flight, and she certainly didn't want to bring it up if he hadn't. She wasn't sure how she felt about it as it was. 'We don't have to practise that bit,' she said hastily. 'We don't have to go that far until we're on stage.'

'Shame,' Aidan replied. 'I reckon he needs the practice!'

'Shut your face, little brother,' Sam good-naturedly threw a patchwork cushion in Aidan's direction. He didn't seem to be fazed by Aidan's ribbing, and, much to Florence's quiet chagrin, didn't even glance in her direction. 'And remember, it's not me she'll be kissing onstage anyway – it's Benedick.'

Florence grimaced. 'Much as I found Tom annoying when we

started rehearsing together, and I still think Josie only cast him to wind me up, I'm actually kind of missing him, even if he has got an ego as big as his nose.'

'Thanks,' Sam said drily.

Florence blushed. 'That's not a reflection on you,' she said. 'It's just that, West End wannabe as he was, we got into the rhythm of working together, and I thought we managed to pull off being Beatrice and Benedick reasonably well. In a way, his acting experience, although he made more of it than it probably was, was quite reassuring. Now I feel like I'm going to be carrying this production because you, through no fault of your own, have been dragged in at the last minute.' Small town production or not, Florence suddenly felt the pressure of being one of the leads come crashing down upon her.

'I promise I won't let you down, Florence,' Sam said softly. 'I know I haven't had as much time to rehearse as Tom, but I really think we can do this play justice. After all, it's hardly the West End, is it?'

'I know,' Florence replied. She grinned suddenly. 'I just sometimes can't help my inner perfectionist. It's not a trait that's terribly helpful as a teacher, and, it seems, as an actor, either.' She glanced up and saw Sam's eyes reflecting the warmth from the open fire in the grate in front of them and felt a little more measured.

'Look on the bright side,' Aidan said suddenly from his spot on the sofa. 'Tom'll have to think of a whole load more excuses to spend time with you now he's not in the play any more!'

'Fat chance,' Florence muttered. 'Besides, he's not interested in me.'

'How do you know?' Sam raised an eyebrow.

Florence giggled. 'Put it this way; he was more excited when he found out you were his understudy than he was that I'd been cast as dear old Bea. I'm not tall, macho and male enough for him.'

'Really?' Sam shifted in his seat uncomfortably. 'Well, that's a turn-up for the books. I had no idea.'

'You surprise me,' Florence replied, conveniently forgetting that it was Josie who'd first brought the question of Tom's preferences to her attention. 'Thankfully, he was very good at acting like he's in love with me, whatever the actual truth to the contrary. Unfortunately, he won't get the chance to show that now.'

'You reckon Tom's gay?' Aidan asked, before Sam could find his place in the script once more. 'How do you know?'

Florence glanced at him, surprised by the question. 'Well, I caught him swiping through a dating app during a break in rehearsal one afternoon. He saw me looking and, rather than try to hide the phone, he asked me what I thought of the next few profiles! I'm not sure he actually contacted any of the guys I suggested, though.'

'Hmmm,' Aidan replied, a little non-committally, before going back to the copy of the script he was holding. 'Interesting.'

'Interesting why?' Florence asked.

Aidan was prevented from replying when the alarm went off on Sam's phone. He glanced at it and switched it off, and looked pointedly at Aidan, who grimaced good-naturedly.

'Bear with me,' Aidan said, rising from the sofa. 'It's tablet time.'

As Aidan wandered off to the bathroom to take his medication, Florence turned back to Sam. 'Thank you for stepping in at such short notice,' she said softly. 'I bet it's the last thing you want to do with your time off, but if we don't put the performances on, we'll lose all of the money for the SAA.'

'I know,' Sam replied. 'I just can't help being a bit nervous about being on stage in less than a week's time.'

'I'll do everything I can to make it as easy as possible,' Florence promised. Just as she was about to take a breath to ask him what, if anything, that kiss this morning meant to him, Aidan came back into the room. She hurriedly turned back to her script.

For a little while longer, they practised a couple more lines from the opening scene, much to Aidan's amusement, and, feeling distinctly peckish after that, Florence got her phone out and idly checked to see if any of the takeaway delivery services had reached Willowbury as yet.

'It's at times like this that I miss living near the centre of York,' Florence grumbled. 'Not even Pizza Hut delivers out this far.'

'The kebab shop does pizzas if you fancy one,' Aidan said. 'And we've got an Indian and a Chinese takeaway in the village, and the chip shop is to die for. Best fish this side of Plymouth, apparently.'

Florence laughed. 'For two such health-conscious blokes, who used to be in the forces, you clearly know your takeaways.'

Sam joined in the laughter. 'I'll take that as a compliment, I think.'

Florence rummaged in her bag for her purse. 'I'm up for sharing a pizza, if you are.'

Aidan batted away the ten-pound note she'd found. 'My treat this time. I'll head out and grab some pizzas if you two sort out the plates.'

'Will you be OK on your own?' Sam asked, which was met with an impatient glance from Aidan.

'Of course,' Aidan replied. 'I think I can make it there and back without getting lost. It is in the middle of the town, after all.'

'OK,' Sam said. 'But call me if...' he trailed off.

'I'll see you in half an hour,' Aidan said firmly.

Was Florence imagining it or did Aidan throw his brother a knowing glance as he left the two of them alone?

As the front door slammed, Sam let out a breath. 'Don't say it,' he said as he got up from where he'd been sitting to watch Aidan wandering down the road from his vantage point at the living room window.

'Say what?' Florence asked gently.

'That I'm being overprotective. I know I am. But old habits and that.' He smiled apologetically.

'I thought he was on more of an even keel these days,' Florence said. 'I mean, he seems very calm and together.'

'When he's taking his medication properly and getting enough sleep, then life is a whole lot calmer,' Sam turned back from the window and sat back next to Florence on the floor. 'But, unfortunately, either the meds upset his stomach or he forgets to take them, and then we take two steps backward. It's a long game. When he doesn't take them... well, you've heard the milder consequences through the wall!'

Florence nodded. 'I guess it's something that changes all the time,' she said softly. 'But I know he must be grateful to have you in his corner.'

'He wasn't always,' Sam replied. 'I think he blames himself for my resigning my commission. He knows how much I loved being in the navy, and he can't quite come to terms with the fact that I left, as he sees it, to be his carer.'

'But that's not quite true,' Florence replied. 'I mean, you're at work full time.'

'Yes, but he can blow things out of proportion sometimes. He had a very dark time when he was first pensioned out of the army. He struggled to process what had happened to his unit; why he had survived when the rest had died in the IED explosion. No matter how many times he was told that his life would be a "new" normal rather than going back to what it was before, it took a long time for him to adapt, to accept that things would never be the same.' Sam glanced around the warm, cosy living room, which was now decked out with a Christmas tree, although no other decorations. 'This place gives him a kind of physical security – there's no mortgage and he has a generous pension because of what happened to him, but emotionally he still has to take one day at a time.'

'As do you, presumably,' Florence said without thinking, and then blushed. 'Sorry, that's a bit personal.'

Sam smiled. 'I won't lie and say it's been easy, making the adjustment to civilian life after being in the navy for nine years. The discipline and routine of what I did embedded some pretty hard-to-break routines, and I miss the constant presence of people, being part of something. But working as part of the air ambulance crew is just as rewarding, especially that team camaraderie when a job's gone well. And no day is ever the same, of course.'

'Do you miss it, though?"

'Of course,' Sam replied. 'Although I'm still part of the Royal Navy Reserves, too, who are based at Yeovilton. I get to keep my hand in for twenty-four days a year at least, and wear the uniform from time to time.' His eyes sparkled in the low light of the fire, the enthusiasm for his old job breaking through.

'You speak really well about it,' Florence observed. 'How would you like to come into my school and talk to some students?'

Sam laughed. 'Are you serious?'

'Sure. We're looking for speakers for the Careers Day in early February. I know the kids would love to hear about your current job, and, if you're happy to talk about it, your former one. Will you give it some thought?'

'I haven't set foot in a school since I left my own,' Sam said. 'And I kind of like it that way.' He paused a little before adding, in a slightly huskier voice, 'But since it's you... I'll definitely think about it. When do you need to know for sure?'

'Sometime in the new term, but definitely by the end of January,' Florence replied. 'We're putting the itinerary together to send home to parents in the first week of February, so you can think about what you might say to them.'

Sam looked at her wryly. 'Why do I get the feeling that you're used to getting your own way?'

Laughing, Florence slapped his bare forearm where he'd pushed up the sleeves of his grey cashmere jumper. 'You make me sound like a right bossy cow!' The contact of the palm of her hand on his warm, bare skin made her hand tingle as the electricity of contact shivered through her.

Sam joined in the laughter. 'That wasn't what I meant, honestly! I just can totally see why I'd be following your every instruction if you were my teacher!'

'Thanks,' Florence said drily. Her hand was still on his arm, and, as a slightly charged silence descended between them, Florence felt herself moving closer to Sam from where they were sitting on the floor by the fireside. The crackle of a log falling in the grate made Florence jump, in her heightened state of awareness of how close she and Sam were getting. 'So, is that a yes?' Florence murmured as her mouth, with a mind of its own, began to move closer and closer to Sam's.

'It's a definite maybe,' Same replied softly. 'If you promise not to give me a massive telling-off if I mess up.'

'As if I would,' Florence's voice grew husky. 'Unless you want me to, that is.'

Sam's breathing was quickening, and she could feel its warmth on her face, sweet from the hot chocolate they'd all been drinking while running lines. The cinnamon undertones of the sweet confection made her senses reel, and they were within a hair's breadth of another kiss. Instinctively, Florence's hand tightened on Sam's arm, and as their lips were a breath from meeting, she felt an incredible sense of rightness, of coming home.

'I'm home!' Aidan announced as the front door banged behind

him. Sam and Florence jumped apart guiltily. Although why Florence felt guilty, she had no idea. She and Sam were two consenting adults, after all.

'That was quick,' Sam said, perhaps a little resentfully, at least to Florence's inflamed ears.

'Tom spotted me on the way out of the pizza place and gave me a lift back,' Aidan replied.

'Should he be driving?' Florence questioned, shifting away from Sam to put a bit more of a respectable distance between them. She hurriedly picked up her script again and pretended to be looking intently at the rest of the scenes she and Sam had to rehearse.

'He's got an automatic car and reckons there's plenty of room on the left for his cast,' Aidan replied. 'And he's only on paracetamol now, since they discharged him, so he seems safe enough.'

'Perhaps he'll be OK for the performances, then?' Sam said hopefully.

'Sorry, mate, doctor's orders are I can't stand for too long on the ankle, even if it is in this wonderfully colourful cast.' Tom Sanderson's voice echoed through the hallway.

'I, er, thought Tom might want to join us for pizza and to help you two to perfect your lines before tomorrow's dress rehearsal,' Aidan said. 'Is that OK?'

Florence sighed inwardly. She'd grown to like Tom in the weeks they'd been working on the play together, but given the seconds-ago near miss with Sam, she was hoping they might get another chance before she had to go home. With both Aidan and now Tom playing gooseberry, that now seemed unlikely. 'Sure,' she said quickly, as she caught Sam giving her a quizzical look.

'Come and sit in the living room, mate,' Aidan called to Tom, who was hovering in the doorway. 'I'll sort out the pizzas and bring them in in a sec.'

As Tom hobbled through the door on his hospital-issue

crutches, Florence felt a surge of sympathy. Tom seemed gutted to be missing out on his big moment in the Willowbury limelight, and it was clear that he still wanted to be a part of proceedings, even if he was no longer going to be centre stage.

'How's it all going?' Tom asked as he sank gratefully into the large, comfortable armchair by the fire. Florence suppressed a smile as she saw the multicoloured cast that was wrapped around Tom's broken ankle. Trust him to pick something so attention-grabbing.

'We're getting there,' Sam said evenly. 'I don't think I'll be a patch on you, though.'

'Well, of course, one can't overestimate the importance of stage experience,' Tom replied, but the tone of his voice made it clear that he was joking. A few weeks ago, Florence would have wanted to thump him for a comment like that, but now she knew him better, she could take it in the manner it was intended.

Florence was saved from replying by Aidan returning with the pizza boxes and four plates. 'Here we go. What are we drinking?'

'Ought we to drink if we're carrying on rehearsing?' Florence queried, and then blushed at how sensible she sounded. Sometimes the teacher in her sneaked out of the classroom a little more than she liked.

'It might help,' Sam said wryly, passing her a plate before standing up. 'We've got a few bottles of lager in the fridge if you want one.' He looked down at her for confirmation, and she felt her heart flip at the sight of his long, muscular legs, encased in slim-fit jeans, in front of her.

'Yeah, OK then,' she said, struggling to focus on his face. 'I guess one, or three, wouldn't hurt.'

'Not for me, thanks,' Tom said. 'Got to drive home after this.'

'You could have the sofa if you want,' Aidan offered quickly. Was

Florence imagining things, or did Sam's younger brother blush as he made the offer?

'Thanks, but I had a night on the orthopaedics ward last night after they pinned my ankle back together, and while I've always had a thing for cotton sheets and hospital corners, I'd quite like to be back under my own duvet tonight!'

'How did you do it?' Aidan asked.

Tom glanced at Aidan and grinned ruefully. 'It was when I was walking Mum and Dad's Jack Russell, Billy, last night. I put a foot down a rabbit hole up on Willowbury Hill. I managed to limp home after it happened, but after an hour or so I realised I might have done a bit more than sprain it. Thankfully, my next-door neighbour drove me to hospital and then looked after Billy when I had to stay there overnight. Mum and Dad picked me, and then him, up early this morning, so I don't have to worry about him today at least. But thanks for the offer of the sofa,' he added, almost shyly.

'No worries.' Aidan busied himself with handing out the plates and soon they were tucking in to generous portions of Meat Feast (with added chillies) and slugging down mouthfuls of cool lager.

Florence, feeling relaxed in the company of these three very different men, took the time as they were eating to observe them. Aidan was chatting away to Tom, who seemed, unusually, not to be trying to get one up on the other two guys. Knowing where Tom's preferences lay, Florence gathered pretty quickly that Tom had a bit of a thing for Aidan. Weeks ago, she could have sworn it was Sam who'd got his interest, but from the way Tom was laughing uproariously at Aidan's every mildly humorous utterance, she figured it was Aidan who was now on Tom's radar. She wondered if Aidan realised. Then, she chided herself; what business was it of hers, anyway?

Sam, on the other hand, was sitting quietly eating his pizza and paying little attention to the other men as he looked at the script in front of him on the floor, clearly trying to memorise as many lines as he could before the next rehearsal. Every so often he'd glance up though; was she imagining it or did his gaze seem to linger a little more on her than his brother and Tom? In the firelight, and from the dim light of the lamp on the side table nearest the door, it was difficult to tell.

Eventually, full from the takeaway, Aidan stretched and got up from his spot on the sofa. 'I'll get this lot away,' he said, grabbing the plates and stacking them on top of the two pizza boxes. 'Anyone want another drink?'

'I wouldn't mind another beer, if there is one,' Sam replied. 'I can't get any worse at this role, so the alcohol might make it better.'

'I'll give you a hand,' Tom made to get up, seemingly having forgotten about his broken ankle, then sighed and sank back down again. 'Maybe not,' he said ruefully. 'Although I must have a pee.' He looked at Sam. 'Is there a bathroom on the ground floor?'

'Yep,' Sam replied. 'Out of here and second on the right.' He passed Tom his crutches, which were on the floor by the fire.

Tom successfully got up and hobbled out of the lounge door, behind Aidan, who'd taken the detritus of the meal out to the kitchen.

'So,' Florence said as she picked up her own script. 'Where were we?'

Sam, intent on studying his own script, glanced up at her as she settled back on the floor. His brilliant blue eyes regarded her levelly. 'I'm not sure,' he said. 'Are we on the same page?'

Florence blushed. 'I think so,' she said softly. The two of them had the booklets open in their hands, but Florence's slipped from her lap as Sam leaned over, closing the gap between them. They were a breath away from another kiss, and Florence's lips parted in tingling anticipation of what was about to happen. Closer, closer...

'I thought you weren't rehearsing the kissy bits!' Aidan called as he came back into the living room.

Sam sprang back from Florence again as if guilty. 'Oh, you know,' he laughed nervously. 'We'll have to do it on the night, after all.'

Florence felt frustrated by the near miss. 'I think I'll turn in,' she said, feigning a yawn. 'I'll see you at the dress rehearsal tomorrow evening.'

'Sure,' Sam threw her a quizzical look as she stood back up again. 'Can I walk you home?'

'No point, really,' Florence smiled briefly. 'It's not exactly miles away.'

Sam paused, as if he wanted to say something else.

Florence headed out to the hallway. 'I'll see you tomorrow,' she called over her shoulder, opening the front door and then closing it swiftly behind her before Sam could follow her. As the night air hit her, cooling her flaming cheeks, she wanted to scream with frustration. They'd spent most of the evening together and yet they'd both, still, not mentioned their kiss at the air ambulance base. She knew she could just have brought it up with him, but then she'd be forced to consider whether she was keen to embark on a relationship with someone with a whole load of baggage. And was she really going to take that step? Not to mention they'd be onstage together playing at being lovers next Saturday night in front of the whole of Willowbury – how were they going to cope with that?

20

'Christ, these breeches are going to castrate me,' Sam grumbled to Aidan as they both got into their fake military uniforms for the first performance. The dress rehearsal the previous Monday had been nothing short of a disaster, with Sam clutching his script like a life-line and the rest of the cast missing cues here there and every-where. To cap it all, Tom had forgotten to pass on the costume to Sam, so it was only now, literally just before the show was due to start, that Sam had got his hands on it. Struggling abortively with the zip on the breeches, Sam breathed out in frustration. 'I can say goodbye to having kids if I have to do the whole performance in these.'

Aidan waggled his eyebrows. 'The front row won't know where to look,' he quipped, buttoning up his jacket and then bending down to pull on his long boots. 'But then Tom's about a foot shorter than you.'

'And he must have lost some weight,' Sam grumbled. He fidgeted uncomfortably in them. 'I might need to find a different pair.'

'At this notice? You'll be lucky.'

'Ten minutes to curtain,' Josie called. Cool and efficient now the cast had been sorted out, she popped her head around the men's changing area. She furrowed her brow at Sam. 'We're going to have to do something about those,' she gestured to his ridiculously tight trousers, which were still refusing to do up. 'Or you'll give the venerable ladies of the parish a heart attack. Can you stick your jeans back on?'

'With pleasure,' Sam sighed, relieved in more ways than one. Whipping off the trousers, he slipped back into his jeans, which, while pleasingly tight, felt like pyjamas after wearing the costume for ten minutes. Then, he had a brainwave. 'My navy uniform's on the back of my bedroom door,' he said before Josie disappeared again. 'I reckon the trousers'll still fit, and they're a similar shade to these, anyway. What do you think? I can pop back home and get them before the show starts.'

'Sounds fine to me,' Josie said, who basically would have agreed to anything to keep Sam as Benedick at such short notice. 'But make sure you're back here before your first entrance.'

Sam coughed. 'Yup.' He darted out of the back door, safe in the knowledge that the trip to his house and back wouldn't take more than eight minutes. He had the uncanny ability to gauge distances rather well since he'd been flying for the SAA.

'Positions, everyone, one minute!' Josie called, exactly nine minutes later, in a voice that would silence even the loudest Year 9 class.

Sam, back and in his dress uniform trousers, which, thankfully, did still fit, suddenly felt like he was about fourteen years old again. His stomach turned over as he contemplated what was to come. What if he really wasn't up to scratch and let everyone down? No matter how many times Florence had reassured him that everyone knew the tricky position he'd been put in, he still felt the old desire to be the best, to be perfect, kicking in. He knew the odds were stacked against him; that sooner or later he was going to fluff a line or miss a cue, and feel that horror of being the one who messed up, but no matter how many times everyone had told him how proud they were that he'd stepped in, he knew it was all on him now.

As if on cue, the door opened again and Sam's stomach turned another somersault. Aidan was off to his left, chatting quietly to a couple of other cast members before they all had to take their places for the first scene. There was Florence, hair tied up in a bun, with tendrils framing her face. Her eyes looked a deeper blue than he'd ever seen them, enhanced by the glittering stage make-up, and her skin glowed with a luminosity that took his breath away. She'd been wearing the costume at the dress rehearsal, but her make-up hadn't been so dramatic. Sam's stomach jumped again as she smiled and met his gaze.

'Are you ready?' she said gently, taking one look at his pale face.

Sam, temporarily incapable of speech, swallowed hard to relieve the constriction in his throat. 'As I'll ever be,' he finally said.

He couldn't take his eyes off her. In addition to the theatrical hair and make-up, she was wearing a white, floaty summer dress that had been artfully unbuttoned a little to show just a tantalising glimpse of her cleavage, and a red, fake-fur-lined cloak that tied with a red satin ribbon at her throat. As she breathed in, her chest rose and he found himself dragging his eyes back up to her own before she clocked his inattention.

'Well, break a leg,' Florence's eyes glinted, as if she'd seen exactly where Sam's gaze had been drawn. 'I'll see you for the second scene.'

'Sigh no more, lady,' Aidan quipped, returning to Sam's side as Florence left. 'Christ, bro, could you have been any more obvious?'

he continued once Florence was out of earshot. 'Short of falling into her cleavage?'

'Oh, shut up,' Sam muttered. 'She looked bloody gorgeous.'

'Yes, she did, didn't she? Do you think you'll be able to control yourself when you stage kiss her?'

Sam tried not to think about that. At least he had the whole of the first half to prepare himself. They'd had a couple of stage kisses during the dress rehearsal, which he'd been too nervous to appreciate, and now they had to lock lips in front of the population of Willowbury!

As he walked out into the wings, he could hear Florence uttering her opening lines and felt the hair rising on the back of his neck. She had a beautiful speaking voice, with a tantalising trace of the broad Yorkshire vowels she'd picked up from teaching in York. Her diction was lyrical. *Emma Thompson, eat your heart out,* he thought.

As the rest of the scene played out, he felt Chris Charlton, the taciturn actor playing Don John, slipping up beside him with Rob Henshaw, who was playing Don Pedro, on the other side.

'Don't worry, mate,' Rob said in an undertone. 'We're all with you. We'll make this work.'

'Thanks,' Sam was touched. Rob was clearly channelling the role of the valiant prince, and he was grateful for it.

'Let's do this,' Chris said, from his other side. Already psyched into the role of the dastardly Don John, his face was deadly serious.

Drawing a deep breath, the three strode onto stage, Sam pulling himself up ramrod straight as if he really was on parade. What was his first line? His mind was a blank. Then, as he saw Florence in the centre of the female cast, chin thrust upwards in a gesture that was pure Beatrice, his heart expanded. He opened his mouth to speak, but nothing came. As the pause descended, he felt a nudge from Rob on his right side.

'Disdain,' he muttered under his breath.

Sam shook himself. Of course!

'I see you've still got that look of disdain, Beatrice!' he called across the stage. 'I thought it would have killed you by now.'

Florence's eyes flashed. 'Sorry? What was that? I wasn't paying attention.'

And they were off, flashing witty repartee between them until the scene's end, when Florence was left to one side, allowing, for a moment, Beatrice's helpless longing to glimmer through the facade of carefully cultivated indifference.

As Sam exited stage left (having been prodded, once again, by Rob, in the right direction), he breathed a sigh of relief. That was Act One in the bag. Just another four to get through.

'Well done, mate,' Chris said once they were offstage. This time, he was smiling. 'The rest of it'll be a piece of cake.'

'I'm not so sure about that,' Sam muttered, still thrown by seeing Florence in her costume, without Josie milling around, cutting in, and the other numerous distractions that had occurred in the dress rehearsal. It was also one thing to have been rehearsing with Florence and Aidan with a pizza between them and a roaring fire, but something entirely different to be onstage for all to see and judge. Why the hell had he ever agreed to be the understudy?

He belted off to grab a glass of water before he was needed for the next act, which was a much more terrifying prospect, being that he had to 'overhear' the other men discussing Beatrice's love for Benedick and then react accordingly, declaring to the audience that he, too, felt the same. Suddenly, flying helicopters on and off ships in stormy seas seemed like a much easier prospect. He wondered if it was too late to re-enlist before the second half started.

'All right, mate?' Rob asked on his way back to take position for the next act.

Sam nodded. Taking a deep breath, he prepared himself for the onslaught of Act Two. Remembering, as the curtain went up, that in half an hour he'd be kissing Florence in public in front of most of Willowbury, he felt his stomach flip again; but this time, he wasn't sure if was nerves or excitement.

21

'Breathe,' Florence whispered to herself from the other side of the wings. The play was almost finished, and in a moment she and Sam would be onstage performing their final scenes, including the kiss that they'd never really committed to in the dress rehearsal.

'Are you OK?' Amy, the student playing Hero glanced at Florence.

Going into teacher mode, Florence tried to smile reassuringly. 'I'm fine.'

But, inside, all she could think about was the kiss that was coming. The prospect of locking lips with him on stage in public was terrifying. She tried to keep telling herself that real actors did it all the time; that kissing someone while acting was just work for them. Somehow, though, given the unexpected circumstances, this felt about as far from work as it was possible to be.

'Come on,' Amy said, taking Florence's hand. 'We're up.'

Florence took a deep breath and strode onstage for the final scene, which, in this version of *Much Ado* involved a proposal of marriage, the villain being ducked in a pan of cider and a tentative but not definite reunion between the play's other couple, Hero and

Claudio. There was no doubt that the marriage proposal was the centre of the action, though, with Beatrice and Benedick literally centre stage for it.

'Take the man away... he needs to dry off before we decide what to do with him tomorrow,' Sam, as Benedick, intoned from the other side of the stage.

A dripping-wet Chris Charlton was pulled from the cider pan and led offstage by Aidan to boos and cheers from the audience.

'And now,' George, the older man who was playing Leonato, said, 'don't you think it's about time you confessed to Beatrice exactly how you feel about her?'

Sam paused for a moment, and Florence's heart lurched as that moment extended into two or three more beats. Had Sam forgotten his line? Had he frozen up now, at the very end of the show? Was it the thought of the stage kiss that had thrown him?

She drew a deep breath as she stood, stage left, waiting for Amy to pull her forward to the centre so that she and Sam could play their final scene.

Just as Chris Charlton, who was waiting soggily in the wings, was about to open his mouth to prompt Sam, he finally spoke. 'I don't know what you mean. There's nothing between Beatrice and me.' He took a step forward, and Florence's knees went weak with relief.

'Of course not!' Rob 'Don Pedro' Henshaw laughed, grabbing the prop mobile phone from the back pocket of Sam's trousers. 'That's why you've been drafting lovey-dovey texts to her ever since you found out she loved you.' There followed a couple of great belly laughs from the audience and the actors themselves as Rob improvised a couple of lines to represent the texts.

'Well, I don't fancy him!' Florence said, when the laughter onstage and off had abated. 'I wouldn't marry him if he was the last person on Earth!'

'Sure,' Amy, as Hero, responded. 'But even you can't argue with the pictures on your Instagram account – or are you going to tell me you've been hacked?' She waved another mobile phone out at the audience. 'This meme in particular's *very* telling... "Love is best when it's found in unexpected places". Awww!'

A hush descended over the audience and the players on stage as Florence took the phone from Rob and Sam took the other one from Amy. Circling around each other, initially with their backs facing, they came together, smiling at the screens, as directed by Josie, for a count of three. Then, in perfect harmony, they raised their heads, their eyes locked and their hands fell to their sides again.

'I think it's time we stopped pretending,' Sam said softly as he slipped an arm around Florence. 'And admitted to everyone how we really feel.'

'I will if you will,' Florence replied, her voice channelling Beatrice, but her pulse jumping wildly in counterpoint.

'Then let's stop talking,' Sam said. And with that, his mouth was upon hers and he was kissing her. Florence gasped as she realised that this wasn't quite what she'd been expecting. Whether Sam was carried away in the moment, or whether he'd just forgotten what they'd talked through, Florence found she didn't care. Responding with equal passion, she kissed him back, until his arms slid around her and, thankfully, as actually rehearsed, he lifted her off her feet. As the hackneyed strains of the 'Wedding March' echoed through the priory performance space, Sam returned her to her feet, and, both smiling, they turned to face the audience, all of whom were applauding rapturously.

As the cast took their bows in turn, the whoops and cheers from the crowd intensified, and Florence was glad to be joined onstage by the rest of the cast, and then Josie. She realised that Sam still had hold of her hand, and she gave him a sidelong glance, tickled and exhilarated to see the relief and enjoyment on his face. They'd done it!

'Ladies and gentlemen,' Josie called over the applause as it started to die away. 'Thank you so much for coming tonight. As I'm sure many of you know, there was a last-minute change of cast, and Sam Ellis here has been thrust into the spotlight.'

Cheers and more whoops greeted this news as Josie turned and gestured to Sam to come forward again.

'I think you'll all agree that he did an excellent job at the eleventh hour, and with great reluctance, so thank you, Sam.'

'Bravo!' came a voice from the front row.

Florence grinned as she saw Tom waving one of his crutches in the air in appreciation. She was glad that he'd taken it all in good humour, given that this should have been his moment in the local limelight.

Florence felt a warmth spreading through her as she saw Sam's smile of embarrassment and pleasure at the recognition. As he stepped back to join the rest of the cast behind Josie, she squeezed his hand again.

'I'm delighted to announce that we're well on the way to raising two thousand pounds from tickets and refreshment sales from tonight, which will benefit the very worthy cause of the Somerset Air Ambulance.'

More applause, and Florence's eyes were drawn to the back row of the performance space, where a small group of people was waving wildly in Sam's direction.

'They must have got wind that I was actually going to be in it,' Sam murmured into Florence's ear as he gave a slight wave back to the other members of the SAA crew. 'I'll never hear the end of it at work!'

'You were great,' she whispered back. 'Really. Well done.'

'Thanks.' Sam's breath tickled her ear. 'So were you.'

The cast headed off stage, and Florence's spine started to tingle. As relieved as she was that the performance was over, she couldn't help feeling a sense of disappointment, too. That kiss onstage with Sam had been breathtaking; but was it the end of something, or just the beginning?

22

'Darling, you were spectacular!' Florence heard Tom say as she saw him rushing as fast as he could to her side as soon as he'd got backstage. Sending several cast members flying with his crutches, he flung his arms around her.

'Thanks,' Florence gasped as Tom finally released her.

'Of course, if I hadn't had to bow out at the last moment, we'd have been epic together,' Tom grumbled, but he brightened visibly when he spotted Sam hovering by the wall with Aidan, both of them cradling glasses of sparkling wine.

As Florence looked on, Tom, who seemed to flush slightly, hotfooted it, despite the heavy cast and his crutches, over to the boys, ostensibly to congratulate them. Florence trailed in his wake, keen to get closer again to Sam after that passionate onstage kiss.

Now that she was away from the stage lights, she felt suddenly chilly in her thin white summer dress. Referencing Tuscany in the summer was one thing, but there was no getting away from the fact it was still wintry outside.

'Well done, mate,' Tom said. Florence had to suppress a grin at the way Tom's voice still dropped in pitch when addressing the two other men.

'Thanks,' Sam said. 'We had one or two hairy moments, but we got through it.'

'More than that,' Tom said, still heartily. 'You did brilliantly under the circumstances.' He grinned. 'Of course, I'd have been better...'

Florence laughed too. 'We'll never know, though, will we?'

'There's always next year,' Tom said. 'I quite fancy Oberon if you want to be my Titania, Florence.'

Florence smiled and shook her head. 'I think that's me all acted out for at least the next ten years. What about you, Sam?'

Sam laughed nervously. 'I hadn't even expected to be acting in this one, let alone the next. I think I might have to avoid Josie for the foreseeable future.'

'Easier said than done, for me,' Florence said. 'Working with her as well as doing this.'

'Good luck,' Sam's laugh got more confident.

Yet again, Florence thought back to that sizzling not-at-all-fake kiss they'd shared onstage. She could feel her face starting to burn at the memory.

'Well, I'd better go and schmooze our director,' Tom said, seeing Josie coming into the room. 'After all, she'll probably never want to cast me again after this.' Moving remarkably swiftly on his crutches, he homed in on Josie as she was getting a drink.

'I almost feel sorry for her,' Sam said wryly, 'except that she got me into this!' He took a sip of his drink and, as he leaned forward to put his now empty glass on the table, Florence could feel the heat of his body, still warm and exhilarated from the final scenes of the show. She felt her own body responding instantly to his proximity.

She drew a deep breath. Perhaps it was the euphoria of a successful performance, but Florence suddenly felt like taking a risk. As Aidan had wandered off in Tom's wake, they were, temporarily, in their own little space, as they had been during the chapel scene.

'Did you enjoy it, in the end?' Florence asked. Her voice had dropped a little, and all she could think about was that final, delicious kiss as the curtain had come down.

Sam's eyes had darkened, his pupils widening as he gazed down at Florence. 'I did,' he said softly.

And with those two words, Florence felt her insides turning to liquid. She'd willingly have done anything at that moment to feel his lips on hers again.

'Florence,' he whispered, drawing so close to her that she could feel his breath growing shorter, the heat emanating from his body, which was only clad in his costume of flowing white shirt and tight naval trousers. The boots he was wearing elongated his legs to an astonishing degree, and Florence felt like some Regency heroine, bosom heaving as her own breaths came more quickly.

'Yes?' she whispered.

'Do you want to—'

'Hey there, lovebirds!' Aidan was back, and Florence felt herself being pulled forcibly from the moment that had enveloped her and Sam. It had been as if no one else in the world had existed until Aidan had broken in. 'Are we going to a post-mortem at the pub? Tom's asked if we fancy it.'

Sam's eyes were still locked on Florence's, and she could feel her own desire to prolong their separateness mixing with his. 'You can go if you want,' he said to his brother, not taking his eyes off Florence. 'I'll see you at home, OK?'

'OK,' Aidan said.

Florence didn't want to risk breaking eye contact with Sam, but if she had, she was sure she'd have seen Aidan grinning like the Cheshire Cat. Had she been thinking straight, she might have wondered about Aidan's sudden interest in Tom, but at the moment Sam was all she could think about.

'Do you want me to walk you home?' Sam said, his voice loaded with promise.

'I'd like that,' Florence replied. 'Do you think you know the way?'

Sam laughed at the joke they'd made a thousand times. 'I should do by now.'

Not bothering to change – after all, the dress was hers anyway – Florence shrugged on her coat. Just as she was contemplating whether she should dash to the loo and see how her face looked (flushed, she suspected), Sam emerged from getting his jacket. She prayed her stage make-up hadn't run under the lights.

They walked briskly home together, the tension palpable between them. Their breath steamed in the frosty night air, and Florence shivered at the sudden drop in temperature. Not missing a beat, Sam slid an arm around her waist, which brought her out in goose bumps that weren't at all related to the outside temperature. She felt the hairs on the back of her neck rising as he pulled her closer and she felt once again the heat of his body.

It didn't take long before they were at Florence's front door. She fumbled for her key, which was buried somewhere deep in her coat pocket, and with not entirely steady hands thrust the key into the lock, before pushing open the door.

The minute the door closed behind them, Sam had pushed her back against the wall of the hallway and was kissing the life out of her. His mouth was hot, and tasted sweet, and Florence's knees started to buckle as the sensations of heat and rightness washed over her.

'I have been wanting to do this since the curtain fell this evening,' Sam murmured between kisses. 'You have no idea how being so close to you on stage has made me ache.' He pushed closer to her, and she felt the sudden, white-hot heat of her own arousal as his became immediately obvious.

'You're not the only one,' Florence replied. She had a hand in Sam's hair, and the other one slid down to the small of his back, pulling him closer to her as their kisses deepened. 'Christ, I just want to have you inside me.'

Sam pulled back slightly. 'There's nowhere else I'd rather be right now.'

With both of them clearly on the same page, Florence pulled Sam's mouth towards hers, shrugging out of her coat as she did so, and thanking her lucky stars she'd left the heating on in the house and the wood-burning stove smouldering away in the lounge. She wrapped a thigh around Sam's waist, and for a moment wondered about the wisdom of making love up against the wall of her great-aunt's hallway. Perhaps it would have been better to at least get up the stairs first. But there was a passion and a desperation in both of them, formed through weeks of dancing around each other, and stoked by the up-close-and-personal nature of the performance tonight, and the kiss at the end of it.

Sam also seemed as carried away as Florence was, and he groaned as Florence pulled him in closer and closer to her body. There were only a couple of layers of material between them and ecstasy now, and the tantalising prospect of making love drove all sense from her mind. The temptation to shed those last layers right there was overwhelming, and as Florence fumbled with the zip on Sam's flies, she felt his hand come down to still hers for a deliciously agonising moment.

'We should probably go somewhere a little more comfortable,' he murmured, pulling back to allow them both to catch their breath.

Florence, lips tingling from the kissing, was more than happy to continue up against the wall, but the practical side of her remembered she had condoms in her bedside drawer. 'Let's head upstairs,' she said, legs still like jelly. She took his hand. 'Come on.'

Needing no further encouragement, Sam allowed Florence to lead him up the steep stairs of the house and across the landing into her bedroom. Florence thanked her lucky stars she'd changed the sheets and hoovered that morning. Pulling the curtains closed, she left the hall light on, and the door open, so it cast a warm glow on the bed. The climb to her bedroom seemed to temper their up-against-the-wall frenzy of a few moments ago, and Florence felt her stomach flutter as Sam paused, glancing at her bed. His hand was still warm in hers, and as he turned to her, she saw the faintest flicker of nervousness in his eyes.

'Are you sure you want to do this?' he asked.

Florence smiled. 'More than anything.'

She stepped out of her shoes and turned so that they were facing each other. Her heart was beating faster and faster, as was a deep, throbbing, insistent rhythm between her thighs. She brought Sam's hand up to her chest, sliding his fingers underneath the thin linen of the white dress until his fingers encountered the peaking hardness of a nipple. She knew he could feel her heart beating, and as his warm hand cupped and caressed her breast, a moan escaped her lips. With eyes half closed, she saw him move closer towards her, until she felt his lips kissing her neck. Glancing down his body, she could see how aroused he was, and as they moved closer again, she could feel his cock pressing through his dark blue trousers.

'Come on,' she murmured, feeling a primeval need to have him inside her. She led him to the bed and, ever in control, she pushed him down onto it, straddling him for a long, delicious moment with just the remaining few layers of fabric between them. As she ground down onto him, she felt his cock move, and the sensation turned her insides even more to liquid. 'I need you,' she said.

She moved down until she was able to unbutton his shirt and

then unzip his trousers fully, and as he wriggled out of them, revealing a pair of blue checked boxer shorts which left very little to the imagination.

Not wanting to be outdone, Sam sat up and, with warm hands, slid Florence's partially unbuttoned dress from her shoulders, brushing her nipples with his fingertips as he did so. Still straddling him, she wrapped her legs tightly around him and kissed him fiercely, relishing the sensation of his warm, bare skin on hers as they drew closer so that there wasn't a breath between them.

It didn't take much, now, for them to lose the last of their clothing, and as she was still sitting in his lap, Florence broke the momentum only slightly to reach into her bedroom drawer and apply, with slightly trembling hands, what she found there. Then, with a gasp and a sigh, she felt Sam thrust up inside her, filling her with his glorious hardness.

As one of his hands tangled in her hair, the other slid downwards to caress her intimately; sensations that were heightened by the deep, warm presence of his cock inside her. She moved sensuously, rhythmically against his stroking fingers until the pulse of an imminent orgasm built up and she felt the warm, tingling sensations break over her, making her sit even more deeply so that he could feel her come around him. The sensations were exquisite, and as she broke, a moment later so did he.

Sweating and still joined, Florence brushed Sam's hair back from his face as they both came back to earth. His eyes were bright and, in their blueness, reminded her of the oceans which he'd travelled in his former job. A small voice inside her head, shushed to the back of her mind for now, questioned how she could have let herself go with a man whose first love had been flying away to sea, but for the moment, she didn't listen to it. It felt so achingly good to be this close to him after they'd danced around each other for weeks.

'What are you thinking?' Sam asked softly.

'You expect me to put that into words after what we've just done?'

'Well, you *are* an English teacher. I thought that's what you did for a living.' His eyes were twinkling, and as he shifted position to slide out of her, Florence laughed.

'Let's just say I wasn't expecting this evening to end up quite like this.' She glanced down, wondering where on earth she'd thrown her knickers. Not that she remembered taking them off. Perhaps Sam had managed to remove them without her even noticing, she had been so swept up in the moment.

Florence, whose knees were just starting to ache, clambered off Sam's lap and settled back against the white pillows. She felt peaceful, sated and quite amazingly tired after the adrenaline rush of the performance and then what had, literally, come after.

'Are you OK?' Sam asked as he sank down on the pillows beside her.

'Yes,' she said softly. Then, a slight frown creased her brow. 'You don't have to go anywhere just yet, do you?'

Sam smiled. 'Even if I did, there's nothing that could drag me away from you and this bed right now.' He raised his arms above his head and settled back, eyes staring at the ceiling.

'I'm glad,' Florence murmured, snuggling into his chest. Talking could come later; for now, basking in the afterglow was her number-one priority.

23

The winter sunlight flickered in shards through the gaps in Florence's bedroom curtains as she gradually awoke to the awareness of someone in the bed beside her. For a moment, caught between that blissful state of sleeping and waking, she luxuriated in the warmth of his body, feeling one arm slung casually over her waist where she was lying with her back to him. Stirrings of another kind were taking place under her thick duvet, and she stretched voluptuously, pressing back into the contours of Sam's body as sleep slipped away from her.

More glad than anything that she'd decided to just have the one glass of Prosecco post-performance last night, Florence felt clear-headed and decidedly right. What had happened with Sam was not entirely unexpected after the sizzling chemistry of their scenes together during the play, and that unexpected onstage kiss, but she was still surprised that they'd both been so *carpe diem* about the whole thing and ended up in bed. She wasn't known for her throw-caution-to-the-wind approach, and Sam had been equally reticent up until recently. But now, with this sleepy, gorgeous man in bed beside her, was not the time to start thinking and overanalysing. There would be plenty of time for that later.

'Morning,' Sam said sleepily as she rolled over to face him. His face looked pleasantly rumpled, with a smattering of brownish blond stubble on his chin and his unruly hair even more dishevelled by a night of passion.

'Hi,' Florence replied. She tilted her face upwards for a kiss, and as he brought his lips to hers, she felt her body, and his own, responding.

'You were amazing last night,' Sam murmured between kisses. 'I feel like I've had the best night's sleep of my life.'

'Me too,' Florence replied. 'Certainly the best sleep since I've been here, anyway. Although now Aidan's stopped blasting my eardrums with Metallica at three a.m., that definitely helps.'

'Oh Christ,' Sam groaned. 'I forgot to check in with him last night. I hope he found his way home.' Casting his eyes around, as if looking for something, his gaze rested on his phone, which had fallen out of his pocket and was resting on the carpet by the bed.

'Do you want to call him?' Florence asked gently. She could see immediately just how guilty Sam felt that he'd broken their routine of check-ins, even if he had just been sleeping next door.

'No,' Sam said firmly. 'He keeps telling me that I have to give him some space, loosen the reins a little. I guess spending the night with you is as good a way to start doing that as any.'

'Besides,' Florence said playfully, 'I think he and Tom had quite a late night of drinking planned. I wonder if they made it back at all!'

Sam laughed. 'Aidan's not much of a drinker these days, because of all the medication, but he's always happy to lead someone else astray if the chance arises.'

'I feel pretty led astray myself,' Florence observed.

Sam grinned. 'You didn't take that much leading, if I remember last night correctly. I think I was following you!'

Remembering the way she'd virtually told him to take her up against the wall of the hallway, Florence blushed. 'Well, we were on a bit of a high.'

Sam stretched out in the bed, raising muscular arms above his head. 'We really were, weren't we?'

There was an almost imperceptible pause. A question seemed to hang in the air that neither seemed ready to ask just yet.

Not wanting to break the moment, Florence snuggled back into the crook of Sam's arm. 'Can I tempt you to breakfast?' she said.

'I'd love that,' Sam replied. 'But I think I'd better pop next door and check that Aidan made it home first.' He sat up in bed. 'Why don't I do that, and then you can come over and I'll make you breakfast at my place? If you can walk that far, that is!'

Florence laughed. 'I think I can manage that.' She definitely felt as though she'd had a night of passion, but it was only next door after all. 'I'll grab a shower and be over in a bit.'

'Great,' Sam said. Pushing back the duvet, he cast around for his clothing. 'I'll do the same. Half an hour OK?'

'Sure,' Florence replied. Part of her wanted to drag him back into bed for another round, but she realised that their night together was as huge a step for him as it felt to her, and she knew she needed a little time to process what it might mean.

Carpe diem, Florence, remember? she thought. Overthinking things at this stage had been her problem before, and she desperately didn't want to fall into the same trap with Sam.

She watched him throw on his shirt and pull on his trousers with a mixture of lust and amusement; he was obviously still reeling a little bit from last night as his boxer shorts were crumpled in a pile at the bottom of the bed. Not that it mattered, particularly. She'd fling them in the wash and give them back at a later date.

As Sam finished buttoning his shirt, he leaned down and gave her a long, lingering kiss. 'I'll see you in a bit,' he murmured, eyes still warm with lust.

'Definitely,' Florence replied. 'I hope you find Aidan where he should be.'

'I'm sure I will,' Sam smiled. 'And he's going to rip it out of me for staying out all night. He's been egging me on for weeks to make a move on you.'

'I'm glad I've got his approval!' Florence laughed. 'I'd hate to think he wasn't in favour of us getting closer.'

'That won't stop him taking the piss,' Sam replied. 'I hope you can take it!'

'Oh, I'm sure I'll manage,' Florence said. 'I've been teaching teenagers for nearly ten years – I know the best responses to those trying to get a rise out of me!'

Sam laughed, and Florence noticed just how relaxed that laugh seemed. She felt a warm glow to think that she was responsible for that. Somehow, she just knew that Sam was the kind of person who didn't let himself go easily, and that last night meant as much to him as it did to her. As he dragged himself away, she lay back against the comfy white pillows of her bed and allowed herself a few more minutes to luxuriate in the afterglow of the night before. Although she'd quite fancied picking up where they'd left off, breakfast at Sam's would be a decent substitute, and it would put Sam's mind at rest about his brother.

24

Sam was glad he'd checked his coat for his house keys before closing the door at Florence's. He didn't fancy knocking at his own front door and facing the embarrassment of Aidan having to let him in.

As he turned the key in the Yale lock and pushed open the wooden front door, which was slightly stiff from the damp and chilly night, it opened with a loud creak. Closing it behind him, he padded through the hallway, feeling the chill in the air compared to Florence's cosy home next door. The ancient boiler needed replacing, and was intermittent about firing up in the mornings. Usually, this wasn't a problem for either Sam or Aidan, as they were both used to the cooler temperatures of ships and barracks anyway, but he noticed the difference between the two houses.

Just as he was about to head through the hallway to the back of the house, where the kitchen was, he was startled by the sound of a loud snore rending the air asunder. The sound seemed to be coming from the living room. Aidan often fell asleep on the sofa, no matter how much Sam tried to ensure that his brother got a good night's sleep, so it was quite a surprise, when he pushed open the living room door, to find it wasn't Aidan lying prone on the settee. There, spread-eagled, broken left foot propped up on the arm of the ancient patchwork sofa, was none other than Tom Sanderson. On the coffee table were several empty bottles of Carter's Eloise Cider, one of their most notorious and alcoholic varieties, and a half-empty bottle of Sambuca, with two shot glasses and a lighter beside it.

For a moment Sam debated whether or not to wake Tom, but judging by the bottles, whenever Tom woke it wasn't going to be pretty. Deciding that perhaps it was better to take breakfast over to Florence's place, Sam grabbed his phone and texted her, explaining that he'd bring over everything they needed. He didn't fancy a post-mortem of last night instigated by Aidan and Tom.

As he wandered up the stairs, he automatically looked through Aidan's half-open door and was relieved to see his brother was also fast asleep, albeit fully clothed, on his bed. Clearly Aidan hadn't been so far gone that he'd neglected to find his own room. It had been a long time since Aidan had socialised, and part of Sam was pleased that he and Tom had obviously bonded, even if it was over an excess of cider and Sambuca. Aidan needed a network around him, having been surrounded by one in the army for so long, and for a long time after he'd been medically discharged, Sam had been the only one in the frame. Although Sam would never begrudge Aidan the support, it would take a little pressure off his shoulders if Aidan started getting out and making friends. Berating himself for still seeing Aidan as the prickly fourteen-year-old whose battles Sam, as the older brother, had had to fight at school, he tried to remember that Aidan was nearly thirty, and, despite everything, was more than capable of fighting his own battles these days. But if he and Tom were becoming friends, it would certainly help Aidan to see Willowbury as home.

But what about me? Sam thought. Would he ever really settle here? Even after a blissful night with Florence, he still couldn't help feeling like a visitor in Willowbury. How long did it take, he wondered, to truly feel like a local?

Trying to shrug off these thoughts, which were deeper and far more introspective than they had any right to be after such a wonderful, passionate night, he peeled off his clothes and waited in the chilly air of the bathroom for the shower to warm up. Thankfully, there was plenty of hot water this morning (since Aidan was, as yet, dead to the world), so before too long he was luxuriating in the steam, scrubbing away the excesses of the night before, but still feeling as though he wanted to do it all over again. Perhaps, now he was taking breakfast over to Florence, they'd get the chance for a repeat performance.

Stepping out of the shower a little time later, towelling himself dry, Sam swiftly pulled on fresh clothes and then headed back across the landing, checking, automatically, to see if Aidan had surfaced yet. Hearing voices downstairs before he got to Aidan's bedroom door, he stopped. He felt a little bit guilty for eavesdropping, but couldn't help himself. Peering around the corner, so that he had a direct view down the stairs to the hallway, he was stunned to see Tom, still hobbling but up and about, and Aidan, looking perkier than he'd have imagined, saying farewell in the hallway.

'Let's do it again soon,' Aidan was saying. 'I had a great time last night.'

'I did, too,' Tom replied. 'Although I'm not sure that either of us should have drunk quite so much Sambuca and lived to tell the tale.'

'Don't tell my brother,' Aidan laughed. 'He's such a fucking nursemaid, he'll only lecture me about how I shouldn't be mixing alcohol with my meds.' Sam felt a little bit hurt at having overheard Aidan talking about him like that, but swiftly put it down to bravado in front of Tom. He was, after all, only thinking a few moments ago about how pleased he was that Aidan and Tom had struck up a friendship.

'Well, you shouldn't really,' Tom chided. There was a pause between them that seemed loaded with some shared knowledge that Sam, as the outsider, couldn't quite fathom. 'I don't want to have to scrape you up off the floor the next time we go out.'

'Let's make next time really soon,' Aidan said.

'I'd like that.' Tom seemed to want to add more, but at the last moment seemed to think better of it. 'I'll, er, see you later.'

As Aidan walked to the front door to let Tom out, Sam wondered what the two of them could possibly have found to talk about all night. They were from completely different places and perspectives, after all. For the moment, though, all he really wanted to do was to check in with his brother and then get back next door to Florence.

'Good night last night?' Aidan asked, as he closed the front door and Sam came down the stairs.

Sam couldn't help the grin that spread over his face at the question. 'You could say that.'

Aidan grinned back. 'You and me both. So, what are you doing for breakfast?'

'Going back to Florence's,' Sam said. 'Will you be OK?'

'I don't recall you worrying about that for the whole of last night,' Aidan teased. 'I'm sure I'll be all right in the cold light of day, too.'

'Point taken,' Sam said, feeling a little bit guilty that he hadn't even texted Aidan before surrendering to Florence's arms. 'But you know where I am if you need me, OK?'

'I do,' Aidan smirked. 'Although I'm not sure you'll want me to disturb you!'

Sam shook his head. 'Oh, you should be all right for the time it takes us to eat croissants and drink tea.'

'Croissants, eh?' Aidan grinned. 'Where did you stash those, then?'

'At the back of the freezer, so you couldn't scoff them all during one of your three a.m. snack attacks,' Sam said. 'A few minutes in the oven and that's breakfast sorted.'

'Well, enjoy,' Aidan replied. Then, with a more serious expression on his face, 'Look, Sam...'

'Yeah?' Sam felt his throat constrict slightly.

'I know things haven't exactly been easy for you since you moved in with me, but it's great to see you actually start living your life again without worrying about me every five seconds. Florence is a wonderful woman. You should go for it.'

Sam felt his face burning under his brother's clear-eyed scrutiny. 'It's only one night,' he said gently. 'It's not like we're getting married.'

'I've seen the way you look at her,' Aidan replied. 'Your face gets all...' he struggled, as he sometimes did, these days, to remember the word, '... different, when you see her. In a good way.'

Sam laughed. 'So not like I'm having a stroke or something?'

Aidan grinned back. 'She's good for you. That's all I'm saying.'

'Thanks, bro.' Sam cleared his throat. 'Well, she'll be expecting breakfast so I'd better get back next door. I'll see you later.'

'Yeah,' it was Aidan's turn to clear his throat. 'I might text Tom and see if he wants to meet for a drink later.'

'Didn't you two put enough away last night?' Sam chided. 'After all, you're not supposed—'

'I know,' Aidan replied. 'I didn't actually drink that much in the end. The Sambuca was nearly all Tom. That's why he passed out on the sofa, I think.'

'He probably won't fancy another drink, then!' Sam laughed. 'But I'm glad you're making friends, too.'

Something Sam couldn't identify passed over Aidan's face at

that moment, and Sam was just about to ask him why when his attention was distracted by the paper bag that held the croissants starting to rip as it defrosted. 'I'd better get going,' he said, giving his brother a final grin. 'I'll see you later.'

'Not if I see you first,' Aidan replied, closing the front door behind him.

As Sam hopped over the wall, he again wondered about that conversation he'd overheard between Aidan and Tom when they'd said farewell that morning. If he didn't know better... But that was stupid, and he was just jumping to conclusions. Just because Tom was gay, it didn't mean he automatically fancied every bloke he saw, did it? And so what if Aidan hadn't had a serious girlfriend since university? With army life and then his injuries, it was hardly surprising he'd not got close to anyone. Besides, he'd know if his own brother was coming out, surely?

Putting Aidan out of his mind resolutely, he pushed the doorbell and waited for Florence to answer. *Carpe diem*, he, too thought, not for the first time that weekend.

_____

25

After the euphoria of the performance of *Much Ado About Christmas,* Florence found herself pulled into the end-of-term celebrations at school. It had always been her favourite time of year to be in school, even if the near-constant chorus of 'can we watch a video this lesson, Miss?' got a little wearing after a while. It was a time for winding up pieces of work, talking to students about their Christmas plans and handing out more Haribo than she could reasonably carry single-handed.

With only three days left of term, the majority of students were excited for the holiday, and Florence found herself getting in the mood, writing Christmas poems with her classes and sneaking in the odd Christmas-themed film.

As the last day of term beckoned, Florence reflected on the kind of Christmas Day she was going to have. Her parents had indeed opted to spend the holiday abroad, and were already in Australia with her brother, who'd emigrated ten years ago. Turkey on the barbecue hadn't really appealed to Florence, so she'd decided to stay at home on her own in Bay Tree Terrace instead of flying out to join them when term ended. In another year's time, when the loft extension was complete and the house was more shipshape, she'd volunteer to do the hosting at her place, but for this year it was just going to be her, her sofa, a fridge-full of party food and *Love Actually* on Netflix. She was content enough with this choice; after all, she'd had a lot of happy times in this house when Great-Aunt Elsie was alive, including one memorable Christmas Day when her mother had been rather over generous with the sherry and Aunt Elsie had been so tipsy she'd taught them all to play poker in the afternoon.

She did, however, find herself wondering what Sam and Aidan were going to be doing for the holidays. She figured that Sam was bound to be on shift for at least some of Christmas, but, even during their breakfast together, he hadn't really said much about his movements over the holiday period. She tried not to be offended or unsettled by this; a childhood of being on military bases, and more than one Christmas of missing her father dreadfully when he'd been deployed in places far away from home, meant that she was accustomed to the uncertainty of jobs like this, and the circumspect nature of those who did the jobs. Sam may not be in the navy any more, but a career of being guarded about his movements seemed to still be having an effect on his communication skills.

Struggling to her door on the day that school ended for the Christmas holidays, she nearly didn't notice the envelope that was sellotaped to it at eye level, with its festively attached sprig of holly in one corner. She put down her box of holiday marking on the dividing wall in order to gently remove the envelope. On the front was simply her name. What could it be?

Standing on the doorstep, she thumbed open the flap of the envelope and pulled out a Christmas card that had a series of penguins doing somersaults on icebergs on it. Inside was a short, but very sweet message that made her heart beat just that little bit faster. It read:

> *If you have no other plans tonight, I would love it if you joined me for a pre-Christmas dinner. I've got the house to myself! My place at 6.30 p.m.?*
> *All love, S xx*

Florence smiled, then panicked. It was gone five-thirty now, which gave her not even an hour to make herself feel less teacher and more temptress. Since, due to school and Sam's shifts, this would be the first time they'd seen each other for any significant amount of time since they'd spent the night together, she wanted to be able to give the evening her full attention. Divesting herself of coat, backpack and box of books, feeling slightly slovenly for not putting them in the right places, she headed upstairs and into the shower. A little part of her felt irritated that Sam had obviously just made the assumption that she wouldn't have made any other plans for tonight, but, she reasoned, it wasn't as if she'd had a roaring social life since she'd moved here, even with the *Much Ado* rehearsals. Shivering with anticipation despite the hot water, she wondered what tonight would bring.

* * *

On the other side of the party wall, Sam was putting the finishing touches to a dinner that he hoped would show Florence that he wasn't just good in the bedroom. He was, tomato soup notwithstanding, a decent cook, and as he checked the temperature of the oil in the fryer for his first course, breaded Camembert, which he would deep-fry and serve with rocket and cranberry sauce, he glanced at the clock. If Florence had got his note, she'd be knocking on the front door in less than half an hour. He'd prepared the main course, a delectable rib eye steak with green beans, which would only take a few minutes to flash fry on the griddle when they needed it. He'd cheated a bit on the crème brûlée and bought it, but, he reasoned, he couldn't make it better than that, anyway.

He'd packed Aidan off on the train to their mother's place earlier that day, having promised his brother that he'd be heading down the day after, which was Christmas Eve. Sam knew that Aidan found the visits a trial, even more so since his discharge from the army, and did feel slightly guilty that he was leaving him to his mother's untender mercies for one night, but, he reasoned, at some point he needed to let go a bit, give Aidan the space to cope with potentially stressful things on his own. It was tricky, but it was a step in the right direction to let Aidan go there before him. To be fair, they weren't going to be at their mum's place for long, anyway; Sam had rostered himself to work on Boxing Day and in that strange limbo period between Christmas and New Year that seemed to disorientate so many people. Since he didn't have any family apart from Aidan close by, he figured he might as well volunteer to work most of the holiday period, although Christmas in Willowbury seemed like a more tantalising prospect now that he'd grown so close to Florence.

Perhaps tonight would be a good time to tell her how he was starting to feel about her. He was, by nature, a private man, who didn't shout about his emotions from the rooftops, but Florence had really got under his skin. As he put some rocket onto the plates for the starter, he found himself imagining what their future might be like together. After all, sharing her house and having Aidan next door where he could keep an eye on him would be perfect, wouldn't it?

He stopped that line of thought abruptly in its tracks. What was he even thinking? He and Florence still barely knew each other, after all. Perhaps it was just the euphoria of being opposite each other in the play that caused them to fall into bed together. Perhaps, when they sat down to dinner, they'd have absolutely nothing to talk about.

Suddenly, he was gripped with anxiety. He shouldn't have just stuck that note to her door and expected her to comply; she wasn't one of his naval subordinates, after all. She was her own person, and, more than likely, she had plans for the last night of term, anyway. He'd behaved like an idiot. And anyway, if he'd wanted to ask her out on a date, why hadn't he just asked to meet her at The Travellers' Rest in town, instead? That place certainly had enough ambience to be a talking point. What happened if they just sat opposite each other in total silence all night, without Aidan to provide a chatty buffer between them?

He was just about to text her and call it off when his phone pinged with a message. Heart thumping, although it was probably just Aidan sending him confirmation that he'd made it to their mother's house and was already stuck into the Scotch, he wandered over to the kitchen table where he'd put it earlier.

Thanks for the invite. Luckily I didn't have other plans! See you in a bit. Love F x

Sam breathed out a long, slow, calming breath. So she hadn't taken the invitation the wrong way, then. Thank goodness for that! She could have just chucked it in the recycling bin, after all. But she hadn't.

Oh God. She hadn't. He'd better stop faffing with lettuce and go up and get changed. Putting down his phone, he raced upstairs.

26

Twenty-five minutes later, Florence put the finishing touches to her make-up and took one last look in the mirror. Dinner at Sam's place wasn't exactly going to be a formal affair, so she hadn't gone overboard, although she had put on a festively patterned dress from Boden that she hadn't been able to resist when they'd sent her a fifty-per-cent-off voucher a couple of weeks ago. Flat boots and a black cardigan completed the look and made her feel dressed up but not trussed like a Christmas turkey.

A thought ran, unbidden, through her mind that perhaps she wouldn't be wearing the dress for very long anyway. She rapidly shushed that thought.

She was hungry after a long day at school, and she couldn't help wondering if, without the context of the Dramatical Spectacular to focus on, she and Sam would find enough to talk about over dinner. Especially since Aidan wouldn't be there. What if it was all a colossal let-down?

It was too late now though. She'd texted her acceptance before she'd got in the shower. If it all got too awkward, she supposed she could just make her excuses and leave. It wasn't as if she had far to walk home, after all.

'Right,' she said out loud, as if she was addressing a particularly tricky class and not staring doubtfully at herself in the mirror. 'You don't have to do anything you don't want to do. It's dinner and hopefully a chat with a man you're seriously attracted to and have already shagged. Chill.'

She laughed out loud as she imagined what Aunt Elsie would say if she could have seen and heard her now. Somehow, she doubted the word 'shagged' had ever been spoken in this house before. To the best of her knowledge, Aunt Elsie had never had any romantic entanglements of her own, or, at least, none that she'd ever shared details of with Florence.

Checking her appearance one last time, she headed down the stairs and, remembering at the last minute to grab her house keys, stepped outside her front door. She glanced around her briefly, ensuring there was no one there to witness her slightly ungainly hop over the dividing wall in a skirt, took a deep breath and then knocked on Sam's front door.

As the door opened, Florence let out the breath. Sam was wearing another beautiful cashmere jumper, this time in a striking midnight blue. She found her left hand reaching out, instinctively, until she realised what she was doing and stopped.

'Hey,' he said, leaning forward and giving her a brief kiss on the mouth. 'I'm really glad you didn't have any other plans tonight.'

'Well, Adam Driver called, but I decided I'd rather spend the evening with you instead,' Florence teased as she crossed the threshold.

'Glad to hear it,' Sam replied. 'Although, since I'm a massive *Star Wars* fan, I wouldn't have blamed you for blowing me out for him!'

'I never had you for a sci-fi geek,' Florence said as she followed him through to the kitchen, which was lit only by the downlights under the units and a rose-coloured candle in the centre of the dining table.

'Are you kidding? I was brought up on the first six films, and Aidan and I have made a date every time a new one comes out.' He turned back and grinned at her. 'I always fancied being a pilot like Han Solo, and even as a grown-up I idolise Poe Dameron!'

'It's Princess Leia all the way for me,' said Florence. 'Although I'm rather partial to the love story between Rey and Ben, too.'

'Oh, you're one of *those*, are you? A shipper?'

Florence laughed. 'Only in a really cool, non-geeky way, you understand.' She'd never admit to Sam the hours she spent reading *Star Wars* fan fiction online after the new films had come out, or the evening may well have ended there and then.

'Of course!' Sam gestured to the table. 'Have a seat if you like. Can I get you a drink? There's white wine in the fridge, or I've got red, or cider if you want.'

'A glass of white wine would be lovely,' Florence replied. She needed one to calm her nerves, which was daft since she and Sam had been far more intimate than this after the play. In a certain part of her mind, though, it almost felt as though the two of them had still been acting when they'd fallen into bed last weekend. Perhaps it really had been Beatrice and Benedick acting out their desires and not she and Sam? She felt another flutter of nerves before she took the glass that Sam was holding out, and thanked him.

As they made small talk about their respective days, whether it was due to the wine or the company, Florence gradually relaxed. Sam had always been easy to talk to, despite his reticence about his personal life, and even though he had a habit of deflecting things about himself and asking her lots of questions, she did sense that gradually, he was relaxing too.

'Are you hungry? I can sort out the starter if you like.' Sam put his glass down on the kitchen table and enquired, his deep blue eyes taking on a shining hue in the candlelight.

'I am,' Florence replied, slightly surprised. 'Actually, I really am. Lunch is always somewhat of a rush during the school day, and even though I never want to see another packet of Haribo or box of Celebrations ever again, I actually do feel hungry now!'

'Glad to hear it!' Sam sprang up from his seat, nearly knocking it over in the process. As he reached out a hand to steady the back of it, Florence realised that he must have been feeling as nervous as she was.

Without pausing too much to think, she stood from her own chair and crossed the kitchen to stand next to him. 'It's all right, you know,' she said softly. 'I came here tonight because I wanted to.' She drew a little closer to him and, as she did so, his left arm slid around her, pulling her even closer. 'What happened after the play was really fast. We can take our time now.'

Sam smiled down at her, his eyes crinkling at the corners as he did so. Florence reached up with her right hand to stroke the creases, and then slid a hand back through his tousled dark blond hair.

'We've got all night,' she whispered. 'There's no rush.'

In response, Sam dropped his head and kissed her, slowly at first and then with a deepening intensity. He tasted of the white wine they'd both been drinking, and the warmth and sweetness of his mouth made Florence's senses reel. She pressed closer to him, feeling the contours of his body moulding into hers, and a warmth of arousal spread through her, wrapping them both up in a sensation of heady emotions.

'I thought you said we had all night,' Sam murmured, breaking away briefly to smile at her again. 'And that you were hungry.'

'I did,' Florence replied. 'And I am. But you just do something to me. Especially when you wear such gorgeous jumpers.'

Sam grimaced. 'Aidan refers to them as my "on the pull" jumpers! Although Mum actually bought the two of them for me a few Christmases ago, I only ever seem to wear them, he reckons, when I want to impress someone.'

'Oh yes?' Florence raised an inquisitive eyebrow. 'And does it work?'

Sam laughed. 'Not until you! Although don't tell him I admitted to that.'

'You were wearing the grey one when you popped into the auditions for the play,' Florence said. 'Were you, er, *on the pull,* then?'

Looking a tad sheepish, Sam turned away and went to the fridge. 'Not exactly, although I was pretty glad I had put it on when I saw you were involved with the play.'

'Smoothie!' Florence teased. She was impressed when Sam brought the Camembert out from the fridge, noting that he'd obviously toasted the breadcrumbs himself. 'Is that our starter?'

'Yup. Is that OK?' Sam asked as he placed it down by the deep-fat fryer, which was now ticking away in the corner of the worktop.

'Absolutely,' Florence replied. 'I love cheese – the smellier the better!'

'Well, this one should whet your appetite,' Sam replied. 'Have a seat, and a top-up of wine if you like. It'll only take a couple of minutes to sort out.'

Florence did as he directed, topping up her glass and Sam's with a generous slug of white wine

'So you said in your note that you've got the house to yourself,' she said between sips. 'Where's Aidan tonight?'

'Gone to Mum's in Cambridge,' Sam replied. 'I only got off shift at seven a.m., so I said I'd drive up and join him tomorrow for Christmas Eve and Christmas Day, and then bring us both back on Boxing Day. I'm working on Boxing Day afternoon, so we can't really stay any longer than that.'

Florence had been in the classroom long enough to know when someone was being a little reticent with details. Although she found Sam quite tricky to read, she was beginning to work out when he wasn't being overly forthcoming. This was one of those occasions.

'Do you both, er, get on well with your mum?' she asked.

Sam looked back over his shoulder and gave her a rueful smile. 'She's changed a lot since Dad died,' he said. 'She lost him to lung cancer so suddenly, and it was relatively soon after Aidan ended up being injured as well, so she's really struggled to come to terms with it all. She can't quite get her head around the fact that, while he looks and sounds OK, the worst injuries are the ones that can't be seen.' He sighed. 'She tries really hard to be accommodating, but in the end, they just frustrate each other. I'm trying not to worry about leaving them alone for twenty-four hours, but it couldn't be helped.'

'Do you visit her often?' Florence asked.

'Generally only during the holiday periods now,' Sam admitted. 'Our sister Kate lives a mile away from Mum and sees her most days, which lets us off the hook, I suppose, and Kate's got three children, which takes Mum's mind off Dad and worrying about Aidan, so she's well looked after, really.'

'You're worried about tonight, aren't you?' Florence said as Sam set the two plates of warm, delicious-looking Camembert down on the table. She could feel her mouth starting to water as she spooned redcurrant sauce onto the plate. Breaking the breadcrumb crust of the cheese with her knife and fork, her stomach rumbled appreciatively as the gooey, warm cheese oozed out over the plate.

'Which part of tonight?' Sam joked.

'Not *this*,' Florence smiled back, in what she hoped was a reassuring way. 'This is all absolutely lovely, and you don't need to keep fretting about that. I mean, leaving Aidan at your Mum's for the night? It's worrying you, isn't it?'

'Maybe a little bit,' Sam replied. 'Is it that obvious?'

'Only from your body language and expression and tone of voice when you talked about it,' Florence said. She took a mouthful of the exquisitely cooked Camembert and nodded appreciatively. 'This is great, by the way. I wasn't expecting you to be such a good cook.'

'Thanks,' Sam said drily. He sighed. 'But, yes, I suppose I am a bit uptight about it. It's the first time I haven't been there to keep an eye on things since his accident. I know it's only twenty-four hours, and that every day, and every step like this, is progress, but I can't help second-guessing things all the time. If Dad had still been around, then it would have been a lot easier; he always acted as a buffer between Mum and Aidan, who had a tendency to rub each other up the wrong way even before Helmand. Now, even when he's having a good day, she seems to know which buttons to press. I hope that, with Kate and the kids visiting tonight, she might act as mediator, since I can't.'

'It's not always going to be your job to keep an eye out for him,' Florence said softly. 'Surely every day is an improvement.'

'Yes, to a point,' Sam said. 'But it's not just about Afghanistan. He's my little brother; I'll always be looking out for him. Not that he sees it that way, of course. I mean, he wasn't exactly thrilled at the prospect of me becoming his housemate, but given the price of property around here, I knew when I moved to Willowbury that I wouldn't be able to buy for a few years, and even Aidan realised it made financial sense to take in a lodger. He gets fed up with me keeping such an eye on him, but he's also grateful to have someone in the house who gets it, who understands what he's seen and the issues he has because of it.'

'I'm sure he is,' Florence said. 'And he seems to cope pretty well most of the time.'

'He's so much better than he used to be,' Sam said. 'The nightmares and the fits of depression were terrible in the beginning. Survivor's guilt, they often call it. Now, with better medication and a decent routine, he's virtually living a normal life, but he still has to be aware of things. He'll never get away from what happened.' He put his knife and fork down on his plate, having wolfed down his portion of the Camembert, even though he had been talking. 'This is the new normal for him. And routine plays a huge part in that. When you're out in the field, when you're in combat, there are just some things you can never unsee, no matter how hard you try.'

Florence wondered how much Sam was talking about himself rather than Aidan at that moment. She recognised, the more she got to know him, that compartmentalising things must have been a huge part of his life in the navy, and just as much now he worked for the air ambulance. The things he must have seen; he would have had to come up with some sort of coping strategy. She knew that Sam had seen active service in the Middle East as well, and coming back to the UK to do a job like piloting the air ambulance seemed to be an extension of that, as far as managing casualties was concerned.

'How do you cope?' she blurted out suddenly. 'I mean, even now you're not in the navy any more, you fly the air ambulance every day, knowing that you're going to see people at their lowest ebb, people seriously injured, those, even, who've lost their lives, and yet you keep doing your job, flying the helicopter, keeping on. I just can't imagine it.'

Sam smiled at her, and reached over to take one of her hands in his. 'Mentally, it's tough sometimes,' he conceded. 'But anyone involved in the emergency services will likely tell you the same thing; it's about doing the best job you can. We think about the bad stuff, of course we do, but we also put it in boxes. When you're working, it's all about being a team, doing the best you can for the patient at the time. I'm a part of a process; I need to make certain calls, and the medical team needs to make other calls. We talk a lot after a job, and during a job we're checking in with each other. After all, if someone's freaking out, it can have a real effect on morale as well as the patient, so we need to be honest with each other.' He considered her for a moment. 'I mean, you must know when a student of yours is feeling below par; you can pick up on that, I'd imagine, and you can support them. That's close to what we do in our job.'

'Yeah, but mine's not a matter of life and death,' Florence said. 'Although you're right, to a point. If a student's come to school without breakfast, with a chaotic home life, or even if something's happened over the weekend, all of these things can have a huge impact on their ability to work well in school. Sometimes it's more about encouraging them, building them up to achieve, than it is the achievement itself.'

'And if you can sense that, and act on it, then everyone benefits,' Sam said. He shook his head. 'Sorry, that got really heavy really quickly, didn't it? And there I was thinking that tonight was going to be about good food, hopefully, a few laughs and a few drinks.'

'It's nice to get an insight,' Florence said. 'I feel like, even though we were involved in the play, we were all so busy learning lines that we didn't really get a chance to actually talk much. It's nice to be able to do that without worrying about what Josie would say if she caught us bunking off!'

And, she thought, *it's kind of nice to have you to myself without worrying that Aidan's going to come in and gatecrash!* Much as she enjoyed Aidan's company, the knowledge that he was in Cambridge, and that she'd have Sam to herself for the whole night, if they both wanted that, of course, was quite thrilling.

'You still talk like a teacher, even on your time off,' Sam teased.

'Thanks,' Florence gave him her best teacher's stare. 'I thought I'd left all that behind for the holidays!'

'I bet you're great at it, though,' Sam replied. 'You have a passion for Shakespeare, at least. I can imagine even the most reluctant English student being caught up in it when you're teaching them.'

'Now you really are trying to flatter me!' Florence laughed. 'But I can't help getting enthusiastic about Shakespeare, in particular. I love him more, the older I get. He just knew humans, you know? Every emotion you can think of is there in a play or a sonnet. Some of the themes, like Hero and Claudio's disaster of a wedding cere-mony, might be a bit archaic now, but the emotions are timeless.'

'Your eyes really light up when you talk about literature,' Sam said. 'I can see why you like to teach.'

'If the marking wasn't such a pain in the arse, it would be the perfect profession!' Florence smiled. 'But it is what it is. I can't imagine doing anything else now, anyway.'

'Now that I'm flying with the SAA, I can't imagine anything else, either,' Sam said, although Florence noticed a slight wistfulness in his expression.

'What do you miss the most about the navy?' she asked.

Sam paused for a moment, and Florence knew he was weighing up what to say in response. She was getting used to his guarded-ness, even if, after all the conversation they'd already had that evening, he'd opened up more than he had before to her. Eventu-ally he replied.

'The relationships you make... they're like nothing else. You know that you're a team, no matter what. That you'd all stand side by side against the hugest of odds. That no one gets left behind. But that's similar to what I do now. I guess I miss the stability of that career, as well as the unpredictability. And I definitely miss seeing different places, even when those places were incredibly stressful places to be. Travelling the world was a real perk, even if I was working all the time.'

Florence felt a prickle of disquiet at his words. She'd sworn, many years ago, never to allow herself to get involved with a military man for the very reasons that Sam had just outlined. The unpredictable experiences, the constant upheaval of being reassigned to new places, sometimes after months, sometimes after years, and, of course, the ever-present threat, when they were on active duty, of someone losing their life. Florence's father had been stationed in Northern Ireland during the 1980s, and although she had been too young to truly appreciate the stress that the posting placed on her mother and the other military wives at the time, in later years she'd come to realise just how uncertain things could be when there was conflict, and you were at the heart of it. If Sam had still been in the navy, no matter how attracted she'd been to him, she'd have been much more cautious about getting involved. Finely tuned as she was to picking up the tones in people's voices, she definitely detected more than a hint of longing in his when he spoke about his previous career.

'Everything OK?' Sam asked, and Florence realised that she'd zoned out, lost in her own thoughts, which had become a little freer with the lubricant of a couple of glasses of white wine.

Florence smiled a little more brightly than she suddenly felt. 'Yes,' she said. She tried to push aside the dark thoughts that Sam's conversations had triggered. He wasn't in the forces any more, and so there was no point dwelling on things. As she sipped her wine and watched Sam clearing the plates into the dishwasher and prepare to fry the steaks in the cast iron griddle pan on the top of the stove, she firmly closed the door on any thoughts like that. Sam might still miss the navy, but he wasn't going to run away and re-enlist, was he? Determined to enjoy this chance to have Sam all to herself, she tried to push everything else aside, for one night at least.

27

The evening progressed, with slightly lighter talk of careers and their respective ups and downs. Sensing, perhaps, that he'd led Florence into darker territory than she'd been anticipating, Sam kept changing subjects, making her laugh with anecdotes.

'I mean,' he said as they finished up their steak and green beans, 'there we were, flying hell for leather to the Bristol Royal Infirmary because the guy's losing so much blood, and all he's doing is making jokes and looking through Tinder for his next date. He's got a chair leg sticking through his abdomen from where he fell off the table during his rendition of 'New York, New York' and he's asking the paramedics whether or not he should message "Melanie, 29, GSOH, stockbroker"!'

Florence laughed. 'Perhaps it was the shock.'

'Well, you'll be pleased to know he made a full recovery, and sent us an update on Twitter a couple of months later, saying that he'd dumped Mel and was now seeing Annabelle, 27, dog lover and accountant.'

'Hopefully he learned his lesson and won't dance on any tables again,' Florence said.

Sam cleared away the plates and then glanced back at Florence. 'Dessert?'

Never usually one to refuse, Florence found that she felt absolutely full. 'Do you mind if we wait a bit?' she said. 'That was great, but I feel stuffed.'

'Sure,' Sam said. 'Shall we go and sit in the lounge? I've been keeping an eye on the fire and it should be nice and warm in there now.'

'Sounds good.'

They stood up and took their glasses, and the now opened second bottle of wine through to the living room. Florence smiled as she saw that the usual detritus of two single guys living together had been tidied away, although there was a copy of *Much Ado About Nothing* splayed open on the sofa.

'I thought it would be nice to read the full version, since I ended up being in the play,' Sam said, clocking her gaze. 'I haven't read any Shakespeare since school, so it's taking a while to get into it, but I'm getting there.'

'You just have to let go and try to enjoy it,' Florence said, picking up the well-thumbed copy of the play. 'Don't try to understand every word, just feel the rhythm, sense the emotion in the words.'

'I bet that's not the first time you've said that about Shakespeare!' Sam laughed. 'I know I asked my old English teacher a fair few times what the flipping point of studying him was, and she came out with something similar.'

'Thanks,' Florence said drily. 'But, honestly, it's not about complicated words, it's about feeling it, living the experience of people who are just like you but are in different circumstances. He shows us that we still had the same preoccupations four hundred years ago, still felt things the same, still loved, got angry, laughed, cried and felt pain, just as he did.' She paused. 'Sorry, I've gone teacher again, haven't I? Must be the wine.'

'I hope not!' Sam grinned. 'Anyway, it's nice to hear you being so passionate about something. And I am trying to get to grips with it, I promise.' He put his wine glass down on the coffee table in front of the sofa and, as he straightened up, he muttered, 'Alexa, play Sam's Soppy Songs playlist.'

Florence burst out laughing. 'Really?'

'Aidan, the tosser, hacked my Spotify just before he left, and I hadn't worked it out until about five minutes before you were due to come over,' Sam said. 'And it's a good playlist, so I thought I'd risk it.'

'I believe you; thousands wouldn't!' Florence sank down onto the sofa and reached for her glass of wine. The soothing sound of the title track of Coldplay's latest album weaved its way through the air.

Sam carefully sat down next to her, long legs bending towards her as he did so. She felt a jolt as his knees brushed hers.

'This is nice,' she murmured, sipping the wine before putting it back down on the coffee table. 'I was, er, a bit worried about tonight.'

'Me too,' Sam laughed nervously. 'Everything's just been so intense, these past few weeks. I wondered how it would be, just talking to you about stuff that wasn't connected to the play.'

'I know,' Florence laughed. 'I mean, it's stupid, really, especially after we've... you know... but I think I was just suffering from cold-light-of-day syndrome.'

'And having my brother kicking around all the time doesn't help,' Sam said. 'I'm trying not to think about what he and Mum will be talking about over dinner tonight!'

'Then let me take your mind off it,' Florence murmured.

She wriggled down the sofa until she was pressed up, side to side, against Sam's long, jeans-clad thighs. Swivelling slightly, she put a hand up to his cheek and pulled his face to hers, luxuriating in the feeling of his mouth, cool from the wine but warm enough to make her gasp, meeting hers in a sweet, leisurely kiss. The kiss deepened, and Florence felt her spine beginning to tingle as Sam raised his hand to caress her cheek and the back of her neck. They drifted gently downwards onto the sofa, until Florence felt Sam's full weight upon her, crushing her deliciously with the contours of his body, and leaving her in no doubt that he was feeling just as aroused as she was.

'You feel so good,' Sam murmured between kisses. 'I've really missed you this week. Knowing you've been literally next door, but out of my reach, has been so frustrating.'

Florence smiled into the kiss. 'We'd better make up for lost time, then.' She wriggled out from under him and stood up.

'Where are you going?' Sam asked.

'Shouldn't we... er, head upstairs?' Florence asked.

Sam grinned. 'It's probably warmer down here, to be honest. The radiators are a bit temperamental on the first floor.'

Florence shook her head. 'You're really taking advantage of Aidan not being here, aren't you?' She glanced at the windows to make sure the curtains were firmly closed. It wouldn't do to be caught in flagrante by a passing parent or student.

'Well, it doesn't happen very often,' Sam kept smiling.

He reached out a hand and pulled her back down onto the sofa. Leaning towards her, he began, very gently, to kiss her neck, until she'd leaned forward and had begun to lose herself in the sensations of his mouth. Pausing for a moment with his hand on the zip of her dress, looking into her eyes for consent to continue, which was swiftly given, Sam tugged down the zip in one fluid motion, eyes growing wider with pleasure as her deep blue bra, a stunning contrast to her pale skin, was revealed.

'You are so beautiful,' he murmured as his lips again began to kiss down her neck and further. 'I can't believe I was so worried about seeing you again.'

Florence arched her back, surrendering to the pleasure of his mouth on her skin, and then, recovering her equilibrium a little, reached under Sam's jumper and pulled it over his head, taking his T-shirt with it. 'Got to even things up a little,' she murmured as she began to kiss his shoulder.

It didn't take long for them to shed the rest of their clothes and, in the warmth and light of the fire, they were more than happy to lose them. Florence stroked inquisitive hands down the length of Sam's lean, toned body, pausing on the way down to caress his cock, causing him to groan and close the distance between them, such as it was. As Sam's warm, sensitive fingers caressed her and turned her insides to liquid, she could feel herself building, already, to a long overdue climax. It wouldn't take much to send her over the edge, lying in his arms, feeling the whole length of his naked body pressed against her. There was just one last thing they needed.

Reading her mind, Sam at least had the good grace to blush. 'In the back pocket of my jeans, if you can reach them.'

'I don't know whether to be flattered or shocked,' Florence laughed gently, which broke the almost unbearable tension. 'Was I that much of a sure thing?'

'Be flattered, but for goodness' sake be quick,' Sam murmured, stroking her belly, as if he knew how close she was, too. 'I'm not sure I can hold out if you keep doing that to me.'

Florence's hands had been at work, stroking and teasing, and she could feel just how aroused Sam was. Reaching down to where Sam had dumped his jeans, she found what she was looking for, tore open the packet and slipped the condom onto Sam's more than ready cock. Pulling him on top of her, she drew a breath as he slid easily and wonderfully inside her, amplifying the sensations and, with the addition of a well-placed thumb, bringing her closer and closer to climax.

As he established a slow, controlled rhythm with his fingers and his thrusts, Florence rose to meet him until she felt her orgasm roll through her abdomen, rushing through her body in a series of pulsing, throbbing waves. Sam took that as his own cue, thrusting deeper to meet her, and, with a subtle shift of emphasis and a firm, beating rhythm of his own, came a few moments after her.

'We are so good at that,' Florence murmured as he collapsed on top of her, bodies entwined in a sweaty but sated heap on the sofa.

'Definitely,' Sam agreed, leaning up to kiss her, and somehow managing to discard the condom at the same time. 'Multitasking,' he smiled as Florence raised a quizzical eyebrow.

Florence burst out laughing. 'I'm impressed.' She shuffled around on the sofa to give them both a little more room, and, despite the warmth of the fire, she was pleased when Sam pulled the soft throw that was draped on the back of it over them both.

'I think I'm ready for that crème brûlée now,' she said softly, snuggling into Sam's chest and wondering if life got any better than this.

28

They did, eventually, make it upstairs to sleep, after demolishing the crème brûlée and a little more wine. As the early morning sun peered warily through the gap in the curtains in Sam's room, Florence stirred first. She took a moment to look at the man sleeping peacefully beside her, and felt a great surge of affection. Even the persistent voice in her head telling her to keep her distance that had, until last night, been nagging at her in quieter moments had been stilled.

As if subconsciously aware of her scrutiny, Sam's eyelids fluttered and he looked up at her. For a moment he seemed surprised to see her there, but that was carefully hidden as he focused his gaze on her fully.

'Hey,' Florence said softly. 'You OK?'

Sam smiled. 'I am. You?'

'Pretty well, thanks.' She glanced at the clock on Sam's bedside table. 'What time do you have to leave to get to your mum's?'

Sam looked over. 'I should probably get off as soon as I can. It's a long drive, and I can't help wondering how Mum and Aidan got on overnight!' He reached for his phone, which was on the other bedside table, and burst out laughing as he saw a rude meme that Aidan had sent him, obviously before he turned in for the night. 'That well, it seems,' Sam said, showing the image to Florence.

'You'd better get your arse in gear and rescue him,' Florence said. 'And I've got some work to do before my Christmas slobfest really begins.' She leaned over and kissed him lingeringly on the mouth. 'I'll leave you to it.'

'You don't have to,' Sam said. 'I mean, don't you want some breakfast?'

Florence smiled. 'To be honest, after all that wine and the post-coital crème brûlée, I think I'll skip breakfast and head home, if you don't mind.'

Sam's brow wrinkled. 'Don't feel you have to rush off on my account.'

'No, honestly, I've got loads to do, and looking at that message, you'd better get going sooner rather than later!' She went to swing her legs over the side of Sam's king-sized bed, but he grabbed her and pulled her on top of him.

'Sure I can't persuade you to stay in bed a little bit longer?' he teased.

'I'd love to,' Florence said softly. 'But we'll have more time when you get back.'

'Is that a promise?' Sam's voice was husky, and for a moment Florence wavered. Things were stirring excitingly below the duvet, and what was half an hour, after all? Regretfully, she shook her head.

'I promise,' Florence replied softly. 'But you really should get going. And all those Christmas films I've got on my Netflix playlist won't watch themselves!' She wriggled out of his embrace with one final kiss, then pulled on her dress, zipping it up quickly and forgoing her underwear for the short commute home. 'Text me when you get to your mum's?'

'Of course,' Sam lay back against his pillows, which were still new enough to have a very enticing bounce. 'But this bed is so warm...' He had a look on his face that could melt butter from the freezer.

'Get up!' Florence chided in her best classroom voice. She was charmed by this new Sam, who seemed so much more relaxed and devil-may-care about his responsibilities, but she wasn't about to be the reason he was late to his mum's place for Christmas.

'OK, OK,' Sam grumbled good-naturedly. 'It's a shame I can't fly there – the Christmas traffic wouldn't be a problem, then.' He threw back the duvet and reached for his clothes, which they'd both managed to bring upstairs before they'd crashed out last night. Pulling on his boxer shorts, wincing slightly at the chill in the air, he padded over to where Florence was standing by his bedroom door.

Florence gasped as he caught her in a tight hug.

'I'll text you the minute I get there.'

'And I'll see you when you get back,' Florence replied. She pulled his head down towards her for a last, lingering kiss. 'Take care,' she murmured.

'You too.'

Florence smiled at him one last time before heading out of his bedroom and down the stairs. This must be the shortest 'walk of shame' she'd ever had to do, she reflected, as she opened the front door of Number 1, Bay Tree Terrace and hopped over the wall to Number 2. Not for the first time, she wondered what on earth Aunt Elsie would make of the whole thing, if she could see her now.

29

'Thank Christ you're here,' Aidan hissed as, a few hours later, he pulled Sam through the front door of their mother's dormer bungalow on the outskirts of Cambridge. 'Mum and Kate are driving me bloody nuts. I've had to resort to letting Tom, Will and Corey beat me senseless on *Fortnite* for the past two hours. At least, with the headphones on, I can't hear them sniping and moaning!'

Sam shook his head. 'Sorry, bro. Duty called. But I'm here now.'

'Duty? Don't let Florence hear you calling her that,' Aidan quipped, then grinned more broadly as he clocked the expression on Sam's face. 'So, I was right, then? You did invite her over last night?'

'No comment, little brother.' Sam brushed past Aidan with a grin and headed into the lounge, where his mother and sister were sitting, sipping a very early glass of sherry and wearing identical, boot-faced expressions. Every time he saw his sister, Sam marvelled at just how much she was turning into their mother. She'd even be dressing like her soon, he thought. As he saw the two of them rising, almost in tandem, to welcome him, he felt a huge pang of loss for his father, who, though basically undemonstrative, had been a gentler, steadying influence.

'You've missed lunch, but dinner's going to be early so Kate can get the kids to bed at a reasonable time,' Selina Ellis said crisply. She walked to the dining table where the sherry bottle stood. 'Drink?'

'I'll grab Sam a beer,' Aidan said hastily. Sam was relieved; his mother had a liking for the sweet stuff and he was definitely in need of something a little more refreshing.

'Good to see you, Mum,' Sam said as she refilled her own glass and then popped it down momentarily so that he could kiss her cheek. 'And you, Katie.'

His sister shot him a 'don't call me that' look over the top of her sherry glass but conceded a hug to him. 'Does this mean I can go off duty and get pissed now you're here?'

'Do what you have to do,' Sam grinned down at his sister. She was the eldest, and wore the mantle like a responsibility. Since Aidan's discharge from the army, she'd tried to help as much as she could, but with three boys of her own to look after, as well as their recently widowed mother, she already had her hands full.

Sam and Kate might not often see eye to eye, but he did admit that it was nice that all three of them would be in the same room, however briefly, for Christmas. He kept grinning as she went to the sherry bottle and poured another generous measure.

As Aidan returned with a chilled lager from the fridge, and was chided by his mother for not bringing a glass to go with the bottle, Sam took a seat and allowed his nephews, who were nine, eleven and thirteen, to explain to him how *Fortnite* worked. He was grateful for the distraction. The gaping hole that his father's death had left in the family was increasingly obvious, and never more so than now it was Christmas. It had been nine months since he'd passed away; this was their first Christmas without him. Sam wondered what he would have made of this situation, where so much could be said about so many things, but everyone was, seemingly with great resolve, saying nothing of any consequence.

He found himself wondering what Florence was up to, and whether she was thinking about him, too. Surreptitiously getting out his phone, he fired off a quick text to her. As he raised his gaze from the screen, he saw his mother scrutinising him, a question in her eyes. Feeling chastised, he shoved his phone on the little table next to the armchair where he was sitting.

'Who's Florence?' Corey, Sam's eldest nephew, asked as he caught sight of the first line of the text Sam received a few minutes later. He grabbed the phone before Sam could, and Sam heaved an inward sigh of relief that it had a lock on the screen.

'A friend,' Sam replied, tickling Corey under the arms and catching the phone as his nephew crumpled in giggles.

'That's an understatement,' Aidan quipped.

'A *good* friend,' Sam replied, shooting a warning glance in his brother's direction. The last thing he needed was a cross-examination about his love life from either Kate or his mother, or worse, both.

* * *

Over dinner, which mercifully, included a lot more wine, Sam began to relax. He felt that, in the presence of his family, he could at least shed some of his self-imposed responsibility for Aidan and his behaviour, and his nephews were good company. After dinner, Kate's husband Phil had collected their three boys so that Kate could stay on for a few more drinks before walking home, and the three siblings sat around the lounge, each of them regressing a little into the teenagers they used to be, as always happened on these occasions. Selina had gone to bed shortly after dinner, claiming a headache, so, after the inevitable squabbles about what to watch on the television, the three had settled back into an easy quiet. When Aidan nipped into the kitchen to get another beer, Kate turned to her brother.

'So how are you really, Sam?' Kate asked, apropos of nothing and into the air that was being warmed by the electric fire.

'I'm OK,' Sam replied. 'Work's hard, but then what else is new?'

'And Aidan?'

'Well, you've seen for yourself,' Sam said. He felt a prickle of irritation. Everything always came back to Aidan.

'He seems OK,' Kate said carefully. 'But there have been one or two moments since he came... I don't know. I keep trying to tell myself he's my brother, that I have to be patient, but it's hard, you know, seeing him so... changed.'

'You should spend more time with him,' Sam snapped. 'Then you'd see it as more of a continuum. Of course he's going to seem different when you only see him once in a blue moon.'

'That's not fair, Sam,' Kate chided. 'I've had my hands full here with the boys, and coping with Mum after Dad died. I can't do everything, you know.' She looked hurt, and Sam immediately regretted his snappish tone.

'I know, Katie, I'm sorry. I guess I'm just tired. I've been doing a lot of night shifts and you never quite get used to them.' He leaned forward and tilted his head with a rueful smile at his sister. 'I know you've got a lot on your plate, too.'

'I just miss Dad, you know.' Kate's eyes filled with tears. 'Mum's pretending she's OK, but she's struggling with losing him and what happened to Aidan... and the boys are growing up so fast. Phil's just, well, Phil, for which I should be grateful, but after all these years, it's just boring, and I wish you two lived closer.'

Sam was shocked by his sister's uncharacteristic admission. She was, like her mother, one for keeping her cards close to her chest.

But then, he figured, it had been a hell of a couple of years for them all. 'I miss you too, Katie,' he said gruffly. 'And the boys are great. You're doing something right, there.' He wondered if he should pick up on the 'boring' comment about Kate's marriage, but, even though she was his sister, he didn't feel as if he should pry. Kate had never been one to confide details about her relationship with her husband, and it seemed weird to start asking now.

'Thanks,' Kate said wryly. 'And I know you're not his keeper, but Aidan's looking really well, too.' She shuddered. 'When I remember what he was like in the hospital after it all happened...'

'Don't think about it,' Sam replied. 'It was the start of a process that he's going to spend the rest of his life negotiating, one step at a time. And he's come such a long way since then.'

'But he'll never *really* get over it, will he?' Kate said, her voice low in case Aidan suddenly made a return from the kitchen. 'When I think about what you've had to manage while you've been living with him; the sleepless nights, the changes of mood, not knowing if it was going to be a good day or a bad day...'

'We can't look back on what was; it's about where he's going that matters.' Sam held his sister's gaze. 'And it's getting easier, believe me.'

'Hark at you, Mr Zen!' Kate teased. 'He's not the only one who's changed.'

Sam's mind instantly flitted to thoughts of Florence, and he knew he was starting to blush.

'So, who's Florence, then?' Kate asked, as if she'd read his mind.

Aidan, who'd come back into the room, answered before Sam could. 'Our brother's got himself a woman,' he said, passing Kate's glass, which he'd refilled with white wine from the fridge, to her.

'Really?' Kate raised an eyebrow. 'First one in ages, am I right?'

'He's had a bit of a dry spell,' Aidan grinned as he sat back down. 'But this one seems to want to stick around.'

Aidan then recounted the story of how Sam had found himself acting opposite Florence in the Willowbury Dramatical Spectacular, but dropped the final bombshell, about her actually living next door, right at the end.

Kate, who Aidan could always make cry with helpless laughter, was wiping her eyes at the end of the tale. 'Won't that get a bit awkward if it doesn't work out?'

'I don't think Sam's thinking with his head right now,' Aidan said, laughing along with Kate at their brother's evident embarrassment. 'Although Florence is a star and he could definitely do worse.'

'It's nothing serious,' Sam muttered, although he could hear the lack of conviction in his own voice. After last night, he definitely felt the opposite.

'And what about you, littlest brother?' Kate asked, turning to Aidan. 'Anyone special in *your* life since the last time I saw you?'

An uncomfortable pause descended between the three of them that Sam was just about to fill when Aidan finally piped up. 'Oh, you know me, sis,' he said, a lightness in his voice that Sam could detect was more than a little forced, 'I'm happy on my own. Nothing to see here.'

'Well, you two had better get your acts together soon,' Kate said, the wine seemingly making her oblivious to the undercurrent of tension she'd unwittingly created by her question. 'The boys want cousins, and Mum's after granddaughters to dress in pink and frilly things, God help them.'

Suddenly, Aidan stood up from where he'd been sitting on the sofa. 'And on that wonderfully sexist note, I think I'll turn in. Night sis, night bro.' He put his virtually untouched bottle of beer on the coffee table, and, without another word to either of them, exited the room.

'Was it something I said?' Kate asked as they both heard Aidan's tread on the stairs.

'Don't worry about it,' Sam stretched his legs out in front of him as he sank back into the sofa, the alcohol and the long drive suddenly catching up with him. 'He can turn on a sixpence sometimes. And you know how he is with Mum. He can't help thinking he's been some terrible disappointment, having to come out of the army the way he did.'

'But that wasn't his fault; he was lucky to survive!' Kate protested.

'He doesn't see it that way at times,' Sam said quietly. 'He's still processing what happened to him in Helmand. I try to help, but, realistically, it's beyond me. Until recently he's been seeing the PTSD counsellor, but his sessions have ended for the time being. It really is one step at a time.'

'All the same, I reckon there's something deeper going on,' Kate said. 'I mean, why terminate the conversation just because I joked about kids?'

Sam shook his head. 'The weirdest things can be a trigger. Imagine, sis, if you'd lost yourself on the battlefield, lost everything that makes you yourself, and then had to fight each day to accept that you're never going to get it all back. Rebuilding yourself from the inside, as well as the outside, can be tiring and frightening. We have to keep remembering that he's fought an internal battle every day to be where he is now.'

'I get that,' Kate said impatiently. 'I don't think this is about Helmand. I don't know... I've always just had this sense with Aidan that I'm missing something. Even before Afghanistan. And now, it's like I just don't even know who he is any more.'

Sam leaned forward and put a consoling hand on his sister's shoulder. 'Just be there,' he said softly. 'That's all you can do.'

Kate shook her head. 'I'm sorry,' she said, with a slight tremble in her voice. 'I'm just so tired, what with Mum, Phil and the kids. I miss you both.'

'I miss you too,' Sam was slightly surprised to hear himself saying it out loud. He and Kate had never really been that close, but perhaps there was still time, after all. He vowed to make the most of this limited time they had together before he had to return to Somerset. 'Look, why don't you bring the boys to stay with us in the new year? I'd love to show you Willowbury.'

Kate smiled shakily. 'I'd like that. And maybe I can meet this Florence of yours, too.'

Sam shook his head. 'One step at a time, Katie, remember? I'm always telling Aidan that – sounds like you need to take that advice, too!'

Kate swatted him playfully with the copy of the *Radio Times* magazine that her mother still insisted on buying every Christmas, despite the fact that no one ever really looked at it any more. 'One step at a time sounds like heaven, when you're the mother of three boys. Someday you might find that out!'

As Sam ducked away from a second onslaught from the listings mag, he thought of Florence, and how nice it might be to settle down with her; the children they'd have, and the places they'd live.

One step at a time, he reminded himself yet again, stopping those thoughts directly in their tracks.

30

Christmas Day for Florence was everything she'd hoped it would be. Rising when she felt like it, she had a leisurely breakfast of hot buttered toast laden with strawberry jam Josie had given her as a welcome-to-school gift in September, followed by a Skype call with her parents and her brother, who, twelve hours ahead in Australia, had spent a wonderfully relaxing day on the beach and were now polishing off turkey sandwiches, and then she settled in with the Christmas television and enough food and drink to sate a small army.

It was the first Christmas she'd ever spent alone, and she revelled in it. After six or so hours of solid Christmas movies and munching, though, she was getting rather restless. She thought about texting Sam again, but he'd sent her a lovely message a few hours ago, which she'd replied to, and not heard anything back, and she didn't want to appear too needy, since he knew she was spending the day alone.

Just as she was thinking about heading out for a wander along the High Street, her phone pinged again. Grabbing it, heart thumping, she wondered if it was Sam. It wasn't, she soon realised, but the text was just as welcome. It was from Josie.

We're going to the pub for a quickie before late dinner. Join us?

Florence was surprised at how pleased she was for the invite. Solitude for most of the day had been lovely, but the thought of a drink or two at The Travellers' Rest with Josie sounded like a good contrast. She loved the pub, with its atmospheric lighting, stained glass windows and quirky rooms and chambers, and at Christmas she was sure it would look even more decorative. She pulled on her yellow raincoat and her gloves and headed out before she could think twice about it.

She could hear the pub even before she got there; The Travellers' Rest was somewhat of a hub on Christmas Day, and the happy burble of people enjoying a festive drink emanated enticingly. As she drew closer, she could see that the landlord had put out a couple of gas patio heaters on the pavement so that people could enjoy their mulled wine or a sneaky cigarette in relative warmth.

Crossing the threshold, she saw Josie and her husband and young son sitting at one of the tables in the corner by the large inglenook fireplace that dominated one wall, with the bar off to the right.

'You made it!' Josie, obviously one or two mulled wines ahead, rose from the table and enveloped Florence in a warm hug. 'I didn't like to think of you spending Christmas Day completely on your own.'

'Thanks for the invitation,' Florence smiled. 'Although I'm enjoying the peace and quiet.'

Josie scooted down the bench she was sitting on to let Florence sit down. 'Nick'll get you a drink – I'm about due another one anyway.' She waved her empty glass at her obviously long-suffering husband, who threw Florence a quick grin and then headed back to the bar. 'The only problem with coming in here is that I keep spotting parents of the kids in my classes!' Josie said. 'But I'm sure they'll give me Christmas Day off, if no other time.'

As if to demonstrate her point, a couple with a glum-looking twelve-year-old in tow drifted past their table to the bar. The preteen pretended to be engrossed in his mobile phone, but his parents gave her a cheery wave.

Nick soon returned with two glasses of mulled wine, and as Florence sipped hers, and soaked up the cheery and festive atmosphere of the pub, she found her gaze drawn to the framed black and white photographs on the walls. Just to her right was a selection of shots of the various festivals that Willowbury High Street had hosted down the years, from the summer solstice celebrations to scenes of the town covered in snow. Hats figured large in all of them, it seemed. There were a couple of photos of what seemed to be local drama productions, too.

As if sensing her question, Josie followed her gaze to the one directly above their heads. 'Years ago, before the luxury of the Priory Visitors' Centre was built with its community space, they used to perform the Willowbury Dramatical Spectaculars right here in the function room of the pub. I bet they managed to grease the wheels with a fair amount of festive booze!' Josie raised her glass.

Florence stood up to get a closer look at the picture behind her. It was a shot of the whole cast of some production or other, and looked like it might have been taken some time in the fifties. The cast were posing, somewhat awkwardly, for the camera, and the costumes had that unmistakable look of post-war austerity about them, but there was something endearing about the make-do-and-mend feeling of the picture. The men stood upright, and some had a distinct military bearing. The women were smiling more broadly, and as Florence looked along the row of faces, suddenly a very familiar one jumped out at her.

'That's my Great-Aunt Elsie!' she exclaimed, nearly choking on the gulp of hot, spiced wine she'd taken. 'I had no idea she acted in the town plays.'

'Looks like you're continuing a family tradition, then,' Josie said, looking again at the picture. 'She looks so different there. I mean, obviously a lot younger, but... happy.' Josie blushed. 'Sorry, that sounds awful. I didn't really know her, but she was well known round here for being a bit stern.'

Florence laughed. 'She really was!' Peering at the photograph again, she was genuinely shocked at the contrast between the seemingly carefree young woman and the old, abrupt and reserved one she knew as her great-aunt. She looked into that face, wondering what had marked the change. Was it just a lifetime of experiences, or was it something more?

'Hey, look at that guy next to her,' Josie said, a thoughtful note in her voice. 'He was a bit of a hottie. Looks slightly like Sam, in fact.' She smiled slyly at Florence, who felt herself blushing.

Josie was right, though. The tall, dark blond man standing next to Aunt Elsie bore a striking resemblance to Sam. But then, perhaps it was just the military bearing. Florence could spot a soldier a mile away, just from the way they stood. She looked more closely at the two of them, noticing that they were standing a little closer together than the rest of the cast. As her eyes travelled from their faces downwards, she gave a little smile as she noticed that, hidden slightly by Elsie's skirt, they were obviously holding hands.

'Do you think they did that for the cameras?' she asked, pointing to the clasped hands.

'I've no idea,' Josie replied. 'Your great-aunt never married, did she? And yet they look pretty happy there.'

'They do.' Florence looked thoughtfully at the photo. 'I wonder if the landlord'll do me a copy?' The romantic in her wondered what the story was, and why she'd never seen any evidence of this man, or this relationship, before. Aunt Elsie had certainly never mentioned anything about a lover; at least not to her great-niece.

Suddenly, she thought back to the loft space at Mistletoe Cottage that she'd so briefly explored a few weeks ago. She'd needed to spend a few hours with Josie's script so she hadn't looked closely at what was really there in the boxes that had been left. Perhaps there would be something up there that might shed a little light on the mystery man in the photograph?

Swigging back the rest of her mulled wine, filled with a sudden sense of excitement; after all, what else was she going to do with the rest of her Christmas Day, Florence stood up from the table.

'Thanks for the drink,' she said to Josie. 'I'm going to head home now.'

'Everything OK?' Josie asked, seemingly concerned by Florence's hasty attempt to leave. 'Seeing that photo hasn't upset you, has it?'

'No!' Florence smiled. 'Quite the opposite in fact. She gave her friend a quick hug. 'I'm going to get into the attic at my aunt's house, see if I can identify the mystery man in that picture. There're a fair few boxes and things up there – I bet there must be a clue somewhere.'

'Ooh, I like the sound of that!' Josie smiled back. 'If I didn't have to get back home, cook a turkey the size of a small dog and entertain Nick's mum and dad, who are descending right at pre-dinner drinks time, I'd be up the ladder with you.' Suddenly she looked concerned. 'You sure you're sober enough to climb in the loft?'

Florence laughed. 'I've only had a couple, and there's a set of counterweighted steps to get up there, so it'll be safe enough. I'll take my phone with me, so if I do get into trouble, I promise to drag you away from your in-laws!'

'Deal,' Josie said. 'Text me if you find anything interesting?'

'I will,' Florence said. She was filled with excitement. Perhaps she was finally going to find out a little more about her great-aunt Elsie, and why she had always been alone.

31

Florence hurried back to Bay Tree Terrace through the chilly winter air, stopping only to wish a merry Christmas to a couple of students who were mucking about by the entrance to the priory.

'Haven't you got homes to go to?' she asked as she passed.

'Been let out for a bit before dinner,' one of them replied. 'Mum forgot the sprouts, so she sent me to the Co-Op to get some before they closed.'

'Best get them back to her, then!' Florence replied, not quite able to turn off her 'on-duty' voice, even on Christmas Day.

'Yes Miss!' the student laughed, then turned to his friend. 'Laters.'

As Florence headed away from them, they called a cheery 'Merry Christmas' after her, and she waved a vague hand in their direction. Her thoughts were still so full of Aunt Elsie and the mystery man, she couldn't concentrate on anything else for the moment. What was the story? And how come none of her family had ever known? She was so caught up in her curiosity that it hadn't even occurred to her that the Co-Op was shut on Christmas

Day, so sprouts certainly wouldn't have been the reason those kids were out and about.

She let herself into the house and, not even stopping to flip on the hall light, headed straight upstairs. Ensuring that her phone was, indeed, in her back pocket, she went to her bedside drawer and got the torch that she kept there. Then, pulling briskly on the cord that brought down the counterweighted attic ladder, intent on her mission, she headed to the roof.

The loft smelt of dust and was chilly compared to the rest of the house, but was, thankfully, dry. Aunt Elsie had obviously had it boarded at some point, too; the roof joists were covered with long, wide lengths of board, which made negotiating the space a whole lot easier. Florence had a memory of poking her head through the loft hatch as a young teenager, when Aunt Elsie had gone out to get some groceries one afternoon and being put off from going any further by the prospect of falling straight through the ceiling. Fear, rather than curiosity, had got the better of her that day. But not today.

Hoisting herself off the ladder and through the hatch, she switched on the torch and took a moment to get her bearings. Several boxes and an old brown suitcase were stacked neatly against the far wall, the ones she'd briefly looked at last time she'd come up here, but the rest of the space was empty. She wondered if, when the house clearance people had come in shortly after Elsie's death, they'd missed them. They certainly weren't easily visible from just poking your head through the loft hatch. She herself had authorised the clearance but, unfortunately, hadn't been able to be present during it, which she regretted deeply. Perhaps if more possessions had been left, she'd have had more of an insight into the mystery of Aunt Elsie's past.

Florence padded carefully over the wobbly wooden boards to the boxes and case. Suddenly and inexplicably, she felt nervous.

What if she didn't like what she found in them? What if the image she'd carried in her mind and in her heart of Great-Aunt Elsie all these years was wrong?

Then she chided herself. Elsie had been a person; a living, breathing person who'd had a whole life before Florence had ever got to know her. What could she possibly discover about her that could sully that?

Taking a deep breath, she opened the first brown box. With the torch in one hand, it was tricky to get a good, clear look at the contents, but from what she could see, it contained mostly birthday cards of a distinct 1970s vintage. Smiling slightly at the array of garish pictures of technicolour flowers, cute-looking elephants and women in flowing dresses, she was tickled to think of Aunt Elsie opening and displaying those on her mantelpiece. She'd see if she could use some of the better preserved examples of cards in a Media Studies lesson at some point. She got to the bottom of the box and put it down next to her, diving into the next one.

As she pulled open the top of the box, she immediately realised that its contents were a little different. Underneath the flaps was a covering of what looked like thick, blue felt. The material felt stiff under her fingertips, and was folded tightly to fit into the confines of the box. Years of feeling that same sort of felted material pressed against her cheek as she welcomed back her father after a deployment made Florence draw a deep breath as she was assailed by her own memories. The pain of seeing him go and the relief of having him back were in tandem. They never went away.

With slightly shaky hands, she carefully drew out the material from the box, propping the torch up on the junction of a roof beam so that she could get a closer look. It had heavy creases from years of being packed away, but as she carefully unfurled it, the flash of colours on the breast pocket and the sheen of silk lining confirmed it. She was holding a piece of not just her aunt's history in her hands, but his, too: the man in the photograph in the pub. It had to be.

The metal buttons on the tunic were dulled from the years, but in her mind's eye, Florence could see immediately how they'd have looked, immaculately polished, done up and gracing the form of the man who had stood beside Aunt Elsie.

With trembling fingers, she placed the tunic to one side and looked into the box to see what else was there. Her heart stopped as she pulled out a mottled photograph of a man in naval uniform, staring directly at the camera. The same man who'd been with Elsie in the picture on the pub wall. Despite the seriousness of the pose, his eyes were shining with laughter, and she knew, instantly, that Elsie had loved him. There were other photographs, tucked in that same box. Smiles so happy they seemed to light up the gloomy attic on their own; laughing eyes and carefree poses, looking as though nothing in the world could touch them. But then Florence found something else that put the photos into sharp perspective.

'Oh Elsie...' she murmured. Tucked next in the box, near to the bottom, was the heartbreaking telegram from the War Office. His name was Henry Braydon and the Korean War had parted him and Elsie forever.

Florence's eyes filled with tears as she next discovered letters from Henry to Elsie, writing that was so warm and passionate that she could feel the love burning from the pages. He spoke of their future plans, the life he so desperately wanted them to have, the things they would do once he got home. The telegram in her other hand spoke volumes about why that could never, ever be. She couldn't imagine the pain Elsie must have been through. Suddenly, she felt a new sense of understanding and sympathy for her great-aunt, who'd never once revealed this enormous sadness; at least not to Florence and her mother.

There was a newspaper article underneath the letters, yellowed with age but still readable, from the *Willowbury Observer*. It seemed that Henry had been shot down south-west of Pyongyang in 1952. He had been one of a hundred thousand British forces who'd supported a joint United Nations task force in the Korean War. At the time of writing, his body hadn't been recovered.

Realising she was shaking, both from the chill in the attic air as well as the emotion, she grabbed the box she'd been looking through and carefully brought it back down the ladder with her. The rest could wait for another day, but she wanted desperately to read the letters from Henry, to get a sense of the love he'd had for her great-aunt. All the summers and school holidays she'd spent with Elsie hadn't prepared her for a revelation of this nature, and she wanted to learn more about her great-aunt in the comfort of her lounge, Elsie's favourite space.

As she pushed the ladder back into place, she jumped as her phone pinged. Her heart leapt again when she saw it was from Sam.

Coming back tomorrow, thank goodness! Working from 2 p.m. through the night, though :(Lunch with me the day after? S x

Florence's heart lurched. She'd missed Sam and she was looking forward to seeing him again, but the emotions of what she'd just discovered about Aunt Elsie were running very close to the surface. She knew that Sam still desperately missed navy life; that much was obvious whenever he spoke about his former career. She would bet her bottom dollar that his commanding officer would have him back in a heartbeat, and his career *had* been cut short. She imagined trying to cope with the uncertainty of waving him off, not knowing if he was coming back. Not to mention the long spells where he'd be away from home. She'd been through enough with her father. And now it seemed that Elsie had suffered the same fate, but with heart-breaking consequences.

Then she chided herself. Sam was out of the navy, he loved his new job and he wasn't going to drop everything and go back. And they were barely a couple yet, anyway!

Florence shook her head. Sometimes she got so lost in the stories of people's lives, she forgot that actual people were involved. All the same, her heart ached for her Aunt Elsie. What could have been if Henry had come back to her, she'd never know. But then, if Henry had returned from war, would she, Florence, be sitting in Bay Tree Terrace now?

Life was confusing, that was for sure. Elsie's terrible loss had, in the end, given Florence a gain.

As she sat herself down on the sofa and prepared herself for an evening of reading the letters, she found she couldn't reconcile those two things.

32

Sam had been keen to make an early start back to Willowbury on Boxing Day, not least because he had a shift at two o'clock. He'd offered to go in a few hours early to relieve the second pilot, who had a wife and two young children, and, barring any major incidents, changeover would go smoothly. It wasn't unusual for an air ambulance team to be working long after their shift ended if they were kept on an incident, but Sam hoped that the holiday season would mean a slightly quieter day. As a consequence, he wanted to get on the road at around eight a.m., to ensure he and Aidan had plenty of time to get back.

Aidan was quiet on the way home, but this wasn't unexpected after a trip to Cambridge. They both loved their mother, but she was adjusting to a reality without her husband, and although it had been nice to be together for a while, the atmosphere was taut with things that could not, or should not, be said. Selina Ellis had never been demonstrative with her emotions, and the strain of filling silences had, in the end, taken its toll on them all. It was with a sigh of relief that Sam had said goodbye early that morning; work was a convenient excuse.

'Mum seems well,' Sam said, a few miles into the journey.

Aidan grunted, head back against the car seat.

'And Katie's managing, despite those boys giving her the run-around.'

'Do you mind if we don't do the family post-mortem right now?' Aidan said gruffly. 'I didn't sleep last night.'

'Sure,' Sam replied, focusing on the road ahead. A faint prickle of unease nagged at him; Aidan had been so upbeat before he'd gone to Cambridge, and now it was like getting blood from a stone. Insomnia was one thing, but he was finely tuned to Aidan's moods. 'Is everything OK?' he tried again.

'I said I'm tired,' Aidan snapped.

Sam left it at that. There would be plenty of time when they got home, and he got off shift, to have any discussions that were needed. For the moment, he needed to focus on the road ahead. The drive wasn't an easy one from East to West, even on Boxing Day with fewer cars on the road.

The miles eventually were greater behind than in front, and Sam was relieved that Aidan did, indeed, seem to sleep more or less the whole way home. He knew he'd have to tackle him eventually about what had happened to cause this change of mood, but a part of him hoped that, back in the familiar surroundings of Willowbury and his own home, Aidan would seem more settled.

He glanced at the clock on the dashboard as he came off the M5 and headed towards Willowbury. He'd just about have time to grab some lunch before his shift started. Maybe he'd even have time to knock on Florence's door and see her before he went. He was shocked at how much he'd missed her, even in the space of a couple of days. He hoped they would be able to meet for lunch tomorrow. That strange limbo period between Christmas and New Year was such an odd time; for people as driven by routine as himself, it was often more stressful to navigate than a working week. Although he was working shifts for a lot of it, he couldn't help worrying about leaving Aidan in post-Christmas limbo at home. Perhaps he should ask Florence to look in on him? No, he chided himself, Aidan wasn't Florence's responsibility.

He shouldn't be yours, either, a small voice spoke before Sam could hush it. There was no point continuing that train of thought.

As he pulled into the driveway at the side of Bay Tree Terrace, Aidan stirred. Sam wasn't sure if he'd actually slept the whole way or not; his brother could sleep like the dead. Either way, it had been clear that he had no desire to talk to Sam until now.

'What time are you on?' Aidan asked as he made a show of stretching, then flung open the car door.

'Two o'clock,' Sam replied. He felt stiff from driving for three and a half hours without a break but also relieved to be home.

Aidan was fiddling with his phone as he walked up the path to their front door, and Sam noticed that he'd had quite a few messages since he'd been asleep.

'Anyone I know?' Sam asked, gesturing to the phone, where Aidan was briskly texting a response.

'Not really,' Aidan replied evasively, but he did, at least, turn to his brother and smile.

Sam felt a small flicker of relief as he did so. Perhaps the visit hadn't been so bad after all.

'What time will you be home later?' Aidan asked.

'About two-thirty tomorrow morning, jobs permitting. Why?'

'I might go out tonight. Tom's asked if I fancy meeting him at The Travellers' Rest for a pint or two.'

Sam still felt a bit surprised that Aidan and Tom had struck up such a firm friendship, but the sense of relief got stronger. If Aidan was with Tom tonight, at least Sam wouldn't worry so much about leaving him on his own.

'OK,' Sam replied. 'Say hi to Tom for me.'

'I will.' Aidan hurried through the door, seemingly having forgotten all about the bags in the back of Sam's car. Since his mood seemed to have instantly improved upon getting back to Bay Tree Terrace, Sam didn't pick him up on it. He was glad Aidan was making friends, and if it meant they pulled him back from a dark spell, so much the better.

As he dumped the bags in the hallway, he took out his phone from his pocket. Ever aware, and having witnessed the consequences for people who texted while driving, Sam always kept his phone in 'Do Not Disturb' mode when he was behind the wheel so he wasn't tempted to check or respond to messages. As he looked at the notifications that appeared onscreen, he was relieved to see that Florence had accepted his invitation to lunch tomorrow. She'd not responded until late this morning, though, which did make him feel slightly nervous. They'd been texting back and forth a fair bit since he'd been away, and to have such a large gap between messages made him worry a little. He tried to dismiss the thought; she did have a life, after all. She wasn't just waiting next door, hanging on his every message.

'I'm going to grab a sandwich before I have to go to work,' Sam called up the stairs. Aidan had vanished like smoke the minute he'd walked in the door. 'Do you want one?'

'No ta,' Aidan replied. 'I'll get something later.'

'OK.'

Sam ate a hastily prepared cheese and pickle sarnie and then glanced at his watch. Norton Magna was twelve miles away, which was about a twenty-minute drive through the outlying villages on a clear day, so he just about had time to pop and see Florence before he left. Seeing her face would be enough to get him through an extended night shift, he was sure.

Yelling a swift goodbye up the stairs to Aidan, who, from the sound of the running water, had taken himself off to the shower, Sam grabbed his keys and slammed the front door shut behind him. Vaulting over the wall, he knocked briskly on Florence's front door.

After a short pause, the door opened, and there she was. Her hair was tied back in its habitual ponytail, and she was wearing a striped jersey and jeans, feet tucked into Ugg boots.

'Hey,' he said softly. 'I, er, just wanted to see you before I start my shift. Is that OK?'

Florence hesitated for a moment, and then smiled. 'Sure.' She shook her head apologetically. 'Sorry,' she continued. 'Late night.'

'Oh yeah?' Sam raised an eyebrow.

'Nothing to worry about, I promise!' Florence smiled at him. 'I'll tell you all about it later. Good trip to see your family?'

'Interesting,' Sam replied. 'I'll try to avoid telling you about *that* later.'

'Everything OK?' Florence asked.

'I think so,' Sam said. Aware of the time, he stepped closer to her and kissed her. It was a long, lingering meeting of mouths that reminded him just how much he'd missed her over the past couple of days. 'I'm working all night, but I'll see you tomorrow for lunch?'

'Definitely,' Florence replied as she moved back from him. 'We can catch up properly then.'

Sam paused for a heartbeat, weighing up again whether or not to ask Florence to look in on Aidan later. Then he chided himself. Aidan was meeting Tom; there was no need to worry unnecessarily. He had to learn to pull back, to let go.

'Penny for them!' Florence laughed.

'Sorry,' Sam said. 'Just wondering what this night shift's going to be like. You never can tell at Christmas.'

'I hope it's a quiet one,' Florence replied. She leaned upwards and brushed her lips to his once more. 'I'll see you tomorrow. Text me when you get home, even if it is the middle of the night.'

'I will.' Sam smiled at her as he turned and headed back down the path from her front door. He couldn't wait for this shift to be over, so he could spend lunchtime, and whatever time after, in Florence's arms.

33

Sam got to work in record time as the roads were so quiet on a chilly Boxing Day afternoon. The sky grew darker as the afternoon wore on, though, and the reports from the weather service warned of snow flurries heading in from the east. Snow was unusual in Somerset, but when it came it tended to come in hard. Sam kept checking in with the Met Office, as it was his duty to keep abreast of the changing weather, and it was his call if the air ambulance lifted or not.

An initially laid-back afternoon briefing had given way to an hour to unwind and get his bearings, and for that Sam was glad. Haleh, Neil and Darren were all on duty with him this afternoon, and Sam was pleased to be working with his regular crew. Often it was the camaraderie during and after a job that got them through.

'Hopefully everyone's decided to stay put in front of the Christmas telly this afternoon,' Neil said, as he sipped his second cup of post-lunch coffee.

'Wouldn't that be nice?' Haleh joined them on the sofa in the lounge area. She was tucking into a turkey sandwich and, as Sam glanced at it, she offered him the other half. 'Go on,' she teased. 'I'm only really eating it to help Mum out with the leftovers! We might be Muslim, but nothing stops us from celebrating the traditional Christmas way as far as food's concerned!'

'Thanks,' Sam smiled back at her and took the sandwich. Breakfast in Cambridgeshire did seem an awfully long time ago, as did the lunchtime sandwich before he'd come to work. Of course, seeing Florence had helped, as the butterflies in his stomach had put paid to any hunger pangs, but now, with a long shift before him, he was glad of the sandwich. The long drive from his mother's place had also taken a bit of a toll, so he hoped he'd have a little bit of time to relax before the inevitable calls came.

As Haleh continued to chat about what sounded like a fabulous but hectic Christmas Day at home with her parents and brothers and sisters, Sam reflected on his own, somewhat more sedate affair. Even his three nephews had eventually conceded defeat and sprawled out in front of the TV, all of the family united in silent appreciation of the *Doctor Who* Christmas special. Sam had found his mind wandering back to Florence during the show, though, as she did bear more than a passing resemblance to the actress playing the current incarnation of the Doctor. Florence's hair was a little longer, but she had the same gentle smile and slender frame.

He gazed out of the windows that looked out across the airfield where the Norton Magna base was situated and started a bit to see that, even in the space of his conversation and sandwich with Haleh, the snow had started falling.

'Oh wow!' Haleh, following his line of sight, rushed to the window, where the sky was rapidly darkening, even though it was barely three thirty in the afternoon. 'We'd better hope we don't get any calls if that gets any heavier.'

Sam stood up to stretch his legs and joined Haleh at the window. He didn't like the look of the grey, heavy sky above. Ultimately, if the call came in, it would be his decision whether or not the team would respond to it. He'd have to check the weather reports carefully. Risking the lives of the crew was definitely not in his remit.

As if echoing their thoughts, the phone rang. Neil, who was closest, picked it up.

'Right. Right. Cheddar Gorge? Called in by a member of the public.' He motioned to Sam, who'd crossed the room again and was quickly looking up the latest weather reports. Putting a hand over the receiver, he glanced at him. 'It's a hypothermia case,' he began. 'Passerby called it in, looks like a head injury, too. Young guy, thankfully no dog or anything. What do you think?'

Sam looked up from the console. 'The Gorge is about eight minutes from here. We've already got spots where we've landed before on both sides. Snow's coming in, but if it's a straightforward case we can do it as the weather stands.'

'Sure?'

Sam paused for a moment, weighing up the options; terrain, weather, the danger that things might change suddenly, and the context of the patient. There was a lot to consider, and he didn't take a decision like this lightly. These processes were familiar to him, though, and he trusted himself and the team. He nodded. 'Yes. I'm sure.'

Neil confirmed the job and put the receiver back down.

Haleh, Sam, Neil and Darren hurried down the steps from the crew room to the hangar, grabbing their helmets and a fresh foil blanket from the medical supply room on the way out. The helicopter was standing on the tarmac outside, and thankfully the snow hadn't settled much as they headed out.

'Brrrr!' Darren rubbed his hands together as they got into the helicopter. 'I wouldn't fancy being out on the gorge in this. Some people have no sense, do they?'

'The weather's come in quickly, to be fair,' Sam said. 'He probably didn't realise when he started how slippery it was going to be up there.'

'Well, let's get out there and bring him in as soon as we can,' Neil said.

As Sam began the pre-flight checks, with Neil calmly confirming by his side, he glanced at the weather updates. The snow was coming in fast. He didn't like it, but it wasn't bad enough to call off the flight. Looking at the projections, it wasn't due to really close in until later that evening, so conditions were still acceptable to fly. The case seemed straightforward enough, providing the patient didn't kick off. He hoped the guy would, if he was conscious, see sense and settle in for the flight.

As the helicopter ascended, and the light began to deteriorate, Sam was glad that Cheddar Gorge wasn't too far to go. It was one thing getting up into the air; it was quite another getting back down again. The gorge was relatively flat on top, but with the snow settling, he'd need to judge the landing carefully. A stray rock, covered with snow, could cause havoc.

The minutes in the air between the two destinations ticked by as the crew prepared the equipment to treat the casualty.

'Do we have road support?' Sam asked as they neared the gorge.

'Not this time,' Neil replied. 'If it's a simple hypothermia case with a head injury, it's best to get him in the air and across to Bristol's Southmead Hospital rather than try to drag him down the Gorge. It's the Jacob's Ladder side and the team could easily lose their footing in conditions like this.'

'Can we sedate him if we need to?'

'Yup,' Darren chipped in. 'But hopefully that won't be necessary.'

Turning his mind away from the patient for the moment, Sam focused on the immediate challenge, which was going to be making a controlled landing on top of the gorge. It was at times like this that

Sam realised just how complex landing even a state-of-the art machine like the air ambulance could be, despite his hours of flying experience. He was used to landing in tricky conditions after years of flying Lynx helicopters onto flight decks of small ships, many of which ended up rolling, pitching or heaving in stormy conditions, but every landing needed his full attention, for the sake and safety of all on board. There was a good reason why the crew instigated a 'no talking under two hundred feet' rule when landing.

Flying through the beginnings of the snowstorm, down at his minimum allowable height to ensure he maintained enough visual references on the ground, Sam was working hard and hoped that he was going to manage to set down safely.

The crew were getting prepared to step out of the helicopter the moment it landed. Carrying with them the foil heat blanket, as well as their med kits, they were performing their final checks as Sam set down on the Jacob's Ladder side of the gorge, about a hundred yards from the cliff edge. He was so finely tuned to the sensation of the helicopter landing, he even felt the crunch as the wheels impacted in the snow. Loose drifts scattered in flurries, caught by the breeze of the rotor.

'OK, we're good,' Sam said as the rotor came to a standstill. He hoped that this would be a swift departure; he couldn't guarantee a clean take-off if the wind kept picking up.

Now the wait came. The temperature inside the cabin would cool quickly now everything had been shut down. Snow was crusting the windscreen already; he hoped they wouldn't be stuck up here too long. He was in radio contact with the team, and as soon as they knew what the state of play was, they'd let him know. If the casualty was conscious and calm, so much the better.

Remembering that he hadn't checked in with Aidan, he pulled his phone out from the zipped breast pocket of his overalls and thumbed the screen to unlock it, just to check to see if Aidan had been in touch. Vaguely irritated, but not surprised his phone carrier didn't have a signal on top of Cheddar Gorge in a snowstorm, he put it away again and decided to contact Aidan, just to check in, when he set down in Bristol or back at base.

Sam was used to waiting around; a lot of the time, the casualty would be stabilised and sent by road, and it was his job to fly the medics safely back out again. That said, he'd also had to acclimatise himself pretty quickly to having a medical team working on a casualty in the main body of the helicopter while he concentrated on flying to hospital without incident. There was more room to work on a patient in the back of a road ambulance than there was in the back of the helicopter, so it was, contrary to the popular perception of the public, often better to take them by road. More than once he'd been hit by the spurt of various bodily fluids, which was something he couldn't quite get used to. He had a strong stomach, but there were limits.

He glanced at his watch; the team had only been gone for ten minutes. Depending on how tricky the snow was making things, it could be a while yet. Unsurprisingly, in this weather at the top of Cheddar Gorge, there wasn't anyone else around. Sam was used to questions from onlookers, too, and to be honest, chatting to people passed the time when he was waiting to see what the situation with the casualty was. No such luck today, though. He couldn't even log into his phone and check his emails.

As the minutes ticked by, Sam's thoughts kept drifting like the falling snow back to Florence. She was unlike anyone he'd ever met before, and he knew, without a shadow of a doubt, that if he let himself, he could quite easily fall in love with her. The other night had been miraculous and Sam could feel his emotions deepening. He had the feeling that Florence was more special than anyone he'd ever met before.

Sam glanced around to see if there was any sign of them, but still nothing.

As if on cue, his radio crackled to life.

'Sam, this is Neil.'

Sam clicked the transmit button. 'Go ahead, Neil.'

'This guy is critical but stable, hypothermic with a cut to his head. We'll need to go to Southmead. ETA to you is five minutes, with the rocks and snow underfoot.'

'OK. See you soon.' Sam clicked the radio back into place on the dashboard of the helicopter and got out of the cockpit, opened the cabin door and moved the patient-loading system into position. The weather was worsening, and he felt a most uncharacteristic tingle of unease at the thought of navigating off the top of the gorge. He'd been in worse, but it still made him mildly anxious. Hours of flight time had taught him to close off, to be in a state of heightened alertness without panic, but it still took a moment to ground himself before taking to the air.

The cabin prepared as far as he could, Sam was relieved to see the team returning, carrying the stretcher between them. They walked at an admirably brisk pace, given the conditions. Sam waited outside the helicopter, shielding his eyes from the snow flurries, which seemed to be growing heavier by the second. Snowflakes stung his face and hands as he waited for the team to get close enough to load the casualty and he wiped the visor of his helmet to get a clearer view.

They drew closer, and it was when they were within a couple of metres that Sam felt his heart lurch painfully and horribly. Surely not? A familiar mop of messy, dark curly hair, some of it crusted with drying blood was visible at the far end of the stretcher. Though his eyes were closed, and the rest of his body was hidden by the straps and blankets, there was absolutely no doubt of the identity of the casualty on the stretcher.

'Oh no...' Sam whispered.

'You all right?' Neil asked, obviously noticing the colour draining from Sam's face but misinterpreting it. 'Is it the blood? Do you need a minute?'

Sam shook his head. 'I'm fine.' His eyes were still fixed on the patient on the stretcher.

'Good, because we need to get this guy somewhere warm, fast.' The three of them lifted the casualty onto the patient-loading system and smoothly moved it back into the aircraft. The minute the casualty was secure, a cannula was inserted into his hand in case he woke and needed to be sedated. The last thing anyone needed was a patient kicking off in the middle of a flight.

Sam's knees were shaking. He couldn't take his eyes off the man on the stretcher, whose skin was an unnatural shade of pale due to the exposure; a colour made all the more shocking in contrast to the drying blood in his hair. He gripped the door of the helicopter for support, trying desperately to get a hold of himself, to be calm enough to do the job he needed to and fly the helicopter to Southmead.

Detach, he told himself over and over again in that endlessly long moment. *Detach and be neutral.*

'Let's get this bloke off the gorge,' Darren glanced over his shoulder, and his face registered his concern. 'Are you sure you're all right, Sam?'

Sam nodded automatically. 'Sorry. Just a bit cold, that's all.' He shook his head and returned to his seat in the cockpit.

'He wasn't carrying any ID on him, either,' Darren continued as Sam slammed the cockpit door shut and started preparing for flight. 'What the hell possesses someone to come up the top of Cheddar Gorge in a snowstorm, wearing only jeans and a jacket, not even a warm jumper, and without any ID or a mobile phone? He's lucky that dog walker found him when he did, or he'd be a whole lot worse.' He shook his head as he straightened the stretcher in the back of the helicopter's cab. 'I suppose that'll be another job someone'll have to do when he's booked in – find out just who the bloody hell he is.'

Sam looked down at the instrument panel in front of him, flipping switches and preparing to take off. *No,* he thought. *I can save them a job, there.* What he couldn't yet articulate, but knew he'd have to when he set down at Southmead, was that the man on the stretcher, currently being treated for a head wound and hypothermia, was his brother Aidan.

34

'Thank God the snow's lighter here than in the countryside,' Neil said as Sam set the helicopter down on the helipad at Southmead.

Sam nodded, concentrating, as always, on landing as neatly as he could. In lighter moments, his team would tease him about setting the helicopter down perfectly in line with the 'H' on the helipad, but they were too preoccupied tonight.

As he cut the engines and the paramedics prepared to disembark Aidan from the aircraft, Neil turned back to Sam. 'This shouldn't take too long. Let's hope we don't get another callout and we can get back to base before the weather closes in again.'

'Definitely,' Sam murmured, but he knew something in his voice sounded off.

Neil regarded him quizzically. 'Everything OK? Is it flying in the snow?'

Sam shook his head. 'No.' He took the helmet off his head and ran a nervous hand through his hair to unflatten it. 'Look, Neil, the guy on the stretcher... I know who he is.'

'You recognise him?' Neil looked surprised. 'Why didn't you say something when we brought him in?'

'I just wanted to get him here as quickly as I could.' Sam looked at Neil, for the first time feeling helpless under the scrutiny of the medic. 'I'm sorry I didn't tell you. He's my brother, Aidan.'

The temperature in the cabin seemed to drop lower than the air outside as Neil and the rest of the team digested this bombshell.

'Shit...' Neil breathed out. 'Why the hell didn't you tell us?'

Sam immediately noticed Haleh, quietly efficient Haleh, shooting Neil a warning look.

'Are you OK?' she asked.

Sam laughed hollowly. 'I got us here, didn't I?'

'You did, and for that I'm relieved,' Neil replied. 'I'd better get him booked in. But, briefly, is there anything we need to know about his medical history?'

Sam nodded. 'He was discharged from the army with PTSD and is on anti-anxiety medication, but nothing that should interfere with pain relief, from what I recall.'

'You didn't think to mention this before we loaded him?' Neil reprimanded Sam. 'What if he'd kicked off in the back of the helicopter?'

'It's unlikely,' Sam replied. But you're right. I should have told you straight away. I just...' he trailed off.

Neil shook his head. 'Let's get him in and sorted, and then we can talk.'

'I'm sorry,' Sam said quietly. 'In the interests of getting us all here, I needed to lock it off, to put it in a box while we got off the gorge.' He slumped in his seat. 'I didn't intend to put anyone at a disadvantage.'

Neil, obviously sensing that Sam was getting pretty close to a precipice of his own, put a hand on Sam's shoulder. 'We got here,' he said. 'And, thankfully, there's no harm done, except what he's already done to himself. But next time, if there ever is a next time, don't hold something like that back.'

Sam nodded and Neil withdrew again, pushing open the heli-copter door, getting ready to admit Aidan.

'Do you want to go with him?' Neil asked as they began to unload.

'I will, but don't worry, I'll fly us home.' He pushed open the door of the helicopter.

Neil laughed hollowly. 'Let's cross that bridge when we come to it.'

Mercifully, there were no other callouts in the time it took to get Aidan into Southmead and, some time later, Sam made ready to lift the helicopter again. As he went through his pre-flight checks, with Neil confirming by his side, he heard Haleh calling his name.

'Are you sure you're OK to do this?' she asked, concern written all over her face. They'd worked a lot of shifts together since he'd joined the SAA and become accustomed to each other's quirks and idiosyncrasies, like any team who worked closely together in moments of stress. In some ways it was like being back in the navy – that sense of comradeship, especially during and in the aftermath of a difficult job, was what kept them all going at times. Sam was grateful for it now.

'I'll be fine,' Sam replied. 'Aidan's stable and his condition isn't life-threatening. When Mathias comes in to take over, I'll drive back here.'

'You know, even at this stage, we can't let you take off if we have any doubt that you're a risk to fly,' Neil said.

'I know,' Sam said. He forced a smile. 'But I learned to switch off when I was in the navy. Even when I was flying injured friends. I'll get us home safely, I promise.'

Haleh leaned forward and squeezed Sam's shoulder. 'We just need to make sure that you're OK. It must have been a hell of a shock, seeing your brother on that stretcher.'

'I've seen worse,' Sam said wryly. 'He looks similar after a skinful of booze. And it won't take long to get back up here on a Christmas holiday morning, anyway. He's safe now.' He was already closing off, mentally, the part of himself that wanted to collapse in anguish at seeing Aidan unconscious on the stretcher when the team had brought him to the air ambulance. The time to rail, scream and panic would be later, when he'd got his team back to base. He glanced at the weather reports. 'We're cutting it close in terms of the snow conditions, but if we get off now, we'll be back at base in half an hour. I'm not sure we'd be safe to get out on another call anyway, tonight.'

'That being said, I'm going to call for one of the relief pilots to come in and meet us back at base,' Neil said. 'The last thing I want is you with your head up here if we get another job in.'

Sam was about to argue, but Neil's set expression brokered no disagreement. 'Fair enough,' he conceded. 'Everyone good to go?'

As they all confirmed, and the crackle came through from Air Traffic Control, they took off. Despite his earlier assurances to the team that he'd put his worries about Aidan on hold, as he saw the Southmead helipad vanishing into the distance, he felt a sharp stab of desolation. Seeing Aidan lying in the hospital bed, knowing how close he'd come to disaster up there on Cheddar Gorge, was difficult to put out of his mind. Sam kept reassuring himself that Aidan was safe now, that he was stable and being cared for, but the minute he set down, and another pilot had arrived to cover the last few hours of his shift, he would head straight back to Southmead.

35

Florence cursed herself as she listened to Sam's voicemail message for the third time. She'd been snoozing in front of *Home Alone* when the phone had rung, but, since she'd already spoken to her folks again from her brother's house in Australia and hadn't been expecting any calls, she hadn't bothered charging her phone. Subsequently, when it had rung, the last of the battery had been sapped and it had taken five minutes to reboot once she'd located her charging cable.

'Oh, Aidan!' she gasped as the realisation hit her about what had happened earlier that afternoon. Sam hadn't said much, merely asked her if she'd mind coming up to Southmead Hospital with some bits and pieces for Aidan since he'd gone straight back there once he'd landed the helicopter and hadn't thought to pick up anything from the house. He explained that there was a spare key above the frame of their back door, and hoped that she'd be able to find everything she needed. He'd mentioned the names of Aidan's medications, which should be in the cabinet in the bathroom, but said he'd leave the rest to her.

Wandering around to the back of the terraces, which were

reached by way of a communal path that bisected the gardens from the back of the buildings, Florence let herself in. The house felt chilly and was eerily quiet. As she crossed the kitchen and headed through to the hall, towards the stairs that led up to the bedrooms, she shivered. The place felt unloved and unwelcoming without Sam and Aidan's presence.

It didn't take her long to find Aidan's bedroom, which was further along the landing than Sam's. When she caught sight of the electric guitar, still with the Bluetooth adaptor for the headphones plugged into the side of it, resting casually against the pine footboard of the single bed, her heart ached.

The room was surprisingly tidy for a single guy, Florence found herself thinking, but then remembered that army discipline must have rubbed off on Aidan during his years of active service. The bed was made, the drawers of the chest by the window were neatly closed, and the wicker hamper for dirty washing had its lid positioned just so. Perhaps this need for control was part of his recovery, or self-preservation, just like Sam's reticence and reserve.

Without wanting to intrude too much, Florence swiftly found a clean set of clothes and some nightwear and popped them into the backpack that she saw hanging up behind the bedroom door. Heading back out to the landing, she paused outside Sam's room. The door was ajar. She couldn't resist pushing it open slightly further, just to take a quick peek. With the newly rising winter moonlight streaming through the window, she saw again a neatly made bed, double this time, a chest of drawers and a wardrobe. On top of the chest of drawers was a photograph of himself and Aidan that she hadn't noticed when she'd been in this room with Sam. Both Sam and Aidan were in their uniforms and Florence caught her breath at how handsome and composed they looked. Sam wore the dress uniform of a lieutenant, and Aidan was in the equivalent for the army. Pride and confidence poured out from their faces and in their stance, and Florence was suddenly kicked in the gut with the realisation that, for both of them, not just Aidan, leaving the armed forces must have been a huge wrench.

Remembering why she was in the house, Florence made her way to the bathroom, where, in the medical cabinet, she found a variety of packets of tablets identified with Aidan's name on pharmaceutical labels. She wasn't completely clear about which were the current ones, so she grabbed all of them she could see and shoved them into a washbag she found in the cabinet under the sink, along with a spare, unused toothbrush as she wasn't sure which of the two in the holder over the sink belonged to Aidan. Scooping up a new tube of toothpaste as well, she zipped up the bag and put it inside the backpack. Then, glancing at her watch, she headed back downstairs and locked up, pausing to nip back into her own house to grab her phone and her handbag.

Setting Google Maps to direct her to the hospital, she contemplated phoning Sam from the car as she began the drive but thought she'd better get to the hospital first; she wasn't the greatest driver and she needed to concentrate if she was heading out on unfamiliar roads. The snow had stopped in Willowbury, and thankfully it was already starting to dissipate, but she wasn't sure how bad it would be as she headed north towards the city of Bristol.

Even on a dusky Christmas holiday evening, it took just over an hour to get to the hospital. Florence quickly parked the car and headed up to the imposing glass doors of the main entrance. With its tall and imposing frontage, the hospital was intimidating in the winter darkness, but as she saw the signs for reception, she felt grateful for the warmth and light inside the building.

Florence walked through the doors of Southmead and paused. From Sam's garbled voicemail message, she realised she had absolutely no idea where to go. Should she ask at the main desk? Would hospital staff divulge patient information to someone who was, to all intents and purposes, a stranger?

The entrance hall was a hive of activity, with medical staff crossing the scrubbed floors, advising patients and relatives and guiding them to the right places. Florence felt a distinct sense of panic. She hated hospitals at the best of times, and all she knew was that somewhere inside this building was Aidan being treated for hypothermia and God knows what else, and Sam, quietly falling apart.

'Can I help you?' A kindly-looking porter came to her rescue. 'Are you looking for a particular ward?'

'Um, yes, I mean, I don't know, actually. My friend came in by air ambulance earlier this afternoon.' Florence wondered if she should mention that Sam had been piloting the air ambulance, but since he'd driven back to the hospital after flying the helicopter back to base, it didn't seem relevant. He was a worried relative now, not a pilot.

'Right. Well let's just see if we can find your friend's details.' He walked her over to the receptionist at the main desk, and then, as she thanked him, smiled and walked away.

The receptionist looked up from her screen and asked for a few details.

'Aidan,' Florence said. 'His name's Aidan Ellis.'

'Ah yes, I've got him. And you are?'

'A friend. Well, and his next-door neighbour, actually.'

'Bear with me,' she nodded and tapped a few keys. 'He's on floor eight, ward four.'

'Thanks.' Hoping that Sam would be by his brother's side, Florence hurried back across the foyer, then, deciding that the lifts were too busy, she started climbing up the stairs. Thankfully, she was in quite good shape, and she was soon up on the eighth floor. As she pushed open the double doors to the ward hallway that housed the lifts, she saw a figure over by the floor-to-ceiling windows that overlooked the road outside. Clad still in his SAA uniform, he had one hand over his eyes as the newly falling icy rain splattered the glass outside. He had, obviously, just dropped everything when he'd landed back at Norton Magna and driven straight up to Bristol.

'Sam?' Florence said softly. 'Are you OK? Is Aidan OK?'

Sam's head jerked up and he dropped his hand limply to his side as he turned around. For a minute he seemed to be confused as to why Florence was standing there, but then he remembered. 'You got my message?'

'Yes. What on earth happened?' She handed him the backpack that she'd filled with Aidan's things. 'I think I got everything he might need. I virtually emptied the medical cabinet!' She smiled weakly.

'Thanks,' Sam said. 'I wasn't really thinking when I put down at base, as you can see.' He gestured to his flight overalls.

'So why are we here, Sam?' Florence asked.

They began to walk to the ward. Florence kept pace easily with Sam, whose back was ramrod straight, the tension obvious in his frame.

'Aidan decided to take himself off for a late walk on Cheddar Gorge this afternoon,' Sam said. 'He tripped in the bad light, knocked himself out and got hypothermia.'

'Christ!' Florence's hand flew to her mouth, but she didn't have time to stop walking. 'And you got the callout.'

'Right.'

'Sam... stop.' Florence reached out and pulled Sam's elbow to arrest his progress to the ward. 'Can we talk about this?'

Pausing, Sam looked down at her, but his face, for the moment, gave nothing away. It was a careful mask of professionalism.

Florence got the feeling that there was a lot going on underneath, though, if only she could get through the layers.

'Do you mind if we don't? Not just now,' Sam said. 'Let's just see him, find out when he's going to come home and maybe talk when we get back?'

'OK,' Florence replied.

They walked onto the ward and immediately saw Aidan, looking as though he was asleep, clad in a hospital-issue gown. As they approached his bed, though, he opened his eyes.

'Hey,' he croaked. 'Fancy seeing you here.'

Florence gave the best smile she could, despite her worries. Aidan's characteristic cheeky glint in the eyes was, blessedly, in place, but she noticed his hands were a little shaky as he reached for the tumbler of water on the cabinet by his bed.

'Let me get that,' she said, hurrying to fill it up from the jug. Since Sam still hadn't said anything, she asked the obvious next question. 'How are you doing?'

'Not too bad,' Aidan replied. 'Although my head's pounding. Must have taken quite a knock on the rocks when I went down.'

'You're lucky someone found you,' Florence reached forward and squeezed his hand. 'In this weather, it was a hell of a risk to take going up there.'

'It wasn't too bad when I left home,' Aidan said. 'Clear enough to ride the motorbike up there, anyway.' He sipped from the tumbler Florence had passed him. 'The weather changed while I was at the top. Stupidly, I only had my old bike jacket on – I didn't bother with the trousers and just had my jeans. When the light started to fail, I lost my bearings and then slipped on the rocks about halfway across the top.' He shook his head, and then winced as the motion obviously hurt. 'That's all I remember until I came round shortly after I got here.'

Florence glanced at Sam's face as Aidan was speaking; she was startled at how extraordinarily bleak he looked. She couldn't fathom the expression at all. He seemed still to be, mentally, at the top of Cheddar Gorge. His hands were clenched at his sides, as if he was trying to keep everything rigidly under control.

'I brought you some stuff,' Florence said, turning her attention back to Aidan. 'Sam called me when he realised he'd shot up here without stopping at home.'

'You're a star,' Aidan said, squeezing Florence's hand where it still lay in his. Disentangling himself at last, he opened the bag Sam had put on the bed and burst out laughing as he saw the T-shirt she'd chosen. 'This must have got into my drawers by mistake,' he said as he held it up; it had the iconic *Star Wars* logo on it. 'Sam uses this to sleep in.'

'Sorry,' Florence laughed too, but a little nervously. Sam was still silent next to her. She had the unsettling feeling that he was trying to bite back so much he wanted to say to his brother, and that her presence at Aidan's bedside was the only thing keeping him from saying it. 'There's a warm jumper in there, too, though, so at least you can hide the T-shirt under it.' She hesitated for a moment, then leaned forward and kissed Aidan's forehead on the side without the injury. 'Let me know if you need anything else.'

'I will,' Aidan suddenly looked a whole lot more serious. 'Look, Florence, I really am sorry my own fuckwitted behaviour dragged you to hospital. I didn't intend for any of this to happen.'

'I know,' Florence said softly, her face still close to his. 'What are friends for?'

'Shit,' Aidan groaned as he sank back against the pillows again.

'What is it? Do you need some more painkillers?' Florence was instantly alert.

'No,' Aidan replied. 'Nothing like that. It's just that I was supposed to be meeting Tom in the pub later. And I guess I must have lost my phone when I fell, so I can't text him and tell him I won't be there.' He looked beseechingly at Florence. 'Can you call him and tell him I won't make it? They've already told me I won't be discharged until tomorrow morning.'

'Of course I can,' Florence said. 'Do you want me to tell him why?'

Aidan hesitated. 'Yes. Probably should. He'll end up hearing through the town grapevine anyway, so you might as well be honest.'

'OK.' There was a perceptible pause between them. Florence turned from Aidan to Sam. 'I'll leave you two to it, then.'

'I'll come back with you,' Sam said, at last. His face gave nothing away now, but Florence wasn't fooled for a minute. 'If there's nothing else you need?' He glanced at his brother, and Florence saw something pass between them as their eyes locked. 'Get them to call me when you know what time you're getting out of here,' Sam said, by way of parting. 'I'll be sure to come and pick you up. Like always.'

Aidan nodded. 'Thanks, bro.'

Without another word, Sam turned away from the bed and strode from the ward. Throwing an apologetic glance at Aidan, Florence hurried after him.

'Thanks for coming up here,' Sam said as they headed back down the flights of stairs to the foyer. 'I know he appreciates it, and so do I.'

Florence paused as they reached the busy entrance hall of the hospital. 'Are you going to be all right to drive home?'

A mixture of expressions flickered over Sam's face before he responded with an unconvincingly neutral 'Of course.'

'OK,' Florence said, not knowing quite what else to say. She was anxious to get back on the road in case the weather turned freezing. The main roads were clear from here to Willowbury, but a hard freeze would make it incredibly dangerous to drive. As she looked at Sam, trying to think about how to say goodbye, it was as if Sam's shutters were coming down right before her eyes.

'Take care,' Sam said.

Feeling more than a little unsettled, Florence walked towards her car, calling Tom as she crossed the car park to relay Aidan's message before heading home.

36

Despite her qualms about the weather, Florence made it back to Bay Tree Terrace in good time, and, realising that she'd skipped lunch and hadn't eaten since breakfast, she was just making herself a slice of toast and a cup of coffee when there was a rap at her front door. Abandoning the toast, with one tantalising bite taken out of it, she hurried through to the hall and opened the door. It was still snowing, and her heart skipped a beat for a million reasons when she saw Sam standing on the other side of it. Despite the literal hop from his door to hers, snowflakes had settled in his hair, and his blue eyes looked as troubled as the sky above.

'Come in,' she said softly.

Without a word, he did as she told him.

'It's been a hell of a few hours,' Florence said as they headed back through to the kitchen. 'Have you eaten?'

Sam shook his head. Florence passed him the other half of the toast she'd made, and poured him a cup of coffee that had brewed nicely in the cafetière. He took a grateful bite before, somewhat awkwardly, taking off his coat and slinging it on the back of one of her pine kitchen chairs.

'How are you?' Florence said gently. She still couldn't fathom what had happened by Aidan's bedside; the interplay between the brothers had baffled as much as worried her.

'I'm all right,' Sam said as sat down.

Realising that she probably wasn't going to get Sam to do a big confession right off the bat, she tried another tack. 'So, what really happened?' Florence took one of the cups of coffee, and felt the jolt of electricity as her fingertips brushed Sam's as he reached for his.

Sam took a sip of his coffee, then winced when he realised how hot it was. 'As you know, he decided to go for a hike on Cheddar Gorge,' he said. 'He often goes up there, up Jacob's Ladder and then across the top. I guess he felt he needed the fresh air after being cooped up at Mum's for a couple of days.'

'It's a nice walk, although a bit treacherous at this time of year,' Florence observed, cradling her coffee cup in her hands.

'Right. Well, he wasn't really dressed for the weather turning, and when the sleet came in, he lost his bearings.'

'That's not like him,' Florence replied. 'He always jokes about how great his sense of direction is.'

'It was...' Sam trailed off. 'But since his GP changed the medicine he's on, he can get disorientated. And without it, it's even worse. I suspect he's been forgetting to take it again.'

'Oh God...' Florence trailed off. 'But when we were rehearsing for the play at your place, he seemed so good about taking them.'

'Well, he stopped being good at it.' Sam's voice was harsher than he'd intended, and Florence knew that his carefully constructed mask was starting to slip again. She ached to reach out a hand to his, but something held her back. Something in Sam's voice suggested that he needed no distractions.

'He's been messing with his doses,' Sam continued. 'He was so pleased to feel better, to be getting involved in the play, that he obviously convinced himself he didn't need them any more. And so he fucked off up the gorge this afternoon without thinking about the consequences if he got into trouble.' Sam's hand clenched on the coffee cup and, mindful that he looked as though if he clutched it any tighter, her bone china would break in his hands, Florence reached out a hand of her own, worrying at Sam's fingers until he unclenched them and put the cup back down.

'We got the call at base to fly out to Cheddar and we knew that we were going to be dealing with a patient with hypothermia and a head injury. It turns out he'd slipped on the rocky ground at the top, which was covered with new snow, and he bashed his head as he fell.'

'How did they know where he was?'

'Another walker and her dog found him and rang 999. Getting a road crew to the top of the gorge in that weather is tricky at the best of times, and because he wasn't conscious, and very cold, they requested us.' Sam shook his head. 'I didn't know it was him until they brought him back to the helicopter, Florence.' He dropped his gaze from hers to his coffee cup.

Florence could see he was struggling and kept her hand on his. She felt his fingers clench around hers.

'I landed the helicopter and the medical team got out with heat blankets and the kit for the gash on his head. All the time I was thinking, what kind of crazy twat goes up the gorge during a blizzard? What a massive waste of money to have to send the helicopter out because someone didn't think and came up here on a crap day.'

'It must be frustrating,' Florence said softly, mindful of just what a knife-edge Sam was balancing on.

Sam shook his head. 'And you know what the first thing I felt was when they brought the stretcher with him on back to the helicopter?'

Florence didn't reply; she didn't need to. Sam was half talking to himself anyway.

'I was fucking angry, Florence. Angry that he'd done this, that he'd brought us all out there, and angry with him for getting the fucking injuries in Afghanistan in the first place.' Sam's jaw was clenched so tightly, he could barely get the words out.

Florence longed to pull him closer and stroke all of the tension away, but now was not the time. He'd turned in on himself, as if his body language was shutting her out, and trying to shut off the thoughts and emotions that were, every moment, rising nearer to the surface.

'For a split second, I felt such a blind rage towards him. So much so, Christ only knows how I managed to pilot the helicopter to Southmead; I can't remember a single moment of that journey. They unloaded him and took him in, and I almost couldn't bring myself to go in with him. Walking with him to get him checked in was so, so hard.'

Florence remembered the shell-shocked tone of Sam's voice-mail and her heart ached.

'They teach us in the navy to switch off; to grind through the gears and go through the motions under the most extreme conditions. That's what I did. But when they brought him to the helicopter on that stretcher, I suddenly got a vision of what it would have been like when he was airlifted out of Helmand. Only... I was still so angry with him, I was wishing, for the first time in my life, that my own brother had been blown up in Afghanistan, so I didn't have to deal with him.'

Florence's heart lurched. Somehow, the stark truth of Sam's confession seemed like the most honest thing he'd ever said to her. 'It's all right,' she said gently. 'You were in shock. That does odd things to people.'

'Can you imagine what that's like?' he whispered finally. 'To wish that your own brother was dead? What kind of a person am I?' He put his head in his hands.

Acting on instinct, Florence got out of her seat and moved around to Sam. Without a word, she put a hand on the back of his neck and pulled him close to her body, running her hand through his tousled dark blond hair and feeling the release of emotions as he wrapped his arms around her, holding her so tightly it felt like he'd never let her go.

Time seemed to stand still as she held him, feeling his shoulders trembling as he finally released everything he'd been holding in check throughout the dreadful flight from Cheddar Gorge to Southmead and back to the base, and, Florence thought, probably longer than that. He made no sound, but his breathing was ragged and Florence's heart broke to listen to him.

Slowly, as his tears subsided, Sam looked up. Florence ran a hand down his cheek, and as he reached up to brush the wetness from his eyes, he caught hold of it and brought it to his lips. Without a word, she dipped her head and brought her lips to his, feeling him sharply inhale as they made contact and the kiss deepened.

'Florence...' Sam murmured as he drew another breath. 'This is a really weird time.'

'I know,' Florence said gently. 'But just for tonight, don't think about it.'

If Sam was surprised by her forthright tone, he didn't show it. Leaning back on his chair, he pulled Florence with him until she was wrapped in his arms and gasping for breath. Looking down at him, eyes still red from crying, more vulnerable than she'd ever seen him before, her heart expanded further than she ever thought possible.

'Come on,' she said gently. 'Let's go upstairs. We don't have to do anything, just hold each other, if you want to.'

Sam smiled shakily. 'I can't be held fully responsible for my actions tonight, you know. As you said, I've been under a lot of stress."

'Just for once, let me take responsibility for both of us,' Florence replied. She stood on rather wobbly legs and held out a hand. 'Come on.'

Sam's hand felt warm in hers as he stood up and momentarily towered over her. 'Are you sure?'

'Completely,' Florence replied. 'And who knows, you might even sleep.'

'Sleep is absolutely the last thing on my mind, now!' Sam gave a low laugh. The sound seemed to surprise him, given the extremes of emotion he'd been going through over the past few hours.

'Then let's see what happens,' Florence said softly.

The stairs to the first floor of the house were steep, and Florence was glad of the old mahogany bannister. She'd toyed with taking it down eventually, but her knees were shaking so much, she needed the support to get upstairs. She could feel Sam's eyes boring into her back as she headed up the stairs in front of him.

This time, when they got to Florence's bedroom, there was a lot left unspoken, unarticulated in the darkness of the night. The truth hung heavily in the air, and as Florence brought Sam down towards her in her bed, both of them shrugging out of their clothes, there was a tiredness and a tenderness that had sprung out of the traumas of the evening. Whereas the night of the play had been passionate and playful, this encounter was slow, tender, healing them both.

Sam lay on his side and brought Florence closer to him until their bodies were joined, and their fingers and mouths touched until both of them reached a deep, infinitely relaxed peak. As Sam came, he buried his face in Florence's shoulder, and once again she could feel him trembling from exhaustion and emotion.

'It's all right,' she whispered. 'I'm here. I always will be. I promise.'

'Thank you,' Sam whispered.

And in the dark, lying together, Florence's mind turned over and over, denying her of the sleep that she, too, so desperately needed. Her own emotions felt torturously close to the surface, not just because of what had happened with Aidan but because of the knowledge she now held about the grief of Aunt Elsie and Henry Braydon's doomed relationship. There was just so much to think about, so much to process about the past and the present, and as she eventually fell into an uneasy sleep, images of Sam, Henry and Aidan all blurred into one in her dreams.

37

The next morning, Sam rolled over in Florence's double bed. For a moment he was disoriented, but slowly the horror of the events of the day and the balm of the night before came back to him. Intermingled with the sense of relaxation that had come from being with Florence, lying next to her all night, came the increasing anxiety and fear about Aidan being in the hospital.

'Shit...' he murmured, as he realised that, on top of having to get back up to Bristol to collect Aidan later that morning, he'd also have to work out how the hell to get Aidan's motorbike back from Cheddar Gorge, where, if Aidan was lucky, it wouldn't have been clamped for staying in the car park overnight.

'What's wrong?' Florence murmured groggily as she came to.

'Aidan's bike's still at the gorge,' Sam replied. 'I really should go and collect it, since he's obviously not going to be in any state to get it himself for a few days.'

'Can you ride a motorbike?' Florence asked.

Sam grinned, despite his worries. 'Yup. We both learned together when we were on leave a few years ago. I haven't ridden much since then though, so it'll be an experience.'

Florence smiled. 'How are you going to get up there?'

Sam looked a little sheepish. 'I was hoping my next-door neigh-bour could give me a lift.'

Laughing, Florence rolled over and pulled him on top of her. 'I'm sure I can sort something out.' Then, her expression grew more serious. 'He had a lucky escape yesterday, didn't he?'

Sam nodded, not trusting himself to speak for a moment. 'It's getting clearer to me that I need to keep a much closer eye on him. The next time he decides to go AWOL, he might not be so lucky.' He glanced down at Florence and couldn't help noticing her expression was, for a moment, unreadable. 'What is it?'

'Have you ever considered that Aidan's not really your total responsibility?' she asked. Her tone was gentle, but the question was direct. 'He is a grown man, after all. He made the choice to go to the gorge yesterday.'

Sam felt a prickle of irritation, as if, whatever else Florence had actually intended, he was one of her students sat in a classroom. It was an odd feeling, he realised, as he was lying naked in her bed. He didn't like it. 'I know that,' he said, a little more sharply than he'd intended. 'But what choice do I have? If I don't make sure he's taking his medication, stuff like this happens. He's a danger to himself.' Sam shook his head. 'He could have died of hypothermia up there. No matter how angry and frustrated I am about what happened, the bottom line is that he still needs keeping an eye on.'

Florence said nothing, but her expression suggested she had more to add.

'What?' Sam asked.

Rolling over onto her stomach, as if she was avoiding his direct stare, Florence took a deep breath.

'Don't get me wrong,' she began carefully. 'It's just that the way you deal with the day-to-day business with Aidan... it's almost as if you're making him too reliant on you.' She glanced back towards him before she continued. 'There's this theory in the classroom. Often, our first instinct, when we know a student is struggling, when we anticipate that they need help, we'll explain something to the whole class, and then, the instant we've finished explaining, we'll make a beeline for them. More likely than not they'll be sat right next to our desks, right where we can keep an eye on them, and, without giving them the chance to digest or process what we've just told the class, we zoom in on them and give them the explanation again, in simpler language.'

'Seems reasonable,' Sam said, irritated but not quite following Florence's line of argument. 'After all, you don't want them sitting there completely lost.'

'Yes, and for years that was the mantra. Get in there with the support so that you knew the student could access the lesson.' She paused again. 'But the problem with that approach, the overwhelming flaw in that way of thinking is that, over time, the student becomes dependent on that second one-to-one explanation and often switches off for the more challenging, whole class one. After all, if your teacher's going to give you your own personal explanation every single time, what's the point in listening to the one that everyone else gets? So you're setting them up to become dependent on you, when really, the aim is to get them to a point where they can work independently.'

'And you think that's what I'm doing with Aidan?' Sam asked as the parallel Florence was trying to make became clear. 'I'm basically setting him up to fail?' He could feel his heart beating more forcefully in his chest, his own breathing starting to shorten a little. Was that really what Florence thought? That he was failing his brother?

'Not intentionally,' Florence said gently. 'You're doing what you think is best to protect Aidan. I get that, I really do. But perhaps you should loosen the reins a little; allow him to manage his own condition without checking up on him. If he knows you're counting his tablets and organising his life, how is he going to learn to do that by himself?'

Sam swung his legs over the side of Florence's bed, slapping his bare feet down on the exposed floorboards a little too roughly. He tried not to wince. 'Well, thank you for that bit of supreme wisdom,' he snapped. 'I had no idea you thought I was doing such a shit job of looking after my brother. At least I know now.'

'Sam, that's not what I meant,' Florence said. She pulled the sheet off the bed and wrapped it around herself. 'I just think that you're taking on too much, and it's going to, eventually, have an effect on your mental health, if it hasn't already.'

Sam pulled on his jeans, in his haste to be out of Florence's room, once again neglecting his boxer shorts. He buckled up his belt and threw on his T-shirt before turning back to her. 'This might come as a bit of a surprise to you, but not everything can be explained by some tinpot educational theory.' He knew his voice was too loud, but he didn't care. 'I let go of the reins over Christmas, and all the time I ended up doing that fucking play, and look what happened; my brother nearly froze to death at the top of Cheddar Gorge. Mum and Kate are too far away to do anything and Dad's dead, so what options do I have? Frankly, if it's the choice between taking a step back and having to deal with what I dealt with last night, or holding on too tightly and keeping him safe and on an even keel, then I know which option I'd prefer.'

'Sam, wait!' He could hear the upset in her voice, but the fight or flight instinct had kicked in, and all he wanted to do was leave. 'Don't you think you're being a bit black and white about all this?' Florence pulled the sheet more tightly around herself as it started to slip, and Sam tried not to be distracted by the thought of her warm, naked body.

'Black and white? He's my brother, Florence, not some random bloke I met on the street.'

'I know that,' Florence said, this time sounding a little more measured. 'But it seems to me as though, at times, you're just using his condition as a rather convenient excuse, too.'

'How can you say that?' Sam felt a spark of temper starting to rise. 'If I step away, if I take my eyes off the ball even for a minute, then something like yesterday happens. I can't cope with that possibility.'

'You mean you're not prepared to give up your role as martyr?' Florence retorted, matching his tone. 'You'd rather play the victim and be seen to shoulder all the responsibility on your own to the outside world because it gives you the perfect opportunity not to have to commit to anything, or anyone, else.' She shook her head furiously. 'Aidan is your out, isn't he? If you keep making him the focus for everything, it's easy for you to pretend you're not missing the navy, too. He's the perfect excuse for you to keep kidding yourself that you can't settle, that you can't put down roots. And actually, Sam, that's what might just be the best thing for him, as well as you.'

'That's not true,' Sam said, but even as he did, he could hear the lack of conviction in his voice. He shook his head, rapidly trying to take down the heat that was flushing his face. 'Look, I think we both need some space.'

Florence, deflated, nodded. 'I'll see you around.'

Desperate for fresh air, he didn't look back as he walked briskly across the landing and down the stairs, pulling open Florence's front door without pause and shutting it, and the conversation, firmly behind him. He didn't want to think about what she'd just accused him of; a small part of his mind was screaming that she'd read him more clearly than anyone ever had. Perhaps his sense of mourning for his naval days really was the root of it all? Perhaps

Aidan *was* just a convenient excuse? But now was not the time to think about that. It was time to compartmentalise again, box away the tough home truths and focus on getting Aidan back home.

Of course, he reflected, the question remained how the hell he was also going to get Aidan's bike back from Cheddar, but he'd work something out. In the meantime, he'd better get showered and up to Bristol to see about the discharge of his brother. And when he got Aidan home, he was damned well going to make sure that everything that could be organised and controlled bloody well would be. There was no way he was going to leave anything to chance any more.

38

'You don't have to keep checking up on me. I'm not a child!' Aidan began to pace the small living room in agitation. Since he'd been discharged from Southmead Hospital several hours ago, Sam had been trying to keep his distance whilst still keeping an eye on Aidan. He'd settled him back in at home as best as he could, but there was obviously something still bugging his brother. Even before the horrendous events of Helmand, Sam had been able to read his brother's moods clearly; there was something on his mind now, he knew it.

'I know that,' Sam said evenly. 'But you've been through a lot in the past twenty-four hours. You can't blame me for wanting to make sure you're on the right track now.'

'I'm fine,' Aidan snapped. 'What happened up there could have happened to anyone.'

'True enough,' Sam conceded reluctantly. Aidan wasn't the first to get caught on high ground in bad weather, and he wouldn't be the last. He'd flown to enough cases himself since he'd been working for the SAA to know that, in this part of the world, bad weather and high ground were a dangerous combination. But he also knew that Aidan would be feeling hugely frustrated and embarrassed about what had happened.

'I don't need you nursemaiding my every movement,' Aidan continued. 'I'm not your responsibility.'

Sam remained seated. He knew the signs, and he knew that it was better to let Aidan have his moment of release now, rather than try to divert it. The counsellor advised acknowledging and dealing with negative emotions at the time, rather than allowing them to be built up and aggravated.

'I know you're not,' Sam said patiently, palms upward in a placatory gesture. 'But you can't get away from the fact that you still need ongoing care. Not just from me but from the professionals. You need to go back to see the PTSD counsellor.'

'What, that creepy old fossil? He hasn't got a frigging clue what we went through in Afghanistan. How can he be any help?'

'He's a trained professional. And I'm not,' Sam replied. 'And, much as I hate to admit it, sometimes even I can't mend what's going on in your head. You need someone with the skills to talk you through it rationally. I'm too close.'

'Then why don't you just bugger off back to the frigging navy?' Aidan's voice was rising. Irrationally, Sam wondered if Florence could hear him through the party wall. 'If you're so fucking useless to me, you might as well get back on the next bloody ship.'

Sam sighed. Enough was enough. He was tired from the trauma of the past couple of days and he wanted nothing more than to spend the next two days asleep in bed. Again, Florence popped into his mind, despite the way they'd parted that morning. He certainly wouldn't mind sleeping next to her, either. But now was not the time to get distracted by thoughts of what he would or wouldn't like to do with Florence. The chances of that happening any time soon after their conversation earlier were remote.

'Aidan,' he said softly. 'You're not forcing me to stick around. I could quite easily have stayed in the navy if I'd wanted to. Christ knows, they tried to talk me out of resigning my commission a thousand times. But you're my brother and I love you, you thick-headed twat. Where you go, I go. That's the deal. No matter what.'

Aidan turned around from where he'd paused to stare out of the window that looked out onto the main road. There was a regular stream of cars trundling past the house, probably all on their way to or from other Christmas engagements. As he looked back at Sam, Sam could see the conflict in his brother's eyes. 'You don't have to be so bloody noble about it. If it wasn't for me getting blown up, you'd still be doing what you love, where you love.' He covered his face with his hands.

Instantly, Sam was up and out of his seat. He approached Aidan carefully, and when he was within touching distance, he reached out and pulled his brother close. He'd grown used to these light-ning changes of emotional state since Aidan had been discharged from the army, and he knew that, sometimes, the best cure was physical contact. Of course, sometimes, he was wrong. He'd sustained more than a couple of bruises where he'd misjudged Aidan's mood and his brother had lashed out at him. But after all this time, he was getting pretty good at gauging Aidan's mood.

As Aidan sagged against him, Sam realised that his brother had lost a little weight lately. He hoped it wasn't the medication killing his appetite again. He made a mental note to check the documenta-tion to make sure weight loss wasn't a side effect.

'Come on,' Sam said gently. 'I could do with getting my head down. Why don't you go and have a kip, too? We'll get a takeaway tonight, eh?'

Aidan nodded into Sam's shoulder. 'I mean it, you know. You don't have to keep micromanaging me.'

'I know,' Sam replied. But even as he said it, he felt the crushing weight of responsibility as tangibly on his shoulder as his brother's head. He knew that, with the right medication, Aidan could live a normal life. But who else was going to make sure that Aidan took the pills that kept the demons at bay? Sooner or later, Sam was going to have to let go; but with their mother and sister so far away, all they really had day to day was each other. And that left no time for anyone, or anything, else.

Sam's thoughts flitted towards the party wall and the woman who lay behind it, the conversation they'd had that morning and the awful way they'd parted. Whatever his growing feelings towards Florence, though, he couldn't allow himself to act on them any further. It wasn't fair to drag her into this situation with Aidan when they were both still finding their way around what the situation truly was.

Then what can *you commit to?* A little voice in his head said, unbidden. With Aidan's condition as it was, Sam figured, not a great deal. It broke his heart to admit it, but letting Florence in, letting her get past his guard, had been a mistake. He couldn't offer her what he knew she would want.

Much later, Sam lay in bed burning with a combination of resentment and frustration. He hadn't had a serious relationship in years; and flings had never been his style. Knowing that Florence was only a few feet away was maddening. For years he'd shut off the part of him that yearned for a settled relationship. Being on a navy ship for nine months of the year wasn't exactly the ideal context for long-term love; although several of his friends had managed it and were now settled with partners and even one or two children. Sam just wasn't the settling-down type. All the time he was a commissioned officer, it had been easy to blame the job for his lack of love; easy to justify being single to his mother, especially, who desperately wanted to see both of her sons settled with, eventually, more grandchildren for her to spoil. The trouble was, Sam had been happy being single. And now he was living with Aidan, there were bigger concerns at play, no matter how much Aidan tried to suggest otherwise.

But Florence... funny, happy, feisty Florence with the waterfall of blonde hair and a smile that could melt the heart of the most hardened sailor. And harden the loins of the most pragmatic one, he thought wryly, feeling his body respond to the memory of her touch. Much as he hated to admit it, she'd had a point about breeding a culture of dependence with Aidan. Sam realised as the night wore on that she had spoken plainly, but, he thought, truthfully.

Rolling over uncomfortably, Sam prayed that sleep would come quickly, before untapped desire drove him up the wall, or even through it and back into Florence's arms.

39

The rest of the Christmas holiday seemed to pass in a haze of marking and seasonal television for Florence. Still shocked by Sam's extreme response to her thoughts on his situation with Aidan, she had absolutely no idea how to approach him again. Perhaps she had been too forthright, too keen to put things into neat little pigeonholes that were, in actuality, un-pigeonholeable. It was the dual curse of a teaching job, she thought; the desire to find solutions, to fix things, whilst trying to accept that some things, and indeed some students, were often unfixable, at least by her. Sam's situation with Aidan wasn't quantifiable, wasn't measurable, and offering her so-called 'wisdom' had created the opposite effect to what she'd intended. She saw now why Sam had felt angry and patronised.

To try to take her mind off it all, she'd spent some more time getting the rest of the boxes and cases down from the attic and immersed herself as best she could in the details of the story of Aunt Elsie and Henry Braydon. They'd both been in their early twenties, and seemed to have been planning for the rest of their lives when he'd been killed in action. From what she could piece together, they'd been part of a group of friends who'd formed the first group of actors for the Willowbury Amateur Dramatics Society, and they'd been particularly fond of putting on farces, with the odd abridged Shakespeare play thrown in for good measure. Among the ephemera that Elsie had stashed in the boxes were several programmes for productions, a few clippings from the local newspaper and even one or two small props, feather headbands and the like, that she'd obviously seen fit to keep.

What a life they would have had, Florence thought sadly, if things had been different. Her vision blurred as she found a note from Henry's own sister, Joan, which she'd evidently written to Elsie when she'd passed on Henry's uniform and the telegram that the family had been sent to inform them of his missing, presumed dead status over Korea. *'Mum would have wanted you to have these,'* it read. *'And I can't bear to look at them any more.'* At some point, Florence thought, Elsie must have felt the same, when she'd made the decision to box everything up and put it in the attic.

She still had trouble reconciling the images of Elsie and Henry with the woman she'd known as Great-Aunt Elsie, but, as she found out more about their brief life together, felt as though she was growing closer to them both, and understanding their decades-old love affair.

Over coffee with Josie, ostensibly to go through their shared classes for the spring term, Florence filled her friend in on what had happened with Sam, as well as what she'd been piecing together about Elsie and Henry.

'I'm not so sure the received wisdom of an education trainer is completely applicable to those boys,' Josie said, 'although, the culture of dependence stuff is thought-provoking.'

'I still think there's something in it,' Florence said, 'but perhaps my timing, since Aidan was still in that hospital bed, wasn't great.'

'You think?' Josie smiled sympathetically.

'So what should I do?'

'Give him time. They've been through a hell of a lot in the past couple of years. Perhaps they both need to heal.'

'Maybe you're right,' Florence conceded. 'It's just, after finding out all that stuff about Aunt Elsie and Henry Braydon, I'm so aware of time not being on *their* side. They thought they had forever; they were so, so wrong.' Florence blinked back sudden tears.

'I think you both need some space to breathe,' Josie reached over the table and gave Florence a gentle hug. 'Give him until the New Year, let him cool down, and then maybe you should talk.'

'Sounds sensible,' Florence conceded reluctantly. 'It's just doing my head in, knowing he's the other side of the terrace wall and I can't reach him.'

'You always said it would be awkward if you dated and then split up, sharing a party wall,' Josie said philosophically. 'But maybe when you've both had the chance to think things through...'

'I hope you're right,' Florence sighed.

Heading home, she tried to put the whole situation out of her mind and focus on planning for the term ahead, which helped, to a certain extent. Eventually, though, she staggered upstairs in need of some sleep.

But it was no good, Florence thought, hours later, as she pummelled the memory-foam pillow for the fiftieth time since she'd turned in. It was two-thirty in the morning and she was just going to have to resign herself to the fact that she wasn't going to get any more sleep. Whether it was the pressures of work that were keeping her up – her target reports for Year 8 were due on the first Monday back to school and she wasn't even halfway through yet – or the more immediate issues with the man on the other side of the wall, she could take her pick.

She'd suffered from bouts of insomnia since she'd begun her teaching career, and although they were far less frequent now, when she felt the work starting to pile up they tended to occur. It was that, or the anxiety dreams when she did sleep, she thought irritably.

And now she and Sam had, it seemed, gone their separate ways, she didn't feel that sense of optimism she'd begun to feel, that flush of attraction that made things all the rosier, and, of course, that post-sex deep sleep that she'd come to enjoy.

Florence glanced at her phone. Two thirty-two a.m. Lying staring at the ceiling wasn't helping at all. With a growl of resignation, she threw back her duck-down duvet and pushed her feet into the cosy slipper boots she kept by the bed. Reaching for her dressing gown, which she'd slung over the pine footboard of her bed, she decided she might as well crack on with those pesky Year 8 reports; then, at least, she'd have some more free time during daylight hours.

A habitual wearer of contact lenses, she opened her bedside drawer and found the tortoiseshell spectacles she kept for hangovers and eye infections (and now, it seemed, middle of the night report writing) and padded downstairs to where she'd left her school laptop on the kitchen table. She made a huge mug of tea while the laptop was booting up, and tried not to think, while the kettle was boiling, of what Sam might be doing right now. Was he even at home? He did rotating shifts, of course, and she couldn't recall what he'd been doing when they'd had that stupid row and he'd stormed out. It still made her angry and very sad to think of it. Both his reaction and her own tactlessness in broaching the subject during an emotionally charged time felt all wrong now.

She imagined him, if he was home, lying in his bed, perhaps clad once more in that shorts and T-shirt combination she'd found so appealing and she had to admit, if only to herself, that she'd fancied him even then. And now, too late and just as they'd ended things, she'd realised that she was actually falling in love with him, much against her better judgement. But there was no point in dwelling on Sam; she had to take a step back from it all, and focus on other things. There was nothing she could do right now to fix the situation.

Tea made, she settled down at the laptop and tried to remember what she was going to say about her noisy but lovely Year 8 class. The trouble was, so many of them were at the same stage, it was a real struggle sometimes to be original and not to repeat herself. She knew that students, as well as their parents, often exchanged notes, and it could get embarrassing if she'd written something similar or even identical for friends, especially as an English teacher.

Setting herself a target to do at least five reports before she headed back to bed to stare at the ceiling a little longer, she started as the security light came on in her back garden. It was probably just the nocturnal wanderings of a fox or the family of hedgehogs she knew lived at the bottom of the garden, but she couldn't help standing up and wandering over to the French windows that opened up directly onto the patio area, the footpath that bisected the back gardens and her stretch of lawn. Hoping to catch a glimpse of the notoriously shy wildlife, she carefully unlocked the doors and pushed one open to let in the cool night air.

Padding out onto the patio, feeling the chill through her slipper boots, she pulled her dressing gown more tightly around her and focused her attention on the sweep of garden in front of her. She couldn't see anything moving, and, somewhat thankful she wasn't coming knees to snout with one of the local foxes, she hesitated a little longer. Perhaps it had been a breeze that had triggered her sensor light. But the night was utterly still and clear, with not even a breath of wind. The stars above looked pricked out by a silver pin, and for a moment she wondered if Sam was up there somewhere, night-vision goggles on, flying to or from an incident, unaware that there was someone down on the ground thinking of him.

She remembered something Sam had told her over coffee after one of the rehearsals for the play, back in early November. That was when she'd found out about the night-vision goggles he had to wear for flying in the dark, and he'd shown her a video on his phone of what fireworks looked like from above. It was one of the perks of the job, he'd said, to be flying above the beautiful explosions of light on Bonfire Night and New Year's Eve. A member of the crew had taken the video of the Guy Fawkes night displays and put it on the SAA's well followed Twitter feed. Seeing it had fascinated her, and, fired up by the video and the conversation, she'd been inspired to create and teach a lesson to her Year 9 class about experiencing events from a different angle; seeing things from an alternative point of view. It had gone down really well with them, and she'd meant to tell Sam about it. But it was probably too late, now.

God, she missed him.

A slight sound to her left made her jump. The night was so still, every sound seemed amplified. She turned her head, not wanting to frighten whatever it was. It sounded like the snuffle of a hedgehog, but she couldn't see anything immediately around her on the lawn or the patio. Often she'd leave out a plate of cat food for the family of hedgehogs who lived at the bottom of her garden, but she'd only actually seen them once. She remembered Aunt Elsie mentioning that hoglets liked the garden, and had taken her word for it that they were, indeed, eating the food she left out and it wasn't just vermin, that was responsible for the empty plates she found each morning. When Elsie was alive, Florence had thought it was probably Hugo the Highland Terrier sneaking out into the garden at night and eating it.

There was another sound, and as Florence moved vaguely in the direction of it, she suddenly froze. There, on the other side of the garden wall, was Sam, sitting on one of the cheap patio chairs he and Aidan had bought at the end of the summer season, his head in his hands.

Ever since Sam had disintegrated so spectacularly and heart-breakingly in her arms the day that he'd flown his own brother to hospital, Florence knew that he would have slowly been building his mental and emotional walls back up. But seeing him looking so desolate, so in need of a friend, Florence's heart went out to him once again. He seemed completely alone, sitting there in his bed shorts in the cold, she just wanted to wrap her dressing gown around him and take him back inside.

Slowly, she approached the wall, but just as she was about to call out to him, his head snapped up and she ducked away behind the protruding wall of the house. It was perfectly obvious he'd been crying from his reddened eyes and Florence knew that tears could be a very private thing, especially for a man like Sam. They weren't always an invitation or a plea for comfort. She'd had a boyfriend once, who, on the death of a close friend, had only ever cried in private, and the one time she'd attempted to comfort him, when she'd visited him unexpectedly, he'd pushed her roughly away and shouted at her to leave. Some people just weren't comfortable with sharing their emotions like that. She sensed that Sam may well be one of them.

Should she reveal herself, or was it better just to pad away, to leave him to it? Drawing a deep breath, and given that the last time they'd been close, things had not ended well, she decided to exercise the unwritten rule of terraced houses, and pretend she hadn't seen what she'd seen. If Sam needed her, he knew where she was, despite the way they'd parted. She was feeling the cold, as well, and really needed to get some sleep.

Reaching out a hand to touch the rough stone of the dividing wall between the two properties, which was as close as she felt she could get, she turned and headed back into the house.

40

Florence slept, eventually, after seeing Sam on the patio, and woke as it was getting light. She decided to venture out onto Willowbury High Street in search of fresh air, and, possibly, a cure for the insomnia. After all, Willowbury was the hub for all things herbal and alternative; perhaps one of the local shopkeepers could point her in the direction of a peaceful night's sleep that wasn't just pills from the doctor.

As she wandered up the street in the crisp morning air, she once again smiled to see all the different winter celebration customs being exemplified by the eclectic mix of shops. Willowbury was a hub for the spiritual, and all manner of believers and religions managed to rub along in the town without conflict. The town had an all-welcoming ethos, and at no time was that more evident than in the winter season. From every doorway hung bits of greenery – holly wreaths, evergreen fronds and bunches of mistletoe.

Passing the doors of The Travellers' Rest, which was already open for coffee, she headed further up the High Street until she came to ComIncense, the health and well-being shop run by Holly Renton, cystic fibrosis campaigner and wife of the local member of parliament. Florence had heard all about Holly and Charlie's wedding that past summer from Josie, who, despite her job as a teacher, was surprisingly enthusiastic about her local MP. In truth, Florence herself had only heard good things, and Charlie had visited the school a couple of times this term, keen to get involved in supporting it where he could.

She stepped through the doorway of ComIncense and was immediately hit by the pleasantly pungent scent of cinnamon and spices, emanating from an electric aroma humidifier on the counter at the back of the shop. It, combined with the decorations on the High Street itself, made Florence feel that Christmas wasn't quite over, despite her tiredness.

'Morning!' a cheerful voice called from one side of the shop.

Florence stepped further in and smiled to see Holly standing on a set of wooden steps, tidying up the top shelf of her selection of well-being books.

'Give me a shout if you need anything.'

'I will,' Florence replied, smiling back at Holly. She hadn't met Holly Renton before, although she'd seen her at a distance. Florence was immediately struck by two things; firstly, her friendly nature, and secondly, that she was about as far away as it was possible to get from the stereotypical image of a politician's wife. With her cascading dark red hair pulled up in a messy bun, her ripped jeans and patchwork waistcoat, she looked stylish but definitely a part of Willowbury rather than Westminster life.

Not quite knowing where to start on her hunt for a remedy for her insomnia, Florence decided just to browse; after all, there was plenty to see in ComIncense. The shop had been transformed for the Christmas season, with seasonally scented votive candles, bags of cinnamon and dried-orange-infused pot pourri and something rather amusing called 'Festive Wellness Tea' on the shelves. Many of these now had discounts, since the day itself had come and gone. Florence wondered if some of the tea might knock her out.

'Is there anything in particular you're looking for?' Holly had come down off the steps and approached Florence. 'Sometimes this place can be a bit overwhelming if you're not sure what it is you need.'

Florence's stomach flipped as the thought ran, unguarded, through her mind that what she really needed to sleep was to be wrapped in Sam's arms. But that wasn't going to happen any time soon. So she smiled back at Holly.

'I'm having some trouble sleeping,' she confessed. 'I should be absolutely shattered each night, but I just keep staring at my bedroom ceiling until about two or three o'clock in the morning.'

'Sounds like a real pain,' Holly said. 'Are you under a lot of pressure at work?'

'I'm a teacher,' Florence replied, 'so pressure kind of goes with the territory.'

Holly grinned. 'Rather you than me! Where do you teach?'

'Willowbury Academy,' Florence replied. 'The new school just on the outskirts of the town.'

'I know it,' Holly replied. 'My husband Charlie's been there a few times to help out. He loves visiting it, as it's so new, and seems to have been a real hit with the locals.'

'It was a great investment,' Florence replied. 'Now the kids can really feel part of their town, instead of being bussed to Stavenham.'

'I'm glad,' Holly smiled. 'I'll tell him you approve.'

'We've still got some teething troubles,' continued Holly, thinking of the somewhat intermittent broadband and the issues with getting the public buses to run at a decent time so that the kids could get to school in time for registration. 'But it's a great asset to the area.'

'He's always happy to hear about local issues,' Holly said. 'Drop him an email or tweet him if you like.'

'My ears are burning,' a voice emanated from the doorway and Florence turned to see the tall, handsome figure of Charlie Thorpe himself crossing the threshold. Reaching his wife, he leaned over and kissed her on the cheek. 'All good stuff, I hope.'

Holly smiled. 'You know me,' she said. 'I can't be seen to be slagging you off in public!'

Charlie grinned back at her, and then at Florence. 'My wife and I don't always see eye to eye on policy,' he said, extending a hand. 'It's nice to meet you.'

Florence shook his hand and also smiled. 'And you. I was just going to say to Holly that I've seen you around school a couple of times. It's nice to see the local MP taking an interest. In my old school, we only saw the guy who held the seat at election time!'

Charlie shook his head. 'I can't vouch for my colleagues, I'm afraid, but I like to keep an eye on things. I can't preach unless I practise, of course.'

Insomnia temporarily forgotten, Florence had a brainwave. She was proud of her ability to ask a cheeky question and seized the moment. 'How would you feel about coming in to talk to our students?' she asked. After all, it wasn't every day you bumped into your local MP, however high his profile in the community.

Charlie considered for a moment. 'In what context? I mean, I'm always happy to chat to people, students included, but what exactly would you want?'

'Well, we've got Careers Day coming up at the end of February, and we're looking for a variety of local speakers with really interesting jobs.' The whole staff had been asked to think about who they might know who might be interested in giving up some time to talk to students about future choices, and even though the new school currently only had five out of seven year groups, it was never too early to think about setting them on a career path. So far, the school had signed up a vet, a doctor, the manager of a mobile phone shop, a baker, and, of course, Sam, but they still needed a few more professionals for the carousel of events on the day.

'Sounds good,' Charlie replied. 'Can you send details over to my office and I'll see if I can get it in the diary.'

'Thanks,' Florence said. She'd kind of expected a little more resistance, a polite but firm brush-off, so she was pleasantly surprised by Charlie's enthusiasm. 'I'll be in touch.'

'Everything OK here?' Charlie asked, turning his attention back to Holly. 'I'm taking an early lunch and wondered if I could tempt you to come with me to Jack's for a bite to eat?' The Cosy Coffee Shop had become a bit of a hub for locals since Jack had introduced a free cup of coffee or tea with every slice of cake for the month of December.

'I'd love to, but Rachel's taken Harry for his eight-week check-up at the cystic fibrosis clinic at the BRCH today, so I haven't got anyone to cover my lunch hour,' Holly smiled ruefully. 'But if you could bring me a takeaway from Jack's I'd love you forever.'

'You mean you won't anyway?' Charlie teased.

Florence smiled. It seemed a bit weird, hearing the local MP being so silly and romantic, but then, she figured, he and Holly could still just about be classified as newly-weds, and it was nice to see them being so affectionate.

As Charlie said his goodbyes to them both, kissing Holly and giving Florence another smile, she made a note to try to remember to email his constituency office when she got home, before tiredness made her forget.

'So, let's see if we can find you something to help sort out those sleepless nights,' Holly said, as Charlie left. 'I'm sure I can find, if not a cure, then a few things to try.' She wandered back to the shop counter on the back wall of the building and glanced up at the shelves of large glass jars behind it, evidently searching for something in particular. 'I can make up a blend of camomile and valerian that might be good to start with,' Holly said. 'Lots of my customers swear by it for its knock-out properties.' She paused. 'It tastes a little bit soapy, but you can always add a slice of lemon to take the edge off.'

Florence nodded. 'Sounds good. At this stage I'll try anything!'

Holly reached up to the second shelf above the counter and pulled down the two jars she needed. Then, on a pair of vintage grocer's scales, she weighed out equal quantities of both, before giving them a stir with her serving spoon. 'Did you want a jar to keep them in?' she asked. 'Only I'm trying to cut down on plastic bag waste, and the paper bags might get damp in this weather.'

'Sure, that would be great,' Florence replied, watching Holly intently as she tipped the contents of the scale pan carefully into a small glass Kilner jar. She then grabbed the calligraphy pen from its place beside the till and carefully wrote the contents and the date on a label, before sticking it to the jar.

'Come back and I can refill the jar if you like it,' Holly said, ringing up the purchase on the till next to the scales.

'Will do,' Florence replied. She noticed there was a pile of gauze bags of lavender on the counter, and picked up one of them as well, to put under her pillow. If it didn't help her sleep, at least it would smell nice. Handing over the cash for her purchases, she bade Holly goodbye.

As she left, Holly reminded her to email Charlie's office again.

'He loves getting involved in student events,' Holly said. 'I think, in another life, he'd have wanted to be a teacher.'

Florence laughed. 'Maybe the two jobs aren't that different, really! I always thought the House of Commons looked like a rowdy school assembly.'

'You're not wrong,' Holly said. 'I've been down a few times and witnessed it first-hand.' She paused, then added, 'I reckon Charlie would be up for organising a school visit to Parliament if you've got some students who might be interested.'

'I'm sure there are plenty of kids who'd love to see behind the scenes,' Florence replied, pleased that Holly had been so forthcoming. 'I'll put that in my email as well.'

'Do,' Holly replied. 'Despite not always agreeing with my husband's politics, his heart generally seems to be in the right place.'

Florence laughed. 'Must make for some interesting dinner-table discussions!'

'Like you wouldn't believe,' Holly grinned. 'We've had to learn to keep our conversations just the right side of shouty on occasion – wouldn't want the press to pick up on our more animated disagreements.'

'Disagreement is healthy sometimes,' Florence said, tickled by the thought of sensible, serious Charlie Thorpe being tackled on issues of policy by his more alternative-thinking wife.

'Yes, but somehow we always manage to find some common ground,' Holly said, somewhat more reflectively. 'That's what it's all about really, isn't it?'

Florence nodded, wondering if she and Sam would ever be able to find their own common ground. They seemed so far apart in their fundamental perspectives on what a relationship needed to be right now, and how responsible you should be for the people you loved. She regretted telling Sam what she thought, but not enough to change her mind on it. They probably had a long way to go before they agreed.

'Have a good day,' Holly said, as Florence turned to wander back out of ComIncense.

'You too,' Florence replied. She decided that she liked Holly, and hoped that, perhaps, they might become friends.

41

In an attempt to take her mind off both the report writing and her estrangement from Sam, Florence decided to explore the rest of the boxes in the attic, to see if she could find out more about Aunt Elsie and her mystery man, Henry Braydon. After the initial emotional discovery of his navy dress jacket and the telegram, she'd been too caught up with Christmas and, later, the trauma with Aidan to really devote that much more time to it. But now, she figured, she'd have plenty of time before school started to find out what the real story was.

When she'd got back from the High Street and stashed the camomile and valerian tea by the kettle for later, she headed back up the attic steps to see what she could find. As she plunged her hands into the musty-smelling cardboard boxes, finding newspaper clippings and assorted militaria, a picture began to form of the man her Aunt Elsie had obviously fallen so hard for. It was chilly in the loft, however, and she wanted to do justice to her research, and to the memory of Elsie and Henry, so she began to carry the boxes down to the newly arrived oak table in the kitchen, a Christmas present to herself in preparation for when the kitchen itself was going to be refitted.

Just as she was spreading out the contents of the first couple of boxes she'd brought down, and trying to make a kind of sense of what she'd found, her heart lurched as there was a soft tap at the door at the back of the kitchen that led to the garden. Looking up from her research, she felt a twinge of disappointment as she recognised Aidan's unruly hair and uncharacteristically tentative smile. She hadn't actually seen him since he'd been discharged from Southmead, and although she was pleased to see him looking better, she wished, rather guiltily, that it was Sam standing on the other side of the glass, instead.

'Hey,' she said as she crossed the kitchen and opened the door. 'How are you doing?'

'Not so bad,' Aidan replied. 'I was at a loose end and thought I'd pop round for a natter, as I haven't seen you since Christmas.' He glanced at the kitchen table with its piles of paper and other bits and pieces. 'That's unless you're busy?'

Florence smiled. 'Nothing that can't be helped by the addition of a chat to a neighbour!'

'What is all this?' Aidan asked as he wandered around the table, picking up various letters and clippings. 'Something for school?'

'Not exactly,' Florence replied. 'I found it all in the attic.'

Aidan studied one of the newspaper clippings intently, pulling out a chair and settling himself in it at the same time. 'So this Henry Braydon was shot down over Korea then? Poor sod. Or, rather, poor those who were left behind without a body to bury.'

'It looks that way,' Florence said. 'And it looks like my Aunt Elsie never really got over it. All this was just sitting in the loft, in boxes, as though she couldn't bear to be reminded of him.' She felt her throat constrict a little at the thought.

'Shows that you really need to make the most of each day,' Aidan said. 'That's a lesson I've learned well over the past couple of years.' He gave a slightly shaky laugh himself. Then, something else caught his eye on the table. 'Looks like you follow in the family am-dram tradition!'

Florence, relieved to be off the subject of Henry's tragic death, smiled. 'I saw a print on the wall of the pub that made me curious – of Aunt Elsie and Henry posing for a cast photo. When I started going through this stuff, I found a couple of snaps of them playing opposite each other, as well. I think this is the best one.' She passed Aidan a snapshot of Elsie and Henry gazing into each other's eyes, both dressed in what looked like Shakespearean costumes. 'I wonder what the play was?'

'Something schmaltzy from the look of it,' Aidan observed. 'Although that kind of passion isn't easily imitated, if what I've seen between you and Sam recently has been anything to go by.' He threw a meaningful look in Florence's direction.

Florence shook her head. 'I'd rather not talk about Sam right now.'

'He misses you, you know,' Aidan said softly. 'I can tell from the way he keeps moping around the house when he's off duty.'

'It's his duty I'm worried about,' Florence said unthinkingly, her last, emotionally charged conversation with Sam still fresh in her mind.

'What do you mean?' Aidan looked blank. 'He can't help the shifts he works.'

'Of course not,' Florence said hurriedly, trying to back-pedal as quickly as she could. 'I just meant, well, that he feels he has a lot of responsibilities.'

'Including me,' Aidan looked down at the table. 'Especially when I end up having to be rescued in a snowstorm.'

'He loves you,' Florence murmured. 'He just wants what's best for you.'

'So he says, morning noon and night,' Aidan said, eyes still cast down. 'But I can't help thinking that sometimes he uses me as an excuse.'

Florence's heart lurched. She knew the answer, but asked the question anyway. 'An excuse for what?'

Aidan looked up at Florence again. 'An excuse not to let anyone in, to get close to anyone. It's all very convenient to claim that I'm his responsibility if it means he doesn't have to commit to anything else, isn't it?' He shook his head. 'It seems like he uses me as a reason to keep everyone at arm's length at times.'

'I'm sure he doesn't see it like that,' Florence put a hand on Aidan's, where it was resting on the table. 'But I do wish he'd give you a little more credit.'

'You and me both,' Aidan gave a hollow laugh. 'For a lot of things. He doesn't know me half as well as he thinks he does.' He glanced at the clock on the kitchen wall and seemed to think better of elaborating. 'I'd better let you get back to all this.'

'Thanks for coming over,' Florence said. 'And Aidan?'

'Yeah?'

'Just because Sam and I aren't, well, you know, any more, that doesn't mean you and I can't still be friends, does it?'

'Of course not. We'll always be friends.' He gave a smile that, had he been Florence's type, would have sent her weak at the knees. For the first time, she could see a resemblance between the two so very different brothers she lived next to. 'I'll see you soon.'

'Take care,' she said as he wandered back out of the kitchen door.

As she settled back down to look at the clippings and photos, Aidan's warning about making the most of each day kept flying around her head and her heart. The parallels between Elsie and Henry's lost love, Aidan's terrible war experience and her own uncertain relationship with Sam all seemed to be there for the making. But for the moment, thinking about them was all she was prepared to do.

42

With the nights still long and the daylight hours short, January drifted past for Florence in a cloud of schoolwork, redecorating and trying to get the odd book read for pleasure. She was surprised how time-consuming sorting out her aunt's house actually was, but was especially pleased when she arrived home one day to see that a package had been left in the garden box by the front door. Ripping open the paper, she smiled as she saw the blown-up photograph, printed onto a rectangular A4 canvas. It was the shot of Elsie and Henry from the play, where they were in costume, looking into each other's eyes.

As she wandered through to the kitchen to get a better look in the sunlight that was streaming through the back window, she smiled. 'I hope you don't mind, Aunt Elsie,' she said softly, 'but I want to have something to remember both you and Henry by.' She knew that no single picture would ever bring her closer to the truth of what had happened with her aunt and Henry, but she felt it was only right that they hung in pride of place in her newly redecorated living room; it seemed a small, but fitting tribute to their brief love affair.

Florence placed the canvas carefully down on the kitchen table, and then, since it was a beautiful afternoon for early February, she made a cup of coffee and threw open the back door to let some fresh air into the house, as the doors and windows had been closed all day.

Wandering out onto the raised patio area outside the back door, she cupped her coffee in her palms to keep them warm and breathed in the twin scents of wintry air and a good brew. Having lived in the north for a fair few winters, she wasn't overly fazed by frost; in fact, she found it invigorating.

After a busy day, she felt the cares of school begin to drift away on the light breeze that curled around her. It had been a hectic week, but at least she had a couple of days at home now.

As she was about to finish her rapidly cooling mug of coffee, she heard Tom Sanderson's strident tones from over the garden wall. Whatever his faults, she thought, as his perfect diction and excellent projection came over the air, his voice would be able to reach to the back of the London Palladium, if he ever got there. They could probably hear him from here. Tom, and Aidan again, had both popped over a couple of times over the past few weeks, trying to convince her to sort things out with Sam, but she'd resolutely ignored all of their well-meaning 'advice'; she just wasn't ready to be the one to break the wall of silence.

'Are you sure he's still hung up on her?' Tom was saying, between rustles of the branches he was obviously chucking into the council-issued green recycling bin.

'Oh Christ, absolutely!' Aidan's voice drifted back across the garden. 'He can't sleep, he can't eat. He's even talking about spending more nights at the air ambulance base because being on the other side of the wall from her is making him mad with lust.' Aidan gave a filthy laugh.

Florence's face flushed as she realised that they were, of course, discussing Sam. She knew full well, from the layout of the houses, that Sam's bedroom was adjacent to hers. She'd had enough trouble sleeping herself lately; the thought of an aroused and lust-ridden Sam barely four feet away from her in bed at night was guaranteed to eradicate any last chances of rest. Holly's tea had helped a little, but she was still waking up early and not able to get back to sleep.

'Well, why doesn't the stupid fucker get his act together, then?'

'He feels as though he can't,' Aidan replied. 'He's too scared to make the first move after they had that stupid row. He's worried about looking like a twat.'

Florence felt conflicted at Aidan's words; not because she was surprised by Sam's apparent thoughts, but because she wondered if eavesdropping on this conversation wasn't the most polite thing to do. However, since she'd seen very little of Sam over the past few weeks, apart from if they happened to be leaving their houses at the same time, she had an urge to know what he'd been up to, and how he'd been feeling. Guilty or not, she had to keep listening.

'But that's daft,' Tom said. 'Anyone with half a brain can see he's still crazy about her. What's he so afraid of?'

'That she'll rip out his heart and stamp all over it,' Aidan said, and Florence was sure she heard him sigh. 'He knows he dropped the ball big time by reacting so badly to her – he struggles to commit at the best of times, but he knows he just ran out on her without really listening to what she had to say and now he's regretting it.'

Florence swore under her breath as the coffee dregs in her mug spilled over her top, her hands were shaking so badly. In at least one conversation she'd had with Aidan, he'd basically called Sam a massive commitment-phobe! This felt like something else, though. Of course she'd made it clear how upset she was, but had she been crosser than she'd remembered during that last conversation with Sam?

'Yeah, that makes sense,' Tom said. 'After all, she's a bit schoolmistressy at the best of times, and she's more likely to give him a hard time if he comes clean now than if he just keeps quiet. I wouldn't want to be on the wrong side of her when she's angry.'

'And he's frightened to death she'll just bawl him out,' Aidan replied. 'He's really fragile at the moment. I don't think lust and failed love are a great combination, to be honest.'

Florence had heard enough. Not even realising she'd just taken a mouthful of tepid coffee grounds, she wandered back into the house, mind and heart awhirl.

* * *

On the other side of the wall, Tom grinned and put his finger to his lips. 'Bait the hook well...' he said, this time in a stage whisper.

'Are you sure about that?' Aidan replied. 'I mean we've basically just told her he's a lovesick schoolboy with commitment issues who's too frightened to fess up to how much he loves her in case she screams at him. I'm not sure she'll find *that* terribly attractive.'

'Trust me,' Tom said airily. 'From what I know about women, and Florence in particular, she'll love the idea of him being vulnerable. Sam needs a third party to interpret for him on occasion, he's that emotionally constipated.'

'I hope you're right,' Aidan said dubiously, 'or you're going to have a lot of explaining to do when they find out we've just made up a pile of emo-schoolboy crap to try to get them back together.' And with that, they headed back into the house.

43

Oblivious to the storm that was breaking on the other side of the party wall, Sam returned a couple of hours later from his shift to find Aidan and Tom having a cosy cuppa over the kitchen table, laughing uproariously at a punchline it seemed only they understood. As he stood in the doorway, he was stunned to see Aidan stand up, drape an arm around Tom's shoulders and plant a tender kiss on the top of his head before reaching for the kettle to put it on again. Coughing to announce his presence, he was unprepared for Aidan's casual response.

'Hey bro,' Aidan said, turning briefly to acknowledge his brother in the doorway. 'Want a tea?'

'Uh, yeah, sure,' Sam replied, head whirling. What had he just seen? Were his brother and Tom *together*? An actual couple? He pulled out one of the other kitchen chairs and sank into it, wondering what to say next.

'Hey,' Tom said, grinning broadly. 'How are you, Sam?'

'I'm good, thanks,' Sam said. 'Busy shift, but that's nothing unusual. You?'

As Tom confirmed that he was, indeed, fine, Sam could swear

he saw a large elephant sauntering around the kitchen. Suddenly the air seemed thick with things unsaid, kisses unacknowledged. He shook his head in total confusion.

'You OK?' Aidan asked as he brought three mugs back to the table, on a tray with a packet of Hob Nobs.

'Fine,' Sam said over-brightly. 'You?'

'We've done that,' Aidan said gently. He reached out a hand to where Tom's lay on the kitchen table. 'I think it's about time we told you what's going on.' Tom nodded in agreement, so Aidan added. 'We're together.'

Sam knew his jaw had dropped, despite his best efforts not to betray any more shock. 'Well, this is, um... Actually, I'm not quite sure what to say.' He stood up from the kitchen table, pushing back his rickety chair and tried to saunter nonchalantly over to the sink for a glass of water, despite the fact that there was tea on the tray in front of him. He wasn't sure he'd pulled it off when he tripped over one of the legs of the other unoccupied chair.

'Let me enlighten you, bro.' Aidan grinned, relenting a little in the face of his brother's confusion. 'I'm gay. Out and proud. Batting for the other team. A full-on homosexual. I fancy blokes. OK? Well, one bloke in particular.' He looked fondly in Tom's direction.

Sam choked on the water that he'd somehow managed to get into the glass without spilling. 'Why don't you just come straight out with it?' he coughed. Then burst out laughing as he realised just how unfortunate that turn of phrase was. 'I mean... are you *sure?*'

Aidan snorted. 'That's like asking you if you're sure you fancy girls. Yes. I'm sure.' He paused, waiting until Sam had sat back down at the table. 'I've pretty much known all my life.'

'But... you've never, er, brought another man home with you. How the hell have you managed to keep it a secret all this time?' Somewhere, deep inside Sam's brain, was another voice wondering quite insistently about why he'd never guessed. How could he have gone all of his life without having a bloody clue?

As if he could read his brother's mind, Aidan softened his tone. 'Look. I know this might be a bit of a shock, but think about it. By the time I started getting interested in relationships you were off at university. And then you were in the navy and off all over the world. I joined the army and was at the other end of that world for quite a lot of the time. And before you ask, yes, you can be gay and in the army. They're not exactly keen on you snogging on the front line, but there's not a lot they can do about it these days. It was easy to keep my private life private.'

'Does Mum know?' Sam asked.

'Christ, no!' Aidan looked horrified at the thought. 'Although I reckon Kate's probably guessed by now. Having said that, I did bring a few girls home on and off when I was on leave back home, but it was really more of a physical thing than an emotional one.' Aidan glanced again at Tom, who, for once, seemed to have the tact to keep quiet. 'Sleeping with women wasn't really ever a problem, and I, er, was quite happy to go through the motions, but I've never really been drawn to a woman on an emotional level. It doesn't take a genius to work out why.'

'So, are you going to tell them? Officially?' Sam pictured their mother, tucked away in her little house in Cambridge, and wondered how she'd react. Although, given Kate's instincts at Christmas, perhaps their sister wouldn't be surprised.

'I might pop over there at some point and enlighten them,' Aidan replied. 'But I'm not in any great rush. Mum's so wrapped up in her adoration of Kate and her boys that I doubt she'd take any notice anyway.'

'Still, you ought to tell her at some point.' Sam glanced at Tom. 'Is this, er, serious?'

Aidan laughed. 'Is anything?'

'You know what I mean.' Since he came out of hospital, Aidan did seem to have been on more of an even keel, and Sam had thought it was because he himself had been keeping a closer eye on him, but perhaps Aidan's new relationship with Tom had more to do with it? From the contented way they were acting around each other, it seemed likely.

'Well, it's about as serious as I can be right now.' Suddenly far more sombre himself, Aidan disentangled his hand from Tom's and squeezed his brother's shoulder. 'You, more than anyone, know how things are. I can't think too far ahead; in case the bad days take over again. But I can say that I feel more settled now than I have in a long time, and it's partly due to having Tom in my life.'

Tom, who was staring fixedly into the bottom of his now nearly empty mug of tea, looked up and locked eyes with Aidan.

Sam cleared his throat.

'I'm glad you feel that way,' he said softly. 'Although, as the older brother, I'm wondering if I have to do the whole "hurt my brother and I'll kill you" routine to you, Tom.'

Aidan grinned. 'I'll take that as a blessing.'

'I just want to see you happy and settled, after everything you've been through,' Sam replied. 'And if Tom's going to be part of that, then I'm happy for you both.' And as he said it, Sam realised that he really did mean it.

'Cheers, bro,' Aidan replied.

'Is it too early to say welcome to the family?' Sam asked, holding out a hand to Tom across the table.

Tom, a look of relief writ large across his face, took the hand and shook it.

'I'm glad you approve,' Tom replied, looking a whole lot less nervous.

'I mean it, though,' Sam said. 'He's, er, special, so watch how you treat him.'

'Special in a good way, I hope!' Aidan chipped in.

'Of course.' Sam grinned. 'Right, well now that's all out in the open, I'd better get in the shower. It was a long shift.'

As he left, he could hear both Aidan and Tom breathing mutual sighs of relief. And then, just as he started walking up the stairs, he heard Aidan muttering, 'Now that's done, we just need to make the stupid twat realise how he feels about Florence. I wouldn't mind her for a sister-in-law.'

'I've got an idea about that,' Tom said. Annoyingly, their voices then dropped to a level that Sam, who was already halfway up the stairs, couldn't interpret. He shook his head. He knew he'd burned his bridges with Florence, and no amount of pep talks from Aidan, and now Tom, it seemed, would make any difference.

44

'But are you sure that Florence is still hung up on Sam?' Carol, who worked behind the counter of the Willowbury Co-Op, called, loudly enough for her already naturally strident voice to carry across the aisles of the village shop. 'After all, from what you told me when you popped in the other day, she seemed pretty definite to me that he'd better leave her alone after their last conversation.'

Sam, who, having taken his shower, was dispiritedly looking in the shop's small freezer cabinet for something for dinner that just required shoving in the oven, went as still and cold as the frozen chickens on the bottom shelf.

'Oh, absolutely,' Josie replied, grabbing a bottle of Chablis and putting it with a clink into her shopping basket. 'She's not been able to sleep for weeks, ever since they had that row that ended it all. She feels so guilty for calling him out about Aidan that she's really off her game. In fact, I overheard my head of department saying that if she didn't get her act together professionally, she'd be out on her ear at the end of next term.'

Sam drew in an involuntary breath and nearly dropped his own shopping basket. Surely Florence wouldn't really lose her job because of their argument? Perhaps it had affected her more deeply than he'd thought. After all, he knew how much it had affected him, even though he tried not to show it, to push it aside, especially at work. But she'd seemed so together when he'd seen her leaving the house. Every day. Not that he'd been looking out for her, from behind the curtains in his bedroom window, or anything.

'But what will she do then?' Carol asked. 'I mean, I know she's got the house, but she's still got bills to pay.'

Josie sighed heavily. 'Well, if she can't get another job, she'll have to rent the place out and go back to Yorkshire. At least that's what she said. After all, the renovations have been costing an arm and a leg, so it's not as if she can just go and do something minimum wage. She'll have no choice.'

'But that won't happen, surely?'

'She's really not in the best place to be standing in front of classes of kids right now,' Josie said. 'She keeps sighing in the office, writing her name and Sam's in the back of her planner like some lovesick teenager... Frankly, I think she's losing the plot.'

'He's going to have to make the first move, then,' Carol said. 'If only there was some way to let him know just how sad she is. That she didn't mean to be so tactless.'

'Well, he's so stubborn, he's not going to take telling,' Josie replied. 'I reckon he's got a bit desensitised after all those years in the navy, and picking up so many broken bodies in the air ambulance. They say it can do strange things to your mind, and your emotions, when you're exposed to trauma all the time. Compassion fatigue, isn't it? We see it a lot in students who've suffered early traumas – it takes a long time to build trust again. Perhaps he's incapable of falling in love, of letting himself go now. Perhaps it really is too late.'

Sam's hands were trembling so badly that he had to put his shopping basket down on the floor beside him, or risk dropping the contents all over the floor. His knees were turned to jelly, too. Is that really what they thought? That he was too remote, too cold, to express his emotions properly?

Stung, he thought back to that last conversation with Florence. Perhaps they were right, he conceded. Perhaps he did come across that way to others. But nothing could be further from the truth.

'Well, it's not like *you* can do anything,' Carol replied. 'If he's too blind to see what's under his nose – well, next door to him, then so be it. You can't push people together who don't want to be together.'

Leaving his shopping basket in the aisle, heedless of the trip hazard it might cause, Sam almost ran from the shop, making sure that he avoided the aisle where Carol and Josie stood, eyebrows raised.

* * *

'That was a pretty barbed trap we just set,' Carol said, her voice laced with concern as she caught sight of Sam's retreating back. 'Do you think we went too far?'

'Nope,' Josie replied firmly. 'It's about time that man realised just what he threw away when he chucked Florence. I'd say he needed a short, sharp wake-up call.'

'I hope you're right,' Carol replied. 'I mean, we basically just accused him of being a cold-hearted bastard who lacks compassion.'

'He'll get over it when he's snuggled up on Florence's sofa, happier than he's ever been,' Josie said. 'In fact, he'll probably thank us.' She grinned. 'I'm off to look at wedding hats on eBay, just in case.'

'I wouldn't go that far,' Carol said as Josie walked to the counter to pay for her shopping.

'Trust me,' Josie smiled. 'I know a good couple when I see one, and if Tom and Aidan did half as good a job with Florence, those two will be back together before the day's out.'

45

Sam hurried home, thoughts whirling around in his head like rotor blades. Was he really that cold? Did he project an image of not caring, even when he cared so deeply? What the hell was he going to say to Florence?

With a shaking hand, he unlocked the door and slammed it firmly behind him. He needed to shut out the world, to think for a while. Or did he? Perhaps that was the problem; that he'd been closing off from emotion for too long. Perhaps what he needed to do was actually the complete opposite.

'Fuck...' the word seemed to echo off the empty hallway and back at him. Tom and Aidan had gone out for a pub dinner, so he couldn't even run what he'd heard past them. His stomach was turning somersaults.

Maybe he should just go next door, he thought. Strike while the iron was hot. Prove to her he wasn't just some unfeeling bastard who couldn't commit to a choice of sandwich. Yes, that's what he'd do.

Opening the front door again, he slammed it shut behind him before he had any more time to think. Without even pausing to consider what he was going to say, he rapped smartly at her lilac front door.

The wait while she answered it seemed interminable, but, eventually, he heard footsteps coming down the hallway, and as the door creaked open, he caught sight of her.

'May I come in?' he said softly. 'I think we need to talk.'

Was he imagining things or did Florence blush? 'OK,' she said guardedly. 'But I've got a lot of work to do tonight, so can we make this quick?'

Sam wandered through the hallway and then into the living room, standing awkwardly in the middle of it, hands in pockets, all thoughts of what he could say suddenly fleeing from his mind.

'What was it you wanted to say?' Florence prompted. Her tone was gentle, calm even. Sam was surprised by this, as, given what he'd overheard Carol and Josie saying in the shop not ten minutes ago he'd expected her to be a bit flustered, a bit self-conscious, but the tone of her voice suggested concern for him, more than anything else. He wondered why.

'Look, Florence, I'm sorry for the way things ended between us,' he began, clearing his throat nervously. He found himself stumbling a bit over his words. 'I mean, at the time I thought it was the right thing to do, but I had no idea... I didn't know that you were taking things so badly.'

Florence's brow wrinkled suddenly in irritation. 'What do you mean? We said what we needed to say; it sucked, but I moved on.'

'Really?' Sam said in what he hoped was a gentle, compassionate tone, but her quick change of facial expression was making him question himself. 'Are you really OK, Florence?'

Florence tossed her head. 'Of course I'm OK. I'm not some stupid schoolgirl who's going to spend the rest of her life weeping over some commitment-phobic bloke, am I?' She raised her chin defiantly, as if challenging him to argue with her.

'Of course not,' Sam stammered, getting really flustered now. This wasn't going the way he'd assumed it would. He'd thought she'd be sadder, more vulnerable somehow, not defiant and angry. He felt his stomach flip in embarrassment.

Then, miraculously, Florence seemed to relent. Her face grew softer. 'Look, Sam...'

'Yes?'

'I'm sorry if I was a bit harsh the last time we spoke. I don't want you to feel you have to spend nights away from home just to get away from me.'

'What do you mean?' Sam was thrown by her non-sequitur.

'I overheard Aidan saying you've been sleeping down at Norton Magna.' She paused. 'I don't want to drive you away from your own home.'

Sam felt a flash of irritation. Why would his brother say that? He'd spent a couple of nights there after shifts, but he certainly hadn't done it to avoid Florence; it was just because he hadn't fancied the drive home after a long night. 'That's not exactly true,' he said grudgingly.

'Well, OK, whatever. I'm sorry, but I really do need to get on.' Florence clearly wasn't in the mood to continue the conversation, from the way she was edging him towards the front door.

'OK, I get it,' Sam held up his hands. 'I just wanted to clear the air between us, that's all. I'll keep my distance from now on. I was just worried. I don't want you losing your job over me, or anything.'

Florence laughed without humour. 'Do you honestly think I'd let what happened between us affect my professional life? You really do reckon a lot of yourself, Sam Ellis, don't you?'

Face flaming, feeling more and more like a schoolboy caught looking up something rude on his phone, Sam couldn't get out of Florence's house fast enough.

Some time later, when Tom and Aidan barrelled through the

front door, they found Sam sitting staring at his phone in the darkness of the living room. The fire had been lit but was smouldering lethargically in the grate, and the curtains were still open.

'Hey,' Aidan said as he flipped on the lights. 'Why are you sitting in the dark?'

'Suited my mood,' Sam said morosely.

'What's up?' Tom had gone through to the kitchen, in search of more booze, so Aidan sat down on the opposite end of the sofa to Sam.

'Nothing. I'm fine,' Sam said, but even he was unconvinced. 'Well, OK, I'm not, really, but I can't do much about that now.'

'Florence?' Aidan asked gently.

Sam nodded. 'I was worried about her. I'd, um, overheard something that concerned me when I was down the shop earlier. Turns out that it might have been the wrong information.'

'Really?' Aidan busied himself with plumping up the cushions next to him. Had Sam been in an observant mood, he might have wondered why his brother wasn't meeting his gaze.

'Yup. And, twat that I was, I raced round there, full of self-righteous concern, only to be told quite quickly that I was barking up the wrong tree, and more or less asked to leave.'

'You never were the best at communicating on an emotional level,' Aidan observed. 'Too many years of buttoning up in the navy, I reckon.'

'Well, anyway,' Sam said, reluctant to get into a lengthy discussion of his shortcomings with his brother, 'I messed up, again, so Florence and I are no better off than we were a few weeks back when this all kicked off.'

'Tell me,' Aidan said gently, 'why was it you walked out on a perfectly good woman again?'

Sam swallowed. 'Because... because she told me something I didn't want to hear.'

'Which was?' Aidan glanced at the doorway to the living room, where Tom was hovering, and Sam saw him motioning for Tom to head back to the kitchen.

'That I was protecting you too much, and as a result making you too dependent on me.' Sam shook his head. 'I told her that, if loosening the reins meant scooping you off the top of Cheddar Gorge, then there was no way I was prepared to do that.'

'Don't you think that's a bit patronising?' Aidan asked. 'I mean, I had two years of intensive physical and psychological therapy after Helmand. And yes, your support since has been a huge help, but you make it sound as though I couldn't have done it without you.' He laughed. 'I know it's been a bit hairy at times, but I don't think you can entirely blame yourself for my shortcomings.'

'You could have lost your life at the top of the gorge,' Sam said gruffly. 'And it was my fault. I should have read the signs.'

'Bollocks,' Aidan said briskly. 'I made a stupid decision that day, one which, if I could go back and do it again, I'd never have made. But, take it from me, you can't live your life looking back on things like that. It'll drive you mad.' He leaned over and put a hand on Sam's shoulder. 'It wasn't your fault.'

Sam dropped his gaze from Aidan's as he felt tears threatening again. 'I know.'

'Then why are you so frightened to admit that maybe I'm not the reason you're holding back from Florence? That you like to think I'm dependent on you because it means you don't actually have to face up to living your own life like an adult? Feeling the things you want to feel? And, maybe, admitting to the fact that you left the navy because you wanted to, not because of me?'

'I'm not quite sure about that last part,' Sam said, 'but maybe you're right about the rest of it.'

'Well, that's a start,' Tom said as, at a nod from Aidan, he slipped back into the room. 'The question is, what are you going to do about it?'

'What *can* I do? She's really pissed off with me. And after what I said to her today, I'm not surprised.'

Tom and Aidan looked shifty.

'Yeah,' Aidan said. 'Sorry about that.'

'About what?'

Aidan's eyes swivelled towards Tom, who grinned and nodded. 'She overheard something we might have, er, cooked up to try to force you two back together, which obviously went a bit wrong.'

'You what?' Sam spluttered. 'No wonder Florence all but threw me out. She must have wondered what the hell I was talking about when I rocked up on her doorstep.'

'And, worse than that, she now thinks you're a mopey emo twat who can't get over her,' Aidan smirked. 'Although, on the basis of what we've talked about tonight, perhaps that's not so far from the truth!'

'Great,' Sam muttered. 'And I've got to go to her school tomorrow and make a bigger fool of myself in front of a load of kids.'

'Perhaps, after you've done that, it might be a chance to be properly honest with her about how you feel,' Aidan said, taking a pull from the beer bottle Tom passed him. 'Forget all this crap about being responsible for me, accept that you're basically a commitment-phobic idiot, but tell her that, if she'll have you for the next few hundred lifetimes, you're hers.'

'No guarantee she'll listen, though,' Sam said, sipping his own beer.

'Well, let's face it, bro,' Aidan said. 'On the basis of your last conversation with her, what the hell have you got to lose?'

Sam, despite everything, had to concede that for once Aidan was right.

46

Shortly after Sam left, Florence gave up any hope of settling down to either work or pleasure for the rest of the day. How dare he come marching over here, patronising her in that way! Their relationship had been a zero-sum game, really, with both of them distancing themselves after it had become clear that neither could come to terms with the bigger picture; it had hurt, but she was used to packing up and moving on. She may not actually be able to move away from Sam, but she could certainly put the distance between them emotionally. She wasn't going to take back what she'd said about him making Aidan dependent on him, even if a small voice was nagging at her that Sam probably hadn't needed to hear it from her. Not so soon after they'd got together, anyway.

Pacing her living room, feeling a restlessness that she knew wasn't just going to go away, she decided to head out for a walk. As she reached Willowbury High Street, now back to what could only be described as normal in Willowbury's own terms after the Christmas decorations had come down, she caught sight of Josie striding back from Willowbury Hill with her dog, a loveable spaniel called Molly.

'Hey,' Josie waved with the hand that wasn't clutching the dog's lead. 'What are you doing out on this chilly February evening when you don't have a dog to walk?'

'Got fed up of staying in,' Florence said morosely.

'And...?' Josie immediately seemed to sense there was more to it than that.

'Oh, you know,' Florence replied. 'Confused, stressed, pissed off... same old, same old.'

Josie reached out and gave her a slightly awkward one-armed hug, while Molly jumped up and put muddy paws all over her knees by way of comfort. 'Come on,' she said. 'I've got time for a quick drink if you promise not to tell Nick. I'm not supposed to be boozing during the week.'

'Deal,' Florence's voice was muffled by Josie's thick, brightly coloured scarf.

They walked into The Travellers' Rest and ordered a couple of glasses of wine, settling themselves at the table underneath the picture of the actors that had caught Florence's eye on Christmas Day. The sight of Elsie and Henry didn't really help, unfortunately. Their love affair, cut short in its prime, was too tragic to bear thinking about.

'So, what's really up?' Josie took a sip of her wine.

'Bloody Sam Ellis, of course,' Florence muttered. 'He comes marching over to mine this afternoon, telling me he's sorry I've taken our break-up so badly, that he doesn't want to be the cause of me – get this – losing my job, and generally being a patronising prick into the bargain! Honestly, the nerve!'

Josie choked on her wine. 'Really?'

'I mean, sure, I'm a bit gutted that it didn't work out, but I said from the start I wouldn't get involved with someone with a military background because of the potential upheaval and commitment issues. Who the hell does he think he is, thinking he's ruined my life?'

'Perhaps you misinterpreted what he was saying?' Josie's face had taken on a most uncharacteristic flush, which was too swift to have been from the wine. 'I'm sure he's just concerned about you. And perhaps he wants to give things another go?'

'Well, he's got a funny way of showing it,' Florence said. 'I mean, he seems to have got the idea that I've been pining away for him on the other side of the party wall, when in actual fact, it's him who's been doing that, if what I'm hearing is to be believed.'

'Oh yes?' Josie raised an eyebrow as Florence briefly filled her in on the conversation she'd overheard between Tom and Aidan in the garden.

'Well, there you go, then,' Josie replied as Florence finished. 'He's obviously projecting his issues on to you.' She shrugged. 'Or perhaps he's just got a communication problem.'

'Well, I won't be wasting any more time communicating with him about anything from now on,' Florence, fortified by most of her large glass of Chablis, declared. 'Indecisive idiots are off the agenda from now on.'

'He's got you pretty fired up again, though, hasn't he?' Josie said. 'Are you quite sure you're as offended as you think you are?'

Florence sighed. 'No, I guess I'm not, really. I'm frustrated that things ended in a bit of a stalemate, and seeing him this afternoon was a good opportunity to vent some of my irritation on him for that, I suppose. He was an easy target when he came round spouting all that nonsense about me feeling melancholic and emotional.'

'There you go,' Josie said stoutly. 'And he's obviously missing you, if what Tom and Aidan said is to be believed. Lust-ridden and moping around? How could you resist him?'

Florence smiled, in spite of herself. 'Quite easily, it seems.'

'Well, it's up to you, of course, but what could he say that might actually change your mind?'

'I just want him to be honest with me, and himself,' Florence drained her glass and contemplated another one, but she wasn't sure how long Josie could be out for with the dog as an excuse. 'I mean, I really think he's just hiding behind Aidan as a convenient excuse not to commit to anything else. It would be nice to know if that were true or not; how he really feels about the future. Is he ever going to want to settle down and lead a life with me in it?'

'Then perhaps you should just ask him that,' Josie said gently. 'Although, perhaps you don't want to have to. Perhaps he needs to be the one to tell you without prompting from you?' She was speaking half to herself now, a faraway look in her eyes.

Florence looked at her, confused. 'What?'

'Never mind,' Josie said hastily. 'I'm sorry, hon, but I've got to get back before Nick sends out a search party. Not for me, mind, but for the dog! She's the most important female in his life these days, or so I've long suspected!' She picked up Molly's lead from where she'd looped it under her chair. 'I'll see you tomorrow at school for Careers Day?'

'Sure,' Florence said, also rising. 'Let's hope Sam communicates better with the kids tomorrow than he does with me!'

As she left the pub, she couldn't help thinking that Josie had terminated that whole conversation suspiciously quickly. Feeling more confused than ever, she wandered back home and tried to get down to a bit more work before school the next day.

47

The Willowbury Academy Careers Day dawned bright and sunny, and as Florence parked her car in her usual spot, the weather felt distinctly at odds with her dark mood. She knew she shouldn't let it get to her, but, despite what she'd said to Josie when they'd met in the pub, the fact that Sam was going to be on site today was really getting under her skin.

As the school had a relatively small population at the moment, initially all of the staff had mucked in to help arrange the Careers Day, although, blessedly, once she'd passed on Charlie and Sam's contact details to admin, that had been the end of her involvement in the arrangements. She was due to meet them both 'officially' during her break time in the staffroom but hoped that, since she had to escort classes to talks immediately afterwards, their communications would be brief. She was a professional; Sam was a professional: it shouldn't be an issue.

As the classroom clock edged towards break time, Florence's stomach fluttered with nerves. She'd had a busy morning, which was about to become busier as she reprimanded a couple of students for chucking pens across the classroom.

'Jake, Harry, see me at the end,' she called. She really wasn't in the mood for her madder Year 8 class this morning. Knowing Sam was going to be somewhere in the building, probably right at this moment, was enough to shorten her fuse.

'But, Miss, I was just giving him his pen back,' Jake protested.

Florence silenced him with a glare that Jake seemed to instinctively know meant *don't push your luck, child.*

By the time break arrived, she had a couple more students lined up for a chat. Perhaps there was something in the air today, knowing that they were going to be off timetable for the rest of the morning and the first afternoon lesson, taking part in workshops and listening to the speakers, or, more likely, it was that Florence had communicated her poor mood to her classes, which, sadly, could be an occupational hazard no matter how experienced a teacher you were. Either way, she'd ensured that, by the time she'd dealt with the students, there wouldn't be time for anything else other than a cup of tea and a trip to the loo before the Careers Day took over. As it was, she didn't even get the cuppa, so was spared the trial of seeing Sam across the crowded staffroom. She felt regretful she didn't get to say hello to Charlie Thorpe, but there would be time later to touch base and say thank you.

'So, you're taking your Year Seven groups to Journalism, Veterinary Science and Medicine, then finishing with Charlie Thorpe and Politics,' Josie confirmed in passing, from her copy of the itinerary that had been popped into all of their pigeon holes that morning. 'Unless you want to do a swap and listen to Sam talking about the navy and the air ambulance?'

'Not likely,' Florence said mutinously. 'I could do without that, after our last conversation.'

'Fair enough,' Josie squeezed Florence's arm as they passed. 'Perhaps that wouldn't be the best time for a tearful reunion.'

'Not going to happen,' Florence snapped, then apologised.

'Sorry. Not sleeping well again. And I've just bollocked five Year Eight students for stepping out of line before break.'

'Don't worry about it.' Josie threw a sympathetic glance back over her shoulder. 'See you later.'

Settling into her seat in the classroom where the first speaker was giving her presentation a few minutes later, Florence was relieved to find the journalist from the local paper was funny and engaging, and she kept the students entertained as well as informed. She couldn't help wondering if Sam was faring as well with his group of older students. A part of her wished he'd crash and burn, before she shushed herself for being a cow. No one deserved to dry up in front of a hall of students, no matter how cross she was with them.

As the end of the first talk approached and she prepared to move her students to the next room, she stood up and glanced through the glass classroom wall. A brand-new build, all of the classrooms had glass frontages that faced out into the corridor, designed as a way of passively supervising students in transition from lesson to lesson and at social time. The class next door had already started to move, and she saw Josie striding past as she shepherded them along the corridor.

Just as she was getting her own students in order to leave the room, out of the corner of her eye, she saw a head of dirty blond hair atop a pair of broad shoulders disappearing round the corner and her heart flipped. She was glad she didn't actually see his face, though, or she'd never have been able to concentrate on getting the students where they needed to go. Glancing at her watch, Florence willed, harder than ever, for this day to be over.

* * *

'Hi,' a deep, but pleasant voice said as she took her class to the hall, where Charlie Thorpe was preparing to give the keynote address to the Year Nine students. It had been a pleasant day so far, all in all, despite the unsettling feeling of sharing the space with Sam, and as she shook Charlie's hand, Florence was pleased that the students had behaved brilliantly, too.

'Hi,' she replied, smiling at Charlie. 'Have you had a good day?'

'Yes thanks,' Charlie said. 'The students here have been great, and they've asked a lot of really searching questions. Thanks for getting me involved.'

'My pleasure,' Florence replied. 'I'd love to stay and listen to your talk, but Years Seven and Eight are back on timetable for their last lesson, and I've got some Shakespeare to teach.'

'No worries,' Charlie smiled, and yet again Florence could see exactly why Holly, and the local voters, had fallen for him. He had an easy charm and a sincere manner, and she instinctively wanted to trust him.

A rare set of virtues for a politician, she thought, amused.

'Thanks again,' Florence replied. 'See you around.'

As Charlie waved, Florence tried to remember how far she'd got in the play she was teaching before she made it back to her classroom. Doubtless, Year Eight would try every trick in the book to distract her from Shakespeare, so she'd have to try extra hard to keep them with her.

Just as she got to the door of her classroom, she remembered, with a lurch, exactly where they'd left off last lesson. Surely, she thought, someone up there was conspiring against her today. Putting all stray thoughts of the last time she'd been working on Shakespeare firmly out of her mind, she took a deep breath and prepared to enthuse her class about the Bard.

48

Sam looked around the classroom where he was going to be giving his talk to the group of Year Ten students and felt his stomach disappear. Unaccustomed to nerves when he was actually doing his job, the thought of talking about it to a bunch of students was a terrifying prospect. That Josie was the one there helping him to set up added to his feelings of unsettlement, as the last time he'd seen her was at the village shop, after which he'd tried, so disastrously, to talk to Florence. The fact that she was doing a great job of multitasking, setting up a laptop and a projector whilst simultaneously lecturing him on his love life, added to his anxiety.

'Look, when are you just going to admit it to yourself, and to Florence? You're crazy about her. You have been since the moment you locked eyes on your doorstep on her first day at work.' Josie kept fiddling with the data projector and her laptop as she spoke, neither of which was communicating with the other. In exasperation, she pulled out the cables, switched both off and rebooted them, all the while with half an eye on the clock, waiting for the students to begin entering the classroom.

'I don't really think this is the moment to be having this conversation, when I'm just about to face your Year Ten students and give them a careers talk,' Sam muttered. 'Can't we talk about this later? Or never?'

'Time, as I'm sure you're well aware, isn't something we have a great deal of in this job,' Josie said briskly, breathing a sigh of relief as the projector finally connected to the laptop, and Sam's slide presentation appeared on the large white screen on the wall. 'So, you'll understand the need to be direct occasionally.' She turned away from the laptop and looked Sam squarely in the face. 'When are you going to stop being such a twat about what happened between you and Florence and apologise to her, and then tell her that you love her?'

Sam could feel the headache that had begun as a dull thump that morning when he woke up beginning to crush his brow. He'd carried the tension with him for weeks, ever since he'd cooled it with Florence, and it was banging away with a vengeance now. 'It's not as simple as that.' The certainty of last night, when Aidan had made it all sound so easy, had drained away as the dawn had broken, and now all of Sam's old doubts and fears about levelling with Florence had crept back into his mind with a vengeance.

'Why not? You live right next door to her, for heaven's sake. All you have to do is jump over the wall and knock on her front door. Seems straightforward enough to me.'

'Been there, tried that,' Sam said wearily. 'And from what Aidan told me last night, I was acting on completely the wrong information, anyway, no thanks to you, him and Tom. She didn't listen to me yesterday, and I doubt she'll have changed her mind now.'

'She got the wrong end of the stick yesterday,' Josie said, and Sam was sure he saw a most uncharacteristically sheepish look pass over her features. 'And I'm sorry for my part in that. We all thought we were doing you a favour by interfering, just like with Beatrice and Benedick, when actually, we probably made it worse.'

'No kidding,' Sam said, raising a wry eyebrow.

'But really, what we did doesn't matter,' Josie said hurriedly. 'You're both crap at communicating. You need to sit down and actually *talk* for a change. After all, as far as she's concerned, Florence thinks you're a commitment-phobe with a martyr complex. You need to show her otherwise.'

'You don't mince your words, do you?' Sam gave a short laugh.

'Being a teacher, I generally have to be direct,' Josie replied briskly. 'It tends to spill over into my social life, too. But you have to admit...' she trailed off hopefully.

Sam sighed. 'Yes, OK. You're right, Josie, I've been a complete twat, and thrown away probably the best, most stable, most wonderful person in my life, because I was too terrified to commit to her. Why should she even give me the time of day any more?' He balled his fists in frustration and began to pace the front of the classroom.

Josie, seemingly aware that putting Sam off his stride just before he addressed Year Ten wasn't exactly a great idea, glanced at the clock again. 'Look, Sam, I know you're afraid of hurting her, and yourself again, but she's stronger than you give her credit for. And the worst thing she'll do is tell you where to go, don't you think? She's pretty much done that already. You've got nothing to lose by giving it one more shot. And if the worst comes to the worst, you can always put up a taller wall between your houses, right?'

'Look,' Sam stopped pacing. 'Just let me get through this presentation first, OK? The thought of cocking up in front of a bunch of teenagers is frightening enough right now. Once this is over, I promise I'll think about sorting things out with Florence so we're not in this weird stalemate.'

'Good enough for now,' Josie said, as the first students filed through the door. 'Oh, and Sam?'

'Yeah?'

'Best do up your flies. You don't want to be laughed off stage before you even begin.'

Cursing as he realised Josie wasn't joking, by the time he'd made himself respectable, she was already welcoming in the front row. Tugging down the panels of his jacket, he prepared to face an audience far tougher than any he'd ever faced in the Royal Navy.

49

Time seemed to have slowed down by torturous proportions for the last lesson of the day. Usually, Florence loved teaching Shakespeare; the words just seemed to fly off the page, the characters coming so wonderfully to life the more years she did it. But not this afternoon. Her Year Eight class was restless, desperate to be out of the classroom and heading home to tea, unrestricted mobile phone use and games consoles. The last thing anyone wanted was to be ploughing through a play that, typically, right at that moment had reached its achingly romantic climax.

'OK,' Florence said wearily. 'Jack, why don't you be Benedick for this scene, and Rosie, you be Beatrice.'

'Do I have to, Miss?' Rosie grumbled. 'I don't get it.'

'You don't have to understand every word,' Florence replied automatically. Over the years she'd got used to this familiar refrain from her students. 'It's about trying to *feel* it. Try to get a sense of the emotion of the moment. Beatrice and Benedick have both suddenly realised that they can't imagine life without each other. That all this time they've been dancing around their feelings, neither of them willing to commit, to back down, and now, after all of the tragedy and the heartache, they're both finally able to communicate how much they really do love each other.'

'Whoa, Miss, you really do like this stuff, don't you?' Kyle, the cheeky chap in the front row grinned at her.

'You could say that,' Florence replied drily. She looked back at Rosie. 'Give it a go, my lovely. If you get stuck, we can do a switcheroo and someone else can read.'

Thus encouraged, Rosie took a deep breath, but before she could start, another voice emanated from the back of the room, by the door to the classroom.

'I do love nothing in the world so well as you. Is not that strange?'

Florence's knees started to tremble as she gripped her annotated copy of the play tightly. Immediately, she could feel a blush spreading across her cheeks, and a flare of something that should be anger, irritation, but instead felt like adrenaline laced with relief, of coming home.

Voice betraying only the vaguest sense of these swimming emotions, she read the next line, eyes still steadfastly on the copy of the play in front of her. 'As strange as the thing I know not. It were as possible for me to say I loved nothing so well as you, but believe me not, and yet I lie not. I confess nothing nor I deny nothing.'

Florence could sense, rather than see, the movement of the interloper in her classroom, by the creak of boots on the tiles and the stir of the air as thirty curious faces turned away from her and in the visitor's direction. Her eyes stayed fixed on the copy of the text in her hands, using it as an anchor as the classroom seemed to shift around her.

'By my sword, Beatrice, thou lovest me.' His voice was low, and had the vaguest semblance of a tremor as he continued his ascent up the aisle between the tables.

'Do not swear and eat it,' Florence replied, not really needing the copy of the play to read from, but holding it in her hands in an effort not to lose control in front of a class of increasingly agog Year 8 students.

'I will swear by it that you love me, and I will make him eat it that says I love not you.'

Florence shook her head, remembering the moment onstage in the priory's performance area when she and Sam had performed Josie's version of this very scene, also in front of an increasingly entranced audience.

'Will you not eat your word?' She was whispering now, trying to stop the tears from spilling over.

'I protest I love thee.' Sam's voice was trembling, and Florence could hear that he, too, seemed to be having trouble containing his emotions in front of this rapt crowd of students.

Florence started as Sam stopped right in front of her. She could see his highly polished boots and the bottom of his trousers, which, incongruously, were the same trousers he'd worn onstage, his naval dress trousers. She dropped the copy of the script, and it bounced off one of Sam's boots and lay, splayed open, off to the side.

'Why, then, God forgive me.' She watched a tear fall onto her hands, which were still held as if they had the book between them.

'What offence, sweet Beatrice?'

Florence shook her head, then jumped as one of Sam's hands closed over hers. Shaken from her momentum by the act, she stumbled and blanked on the words. 'I... I'm sorry... I can't ...'

'Then let me.' Sam raised his other hand and brushed her tears away. 'I don't think this lot will mind too much if we swap a line or two.' He drew a deep breath, and Florence could feel his hand trembling against her cheek where it still rested.

'I was about to protest I loved you,' Sam said softly. 'I love you with so much of my heart that none is left to protest.'

'Oh Sam...' Florence whispered. 'I've missed you so much.' She reached up a hand to his face, and as she did so, looked up for the first time. The classroom was so silent; you could have heard a pin drop. Sam's eyes were filled with such tenderness that Florence's tears spilled over again.

'I've missed you too,' Sam replied. His eyes flickered from Florence's eyes to her trembling mouth and back again. 'And I mean it. I love you. More than anything. I'm not afraid of it any more. I don't think, really, that I ever was. I've never felt afraid when I've been with you.' He slid an arm around her waist, and, mindful of his audience, he dipped his head and gave her a very light, very gentle kiss.

A chorus of oohs and ahhs, interspersed with the odd self-conscious giggle, met this action, and, encouraged, Sam wrapped his arms around her and gave her a huge hug, as the room exploded into raucous cheers.

'Whoo! Get in, Miss!' came a voice from the front row, but Florence was past noticing.

Eventually, they broke apart again, and as they turned to face the class who had become their impromptu audience, Florence's jaw dropped as she saw none other than Josie standing in the doorway of the classroom.

'Well, I couldn't let him get away without telling you how he really feels,' she said drily. 'Especially while he's wearing such a wonderful uniform!'

'I'm glad,' Florence said. 'Even if, thanks to you and this lot, I'm never going to live this down.'

'We won't say a word, Miss,' fibbed Kyle happily. 'After all, you were only teaching us the play, weren't you? You're always going on about how it's meant to be seen and heard, not read.'

Josie wandered up the aisle and glanced at the remainder of the PowerPoint presentation on Florence's laptop. 'Go on, get lost,' she said, looking at the two of them in amusement. 'It's nearly home time anyway. I'll finish off with this lot.'

'Are you sure?' Florence asked.

Josie grinned. 'To be honest, I think you've probably lost your audience now.'

It was ten minutes to the bell, and Florence definitely felt as though she needed some fresh air. She reached out and squeezed Josie's hand. 'You're a star, thank you.'

'No worries. Get out of here,' Josie replied. 'But remember you've got double Year Seven in the morning, so no flying off into the sunset just yet.'

'We won't.' As Sam slipped his arm around her again, and the catcalls and wolf whistles surrounded them once again, Florence wondered if she'd ever be able to face 8E2 again.

50

'So, what *really* changed your mind?' Florence asked as, a little while later, they were ensconced behind a table in The Travellers' Rest, sipping a glass of something to fortify them both.

'Aidan did, finally,' Sam said. 'He told me what a twat he thought I was being. Although, to be honest, I'd kind of worked it out by then already. I just didn't quite know how to tell you. Or if you'd even listen to me.'

'No, I'm not buying that for one minute,' Florence said. 'He's been telling you for weeks that he thinks you made a mistake, and I know for a fact you've not listened to him at all.'

'How?'

Florence smiled. 'He and Tom visited me a couple of times during your evening shifts. They made it their mission to get us back together pretty much since we stalled. But they were getting more and more pissed off that none of their pep talks seemed to be working with either of us. I wasn't going to push you, and I was still stubborn enough to believe that you were going to up and leave, and you'd just closed down and wouldn't discuss it, so we were at a standoff. They'd basically given us up as a lost cause.'

Sam started. 'Do you know they're... together, then?'

'Yes,' Florence grinned. 'They told me a couple of weeks ago.' She paused, looking at Sam speculatively. 'Aidan was quite nervous about levelling with *you,* though. He wasn't sure how you'd take it.'

'It was a bit of a surprise,' Sam admitted. 'I felt like a complete idiot for thinking I knew him so well and not realising that he was gay.' He waved away Florence's attempt to reassure him. 'No, it's OK – he made it clear that it was up to him to tell me, at a time of his choosing. I still can't quite believe I missed something so important about him, but at the end of the day, he's my brother, not my other half. He's entitled to keep his private life private.'

'Unlike you and I, it seems,' Florence said wryly. Thanks to Josie and Tom's interventions, and now Sam's declaration of love in front of her Year 8 students, she felt as though her entire love life had gone public.

'Yeah, sorry about that,' Sam said, smiling broadly. 'But something, or rather *someone*, told me that I had to take matters into my own hands a bit more dramatically, if I was ever going to convince you I was serious about committing to you.'

'Was that someone Josie by any chance?'

'How did you guess?' Sam squeezed Florence's hand, where it lay on the tabletop.

'Well, I think you've proved that now, in front of thirty witnesses!' The warmth of Sam's hand over hers was both reassuring and wonderfully distracting.

'Are you OK about all this?' Sam asked, seeing the somewhat harried look that crossed Florence's face at the memory of falling apart in front of her Year Eight class. 'I mean... it was a spur-of-the moment thing. I didn't mean to put you under pressure in such a public way.'

In response, Florence leaned across the table and planted a

gentle, wine-infused kiss onto Sam's lips. 'Please don't ever worry about that. You were, as ever, in exactly the right place at the right time.'

EPILOGUE

'Right, I think that's everything.' Sam looked around what used to be his bedroom and smiled. He'd enjoyed living with Aidan, but it was definitely time to move on. As he double-checked the ensuite bathroom, he reflected that Aidan didn't exactly have far to walk to return anything he found, anyway.

Moving in with Florence had been a gradual, organic process that had taken most of the year; mostly because Florence was still finishing the renovations to her house, but somewhat because Sam was still coming to terms with not quite being the port of call he had been for the past two years for Aidan. It was when Aidan himself had started making more definite noises about setting up a permanent home with Tom at Number 1 Bay Tree Terrace that Sam had finally made the decision to move to Number 2.

Sam had to admit that it was strange not to be Aidan's go-to any more; and in some ways he had felt jealous that Tom had fitted in so easily to Aidan's life. But he acknowledged that Tom understood the rise and fall of life with Aidan, and he couldn't help feeling a release of pressure as he felt a little freer to pursue his own life, especially the one that he was now tentatively starting to build with Florence.

As he headed down the stairs, he checked the pocket of his jacket for the ring he'd bought a couple of months ago. Now, having spent so much more time with Florence, he finally felt secure enough to give it to her, should she wish to take it. He felt as though he'd got to know her well enough over the past year to take a chance on the style; he'd chosen a simple platinum band inset with a single, respectably sized diamond.

Wandering into the kitchen, he saw Aidan emptying the dishwasher. 'Tom's finally getting you house-trained at last, is he?' he joked, taking the clean mugs from Aidan and stacking them neatly in the cupboard. 'Don't remember you ever doing that when I lived here all the time.'

'That's because you did it all for me,' Aidan grinned. 'Why own a dog and bark yourself?'

Sam thought better of swatting Aidan with the tea towel on the kitchen table; he had a proposal to deliver. 'I, er, guess this is officially it, then,' he said instead. 'I'm moving out.'

'About bloody time!' Aidan replied. 'At least Tom and I can wander around starkers now without worrying about shocking my big brother's sensibilities!'

'I hate to tell you this, but I've seen it all from you before, and Tom's not my type,' Sam replied. 'But thanks for the consideration up until now.'

'Are we meeting later for a pint or three?' Aidan asked. 'Make your new living arrangements official?'

'Yeah, why not?' Sam replied. 'But can you, er, text me first? Depending on what Florence says when I pop the question, I could be celebrating or drowning my sorrows.'

'You don't honestly think she'll say no, do you?' Aidan finished unloading the dishwasher and pushed the door shut. 'I mean, joking aside, you're a pretty decent bloke, and you've been virtually living there for ages anyway.'

'I know, but there's always that doubt, isn't there?' Sam looked away, embarrassed to be having this conversation. 'At least there's a spare room here if it doesn't go to plan!'

'Not a chance!' Aidan laughed. 'Tom wants it to be a music room – says he's fed up of the guitar at the bottom of the bed.'

'And you're too in love to refuse him anything,' Sam said wryly, enjoying the fact that it was now Aidan who looked more embarrassed.

'He'll do for now,' Aidan said, but the affectionate tone of his voice belied the words. Sam realised, once again, just what a good place Aidan was in now. His brother was happier than he'd been for a long, long time. Aidan's relationship with Tom had a lot more to do with it than Sam had, and Sam felt as though they'd both turned a corner.

'You could always do the same and ask Tom to get hitched,' Sam said, by way of breaking the silence. 'Although I'm not sure how Florence would feel about a double wedding!'

Aidan laughed. 'I think we're happy enough as we are for now. And I wouldn't want to come to blows over planning the wedding. I'll leave all that to you and Florence – if she says yes, of course!'

'And on that note...' Sam wandered back to the hallway. On the other side of the party wall lay his future, and for the first time in his life, he felt as though he was truly going home.

AUTHOR'S NOTE AND ACKNOWLEDGEMENTS

With every book, there are always so many people to thank, and this one is no exception. First of all, thanks, as ever, go to my agent Sara Keane, my editor Sarah Ritherdon, Amanda, Nia, Caroline, Megan and the rest of the team at Boldwood, who have supported this book so wholeheartedly, and eagle eyed copy and proof readers Jade Craddock and David Boxell.

Research is always a key aspect of the writing process, and I am incredibly grateful to the Great Western Air Ambulance and the Dorset and Somerset Air Ambulance charities for being so helpful and approachable, and hugely generous with their time and expertise. The work that the air ambulance does is absolutely vital, and learning about this was a real privilege. Special thanks to Ian Cantoni, Anna Perry and Jim Green from the GWAA, who, along with answering endless questions, allowed me to get up close to the GWAA's impressive helicopter at their base, and gave me such an insight into the working life of my local air ambulance organisation, especially the role of the pilot in the team. Massive thanks, also, to the wonderful Mario Carretta, chief pilot of the DSAA, who, even after a very late night on duty spent so much time showing me the base and its technology, and answering all manner of bizarre questions, including whether it was possible to land a helicopter on Cheddar Gorge in a snowstorm! His bumblebee metaphor, and the footage of the fireworks from above were two of the many things I just had to include from his wide and varied experience of flight. I learned so much from the very knowledgeable and friendly personnel from both of these important organisations, and I can't tell you how useful it all was.

In addition, huge thanks to Chris Whittington, of HM Coast-guard Search and Rescue, who mutual friend Rose Nicholls put me in touch with. Chris was an absolute fount of information on so many aspects of his career. He not only answered my questions, large and small, serious and frivolous, but also scripted the conversation that Sam has with ATC when he takes Florence flying, for which I am incredibly grateful. Both Chris and Mario provided a vital context for Sam and his experiences, and also checked over my more technical chapters, which was enormously helpful and ensured that I was on the right lines. It goes without saying that any errors or occurrences of poetic licence in the novel's flying scenes are down to me alone!

Florence is, of course, an English teacher, and I must give yet another shout out to the wonderful Department of English at Backwell School, who really are the very, very best at what they do, and have been so patient with a colleague who spends half her working life in her head, and the other half in the classroom. You truly are a second family, and your support and encouragement mean the world.

Thanks, as always, to the friends and family who have coped with my tunnel vision, once again, while I've been writing this book. I definitely couldn't do this without you. These include the members of the Romantic Novelists' Association, the Mums'

Hotline Bling Ring, my parents and siblings, my husband Nick and our daughters Flora and Rosie, who have to live with me during this process every single time – I love you.

Finally, thank you, the reader, for reading this novel and for staying with me on this journey – I hope you've enjoyed the ride!

MORE FROM FAY KEENAN

We hope you enjoyed reading *Snowflakes Over Bay Tree Terrace*. If you did, please leave a review.

If you'd like to gift a copy, this book is also available as an ebook, digital audio download and audiobook CD.

Sign up to Fay Keenan's mailing list for news, competitions and updates on future books.

http://bit.ly/FayKeenanNewsletter

A Place To Call Home, another heart-warming read from Fay Keenan, is available to buy now.

ABOUT THE AUTHOR

Fay Keenan is the author of the bestselling *Little Somerby* series of novels. She has led writing workshops with Bristol University and has been a visiting speaker in schools. She is a full-time teacher and lives in Somerset.

Visit Fay's website: https://faykeenan.com/

Follow Fay on social media:

- facebook.com/faykeenanauthor
- twitter.com/faykeenan
- instagram.com/faykeenan
- bookbub.com/authors/fay-keenan

AIR AMBULANCE CHARITIES

ABOUT BOLDWOOD BOOKS

Boldwood Books is a fiction publishing company seeking out the best stories from around the world.

Find out more at www.boldwoodbooks.com

Sign up to the Book and Tonic newsletter for news, offers and competitions from Boldwood Books!

http://www.bit.ly/bookandtonic

We'd love to hear from you, follow us on social media:

 facebook.com/BookandTonic

 twitter.com/BoldwoodBooks

 instagram.com/BookandTonic

Lightning Source UK Ltd.
Milton Keynes UK
UKHW011554241121
394505UK00007B/251